BY THE BOOK

A MEANT TO BE NOVEL

JASMINE GUILLORY

SCHOLASTIC
SYDNEY AUCKLAND NEW YORK TORONTO LONDON MEXICO CITY
NEW DELHI HONG KONG BUENOS AIRES PUERTO RICO

Cover design by Marci Senders
Cover art by Stephanie Singleton

Published by Scholastic Australia in 2022.

Scholastic Australia Pty Limited
PO Box 579 Gosford NSW 2250
ABN 11 000 614 577
www.scholastic.com.au

Part of the Scholastic Group
Sydney • Auckland • New York • Toronto • London • Mexico City • New Delhi
Hong Kong • Buenos Aires • Puerto Rico

ISBN 978-1-76129-225-5

Printed in Australia.

Scholastic Australia's policy, in association with its printers, is to use papers that are renewable and made efficiently from wood grown in responsibly managed forests, so as to minimise its environmental footprint.

FSC www.fsc.org MIX Paper | Supporting responsible forestry FSC® C001695

The paper in this book is FSC® certified.
FSC® promotes environmentally responsible, socially beneficial and economically viable management of the world's forests.

To all the Black girls who loved books
and wanted to be princesses.
This one's for you.

© ANDREA SCHER

JASMINE GUILLORY is a *New York Times* best-selling author of novels including *The Wedding Date*, the Reese's Book Club selection *The Proposal*, and *While We Were Dating*. Her work has appeared in the *Wall Street Journal*, *Cosmopolitan*, *Bon Appétit*, and *Time*, and she is a frequent book contributor on the *Today* show. She lives in Oakland, California.

PROLOGUE

Isabelle Marlowe smiled at the world as she walked down the bustling, crowded Manhattan street. She couldn't help it. She knew she should be chill and cool and act like she wasn't excited about her first day of work, but she just couldn't do it. She was so thrilled she could hardly stand it. Wouldn't anyone be? It was a bright, sunny February day in New York City, spring was on its way, and in about thirty minutes, she would officially become an editorial assistant at one of the biggest publishing houses in the world, Tale as Old as Time Publishing. She couldn't wait.

She was early for her first day—she hadn't wanted to risk delays, because she'd had to take the train all the way from her parents' house in New Jersey—so she stopped at the coffee cart across the street from the office to get another cup of coffee to pass the time. Miraculously, there was almost no line.

"Good morning!" she said to the coffee cart guy. "I'm Isabelle. Well, my friends call me Izzy, but probably at work I should just have them call me Isabelle, it sounds more professional, don't you think? Anyway—"

"Coffee?" he barked.

"Oh! Yes, coffee, definitely. Milk, just a touch, but no sugar, please. Thank you!"

He handed her the coffee with a grunt, and she beamed at him. He didn't smile back at her, but she barely noticed.

She took a sip of her coffee. He'd added too much milk, but people usually did, that was okay! She glanced around—maybe she should wander around the neighborhood a bit as she drank her coffee, to investigate what was there and kill a little time. When she'd come in for her interview, she'd been too nervous to really notice anything.

Look, a bakery! And it looked like a great one, with a line out the door and lots of baguettes and pastries in the window. She would probably get a lot of late-afternoon snacks there. Oh, and a drugstore on that corner—that would be very useful.

Oooh. A bookstore! It was still closed at this hour of the morning, but she looked at the books in the window, most of which she'd read. She'd just quit her part-time job at her local bookstore, which had given her access to—and a helpful discount on—all the latest titles. She tried to peek in through the darkened windows to see what was on the front tables. She saw a few of her favorite authors; she'd recognize their book covers anywhere. And there was *It's My Favorite Part!* It had come out after she'd left the bookstore job, and she was dying to read it. She was trying to budget, so she hadn't bought it yet, and she was like sixtieth on the waiting list for it at her library. At this rate, it would take months to get it. She might have to crack and buy it anyway.

She pulled her phone out of her pocket to check the time and saw that her parents had both texted.

From her dad:

Good luck on your first day, Isabelle!

From her mom:

Yes, good luck honey!

She smiled at her phone.

Thank you!!! I'm so excited!

She was still living at home with her parents, but just for now. Her salary was on the low side—though she was thrilled to have one at all!—and it seemed to make the most sense to live with them in New Jersey and commute. But she got along great with her parents, so she didn't mind that at all. Plus, she was sure it wouldn't be for long.

At ten minutes to nine, she decided it was time to head toward the office. She looked at her reflection in the window, smoothed down her favorite blue dress, and adjusted that one bobby pin in her hair. She made her way to the Tale as Old as Time building, snapped a selfie in front to send to her parents, and walked inside.

"Hi," she said to the security guard, unable to suppress the big smile on her face. "I'm Isabelle Marlowe, it's my first day here?"

He smiled back at her.

"Hi, Isabelle. Welcome. Let me take a look at your ID and I'll send you upstairs."

After a glance at her ID and a quick phone call, the security guard—his name was Frank, she saw on his name tag—waved her toward the elevators.

"Good luck on your first day," he said.

"Thank you!" She took a deep breath and walked into the first elevator.

A woman with dark hair and glasses was waiting when Isabelle got off.

"Isabelle? Hi, I'm Rachel. Nice to meet you in person finally after so many emails. Marta won't be in for a while today, so I'm going to show you around."

Marta Wallace was one of the top editors here at TAOAT, and Izzy's new boss. Izzy was sort of glad Marta wouldn't be at the office right at the beginning—she'd been very intimidating in the interview, and Izzy had been sure she wouldn't get the job. She'd been shocked when she'd gotten the call from HR a few weeks later, and it had taken her many emails before she'd been convinced this whole thing wasn't a trick.

She'd really thought she'd get a job at a different publishing house. When she'd still been an intern, she'd gone to a mentorship event and met Josephine Henry, an editor over at Maurice, and a Black woman like Izzy. Izzy had gotten up the courage to email Josephine later to ask her for advice. Josephine had done far more than that—she'd taken Izzy out first for coffee, and then lunch, and given her a lot of advice on how to get a job in publishing. When a job as an editorial assistant was posted at Maurice, Izzy had applied immediately. She'd been crushed when she hadn't gotten it. But then the offer had come from Marta here at TAOAT shortly afterward, and she'd been overjoyed.

She looked around as they walked down the halls, and her eyes widened. There were books *everywhere* here. Being surrounded by books like this had been her dream since she was a little girl. She couldn't believe she'd gotten here.

Rachel gestured to a cubicle. "This one is for you," she said to Izzy. "Marta's office is right there." She pointed at the dark office down the hall from Izzy's desk.

Just then, a white guy with lots of dark hair, glasses, and what even Izzy could tell was a very well-cut blazer walked by.

"Oh, hi, are you Marta's new assistant?" he asked her.

She nodded and smiled at him. "Yes, hi! I'm Isabelle Marlowe, nice to meet you."

He looked over his glasses at her and smiled. "I'm Gavin Ridley. I sit right over there," he said, pointing to a desk not far away. "I was Marta's assistant up until recently; I'm an assistant editor now."

"Oh wow, congratulations!" Izzy said.

"Thank you," he said. "And really, feel free to ask me for any advice about working here. Happy to help." He waved at Izzy as he walked toward his desk.

Izzy smiled to herself. People were so nice here.

Rachel patted a stack of papers on Izzy's desk. "There's some paperwork here, along with a temporary badge and a few fun gifts for your first day—why don't you go through this and then you can come find me and we can get your picture taken for your ID badge and all that good stuff."

Izzy nodded as she sat down at her desk. "Sounds great. Thank you!"

She took her favorite pen out of her purse and diligently filled out all the paperwork sitting on her desk. Once that was done, it was time for the fun stuff. She picked up the bulky Tale as Old as Time tote bag and beamed at it. A new tote bag! She could just see herself taking this bag with her to the park on the weekends, her notebooks and pens and laptop inside, and working on that novel she'd started writing last month.

She reached inside the bag. A water bottle, a coffee mug, and . . . oh my God, a copy of *It's My Favorite Part!* She'd been dying to read it, and they just gave it to her? Had she entered a wonderland of free books?

She grinned as she got up to go find Rachel. She couldn't wait for her new life to begin.

CHAPTER ONE

Two years later

Izzy walked into work on Monday morning, flashed her badge at the security guard, and made her way into the elevator. She glanced down at her phone. Thirteen more emails had popped up, just during her walk from the subway to the elevator. Five of them were from Marta. Those could wait until she sat down at her desk. Preferably after she'd downed at least half the large cup of bad coffee she was holding, but that might be asking for too much. She sighed as the elevator stopped at her floor, a sigh echoed by at least three other people in the jam-packed elevator.

She pulled her hat off on the way to her desk and shook her long braids loose. The hat had only been partial protection from the freezing-cold air outside. February in New York was so depressing. It should feel better, shouldn't it? Winter was almost over! But instead it was cold and dreary and endless, despite being the shortest month of the year.

Her friend Priya Gupta waved at her as she walked by. Priya was another editorial assistant—she'd started at TAOAT just a few months after Izzy and she worked for Holly Moore, one of the other big editors at the company. During Priya's first week, there had been an editorial meeting where one editor had waxed poetic about how diverse their books were that season. Of the twenty-five books in their imprint, there were three whole authors of color, none of whom were Black. She and Priya had locked eyes from across the room. They'd been friends ever since.

"I cannot WAIT until we're in California next week, can you?" Priya said.

Izzy closed her eyes and let herself smile. "California. It's going to be warm, and we're going to take books out to the pool, and relax on lounge chairs in the sun, and let our skin get browner. Aren't we?"

Priya nodded. "Oh yeah, definitely we are."

They both knew this was mostly just a fantasy. They were going for a conference, so they'd be running around carrying boxes full of books or stacks of name tags or escorting authors from place to place nonstop. But it was nice to dream. Plus, editorial assistants almost never got to go to conferences like this. Izzy and Priya only got to go because their bosses' most demanding authors were going to be there, the ones who basically needed a door-to-door escort in every situation. Sure, she'd be dealing with huge egos all week—even more than usual—but she was grateful for the short break from the office.

She also needed a few days away from her parents, whom she was so very sick of living with. She loved them, she did! But they always talked to her first thing in the morning and asked so many questions at all times of day, and she felt like she had to text them when she was going to be out late. It all made her feel stifled, frustrated.

Izzy got to her desk and sighed. Another stack of books had appeared there overnight. Great, more books for her to deal with. She pushed them aside.

She spent her first hour doing all the work she always started her week with—checking her own email, skimming through her boss's email for any manuscripts that had come in overnight or fires she needed to put out, checking sales numbers for their releases from the previous week, reassuring authors and agents that yes, Marta would get back to them eventually (that was . . . mostly true), the usual.

Oh, she also had to send a slightly different version of the email she sent every two weeks to Beau Towers. Beau Towers: former child star, son of two celebrities, famous first for being a teenage heartthrob, then for his general rich-kid dirtbag-type behavior—fights in nightclubs, crashing sports cars, smashing paparazzi cameras, etc. And then there had been the multiple screaming matches he'd gotten into during and after his father's funeral; they'd been all over the tabloids.

Almost immediately after the funeral, Marta had given him a splashy book deal for his memoir. But well over a year ago, Beau Towers had basically disappeared. He was definitely still alive; his agent periodically sent emails swearing Beau was working on the book, though his deadline had long since passed. But Marta had told her to email him regularly to check in, so she sent him an email every other Monday at 9:45, like clockwork. He never emailed her back, but she'd stopped expecting a response long ago.

She reread the email that she'd sent two weeks ago. When she'd first started sending these emails, they'd been polite, professional, earnest queries asking him to check in with her, or with Marta, or to reach out if he had questions, or offering to set up conference calls with potential ghostwriters—all basically ways of saying, "Please, please, please email me back!!!" without actually saying those words. But after many months of sending the messages with no response, and as everything in her job got more and more stressful, she'd cracked.

Now she had fun with these, since she was certain no one but her read them—not Beau Towers, not his agent, and not Marta, whom she always cc'd.

To: Beau Towers
CC: Marta Wallace, John Moore
From: Isabelle Marlowe

Mr. Towers,
Happy February! February is the shortest month

of the year, along with being Black History Month, American Heart Month, National Bird Feeding Month, and National Snack Food Month! (I knew about the first two, but not the second two—we learn something new every day!) I hope the transition to a new month is treating you well! I just wanted to reach out again to check in and say I hope the writing is going well, and that if you need any assistance as you work on your memoir, you shouldn't hesitate to email or call me. Please let me know if Marta or I can help you with anything at all.

Kind regards,
Isabelle Marlowe
Editorial Assistant to Marta Wallace

She let herself grin at that. Look, she had to find her fun where she could in this thankless, stressful, overwhelming job, okay?

She put her fake cheery email persona back on and typed Beau Towers's email address into the TO box.

To: Beau Towers
CC: Marta Wallace, John Moore
From: Isabelle Marlowe

Mr. Towers,
Have you read any good books lately? I've read a number of excellent celebrity memoirs in the past few months—Michael J. Fox, Jessica Simpson, and Gabrielle Union all have fantastic memoirs out! People insist on giving me books for Christmas, even

though I work in a place where books literally fall out of the sky, but I didn't have any of those books before and was both surprised and delighted to find that I was absorbed by them. Just in case you're struggling with anything in your memoir, I thought maybe you could read one of those for inspiration! I'm happy to recommend more books to you at any time, or offer you any other assistance that you need. (FYI, Barack Obama's is far too long, though Michelle's is great! But really, would you want to edit a former president?) Looking forward to talking to you soon!

Kind regards,
Isabelle Marlowe
Editorial Assistant to Marta Wallace

She almost laughed out loud at that last line. She didn't think that she'd ever talk to Beau Towers, let alone soon. She'd probably be sending him progressively more and more unhinged emails every two weeks for years to come.

The thought of that made the smile drop from her face. How much longer could she do this?

Her first year at TAOAT had been hard, yes, but still new, exciting, thrilling every day to work with books all around her. But as certain parts of her job got easier, other parts got harder and more overwhelming. Marta gave her more and more work to do—more details to manage, more manuscripts to read, more authors to talk through their work with, cheer up, or get to chill out. And all those new responsibilities were great, and she felt like she was good at most of them, but they were all in addition to her regular work, and sometimes she felt like she was drowning. And since she was one of the few employees of color here, on top of everything else, she was always getting pulled in to give advice about diversity this or inclusivity that or to meet that one Black author who was visiting that day. She had to put a smile on her face and do it all, but it was exhausting.

Plus, what really mattered was whether Marta thought she was good—and when it came to that, Izzy had no idea. She tried to remind herself every day that Marta was brilliant, that she'd learned so much from watching her and listening to her, that she was lucky to have this job. But while that was all true, it was also true that Marta was hard to work for—often curt, not at all friendly, not particularly encouraging, and she rarely, if ever, gave out compliments. What Izzy wanted was to get promoted to assistant editor, and then, eventually, to editor. Not immediately, but someday. After all, Gavin had been promoted after two years, and her own two-year anniversary was fast approaching. But Marta hadn't dropped a single hint to her that promotion was in the cards.

Very occasionally, Marta would throw a "Good job" in Izzy's direction, and each time it would thrill her. She would work harder for the next few weeks, in the hopes that Marta would notice her and praise her again, and when no praise came, she would give up in despair. One time, after a particularly curt email from Marta on an edit she'd worked so hard on, Izzy even went so far as to update her résumé. But she'd never done anything with it. Why would she, when she had no idea if she was doing anything right? And that was one of the most depressing things about this job—she wanted guidance, mentoring, a way to get better at her job, a way to someday become the kind of editor Marta was. She wanted to edit great literary fiction, commercial fiction, and memoirs. But she had no idea if she'd even been learning anything.

And, yes, she'd wanted to write some of that great literary fiction herself. But she hadn't written a word in months.

She'd started to question if she really belonged here, if this job, if this career, was really for her. Something she barely wanted to admit to herself was that working at TAOAT had spoiled her previously uncomplicated love for books and reading. Reading used to be her greatest hobby, her source of relaxation, comfort, joy. Always reliable, always there for her. Now reading felt like homework, in a way that it never had back when she was in school. Now she felt guilty when she read for pleasure, because she knew there was always something else she should be reading, always another manuscript out there, always something Marta was waiting on, an author was waiting on, an agent was waiting on. It made reading stressful, when it never had been before.

Izzy sighed. She might as well deal with that pile of books she'd shoved to the side of her desk.

A few minutes later, Marta walked in, chatting with Gavin. As they got closer to her desk, it was clear they'd run into each other skiing over the weekend. Ah, that's why they'd both left early on Friday.

Izzy couldn't help but envy Gavin's relaxed, easy relationship with Marta, who still completely intimidated her. Even though Marta stressed her out constantly, Izzy wanted so much to impress her. She wished she had any idea how to do that.

Marta nodded at Izzy on her way to her office. That was more of a greeting than she usually got; Marta often didn't even seem to notice her there. Gavin stopped by her desk on the way to his own.

"Hi, Isabelle. How was your weekend?"

Izzy smiled at Gavin. "Good, thanks. How was yours? Did I hear you saying you were skiing?"

Izzy had heard the whole conversation—they hadn't been quiet—but she'd let Gavin tell her about it. He was always a little pompous and long-winded, but he'd also always been kind to her—he'd given her lots of advice about working with Marta and had always been something of a mentor for her. Lord knows Marta wasn't.

Months ago, Gavin had found her in the office, after hours, printing out the draft of her manuscript, and had asked to see it. She'd been nervous to show it to him—she hadn't really shown it to anyone at that point and had only really told Priya about it, but she'd handed the printed copy over to him then and there. He'd given it back to her a week later without any notes on it and a pat on the shoulder. She shouldn't have asked him what he thought; she'd known from the look on his face, but she couldn't help herself.

"It's a really sweet first effort, Isabelle," he'd said. "But . . . I'm not sure this is your path. I . . . could tell you were trying to be literary, but, well . . ." He stopped himself. "I don't want to hurt your feelings. I shouldn't say anything more."

And because Izzy was a glutton for punishment, she'd asked him to say more, and he had. At length. She hadn't written a word since.

Izzy shook that memory off and tried to pay attention to whatever Gavin was saying about Vermont or wherever he and Marta had been.

"Oh," he said after a few more minutes of talking about how he'd ridden up a ski lift with Jonathan Franzen. "You know how you were wondering last week about whether you'll get promoted this year—when I saw Marta on the slopes, we talked a bit about that, and . . . don't tell Marta I told you this?"

Izzy could barely breathe all of a sudden. "Of course not, I wouldn't," she said.

He smiled at her, but she could tell from his smile the news wasn't good. "Not this year, Isabelle. Maybe not at all, from the way Marta talked about you."

Sudden tears sprang to her eyes. Why did that hurt so much? She hadn't realized how much she'd still hoped until just this moment.

"But you know how she can be," he said. "Are you okay?"

Izzy refused to let anyone here see her cry. She put a smile on her face. The bright, cheerful one she always wore at work. The one she knew she had to wear.

"Oh, I'm fine. Yeah, I know how she can be. Thanks, Gavin, for letting me know what she said."

He smiled at her one more time and walked over to his desk.

Izzy turned to her computer and let the smile fall from her face. She wanted to leave the office, go outside to scream or cry, but it was too cold outside, and she couldn't cry in the bathroom where everyone could hear you. Instead, she clicked over to her travel itinerary. That made her smile for real. She needed some sunshine, she needed an adventure, she needed an escape. Even though she was only going to California for a few days, she would do everything she could to make them count.

CHAPTER TWO

Izzy and Priya walked into their hotel room and turned to each other with huge grins on their faces. There were palm trees and sunshine, right outside their hotel room. When Izzy had seen the Pacific Ocean out the window of the airplane as they'd descended into Los Angeles, she'd determined that she was going to enjoy this trip, no matter what.

Izzy unzipped her suitcase, and Priya laughed.

"You know we're only here for four days, right? I thought *I* packed a lot!"

Izzy shrugged. "I like to be prepared." Okay, sure, she'd definitely overpacked, but still, she liked to have options! Clothes for the conference, all her favorite pairs of pajamas so she could truly enjoy this hotel room, the workout clothes she knew she wouldn't wear but had packed anyway, a few sundresses out of sheer optimism that she'd get outside and have a chance to experience LA weather and not just hotel-ballroom air conditioning, the notebooks that she brought everywhere out of habit, even though she hadn't written in them in months, a few pairs of flats, and . . . yeah, nope, she was definitely not going to work out, she'd forgotten to pack her sneakers. Oh well.

Izzy looked around the room and sighed a little. She wished she'd had her own hotel room. She loved Priya, but after living with her parents for the past three years, she just wanted a place for at least a few days where she wasn't sharing space—or a bathroom!—with anyone.

After an afternoon where they'd both run back and forth and back and forth across a convention center at least a dozen times, Izzy and Priya returned to their room to change for the conference cocktail party.

As Izzy swiped some lipstick on, Priya grinned at her.

"I, for one," Priya said, "am ready for some free wine and tiny snacks. Are you?"

That sounded absolutely fantastic.

"I definitely am." She checked out Priya's outfit—a deep red dress, huge dangly gold earrings, and flat gold sandals. "Has anyone ever told you that you're devastatingly beautiful?"

Priya tossed her hair so her earrings jangled. "I was just about to say the same thing to you."

They both cracked up. A very drunk guy at a bar a few months before had told them each, separately, that she was devastatingly beautiful, and they'd been trading the compliment ever since.

"But really, that lipstick is amazing. Hot pink is good on you. And obviously I love the dress."

Izzy smiled as she looked at herself in the mirror. She liked this dress too. Priya had helped her buy it last summer. It was color-blocked, red and pink—a combination that she hadn't been sure she could pull off until Priya had gasped in glee when she'd come out of the dressing room. But Priya had been right, these colors looked great against her brown skin, especially with the hot-pink lipstick.

"I figure we're in California, might as well wear something other than black." She tucked one of her braids back into her big topknot and slung her badge over her neck. Okay, she was ready. "Come on, let's get there before people eat all the good snacks."

They made a beeline for the bar as soon as they walked into the cocktail party and managed to immediately snag glasses of the cheap white wine the bar was serving. Izzy turned around to tell Priya they should go find some of their other friends from TAOAT—and the snacks—when she came face-to-face with Josephine Henry.

“Isabelle, hello,” Josephine said. “So nice to see you again.”

“Hi, Josephine,” Izzy said. Did she sound normal? Probably not. She’d wondered, too often, how different things might be for her if she’d gotten that editorial assistant job with Josephine instead of with Marta. How much better Josephine would have been as a mentor, how much more she would have learned, how much more comfortable she’d be about speaking up.

Maybe none of this would be the case. Who knew? Maybe this was all about the grass being greener on the other side. But she didn’t think so.

Izzy shifted her wineglass from one hand to another and tried to look casual. “It’s great to see you,” she said. “How are you?”

Josephine smiled at her. “I’ll definitely be better once I have a glass of wine, you know how the first days of these things are, so rushed and busy.” She glanced down at Izzy’s name tag. “Oh, that’s right, you’re over at TAOAT now. Who are you working for?”

Priya melted away. She knew Izzy’s history with Josephine.

“Marta Wallace.” Izzy gestured to the room. “She’s here somewhere.”

Josephine laughed. “I’m sure I’ll run into her at some point tonight. It’s always so funny at these things—we all work just blocks from one another in New York, and yet we’re on the other side of the country and I run into people I haven’t seen in nine months.”

The bartender handed Josephine a glass of wine, and she nodded her thanks. Izzy started to back away—she assumed Josephine would need to go talk to more important people. But instead, Josephine stepped to the side and motioned for Izzy to follow her.

“I haven’t seen you for a while. How’s it going for you, Isabelle?”

Izzy knew how she was supposed to respond to questions like this, what people wanted to hear. She did it all the time.

“Oh, everything is great! Busy, but a lot of fun! Working in publishing is a dream come true, and it’s so exciting to be here!”

Whenever she said this, she put on a bright smile, she threw conviction in her voice, and her audience was satisfied. But somehow, this time, her heart wasn't in it. Maybe she'd done it too many times, maybe it was because she knew Josephine, at least a little, maybe it was because of what Gavin had told her the week before, but her words came out flat, almost angry.

Josephine winced. "Oof, that bad?"

Oh no. She had to recover from this. She didn't want Josephine to think she was ungrateful.

"I didn't mean to say it like that! It's just—"

Josephine stopped her. "Yes you did. Come on, this is me you're talking to."

Izzy was surprised into laughter. Josephine grinned, too, but from the look on her face, Izzy could tell she really wanted to know the answer.

"I'm okay," she said, after thinking about it for a little while. "There's a lot I love about working in publishing. But it can be hard sometimes. For . . . a lot of reasons."

Izzy could tell from the look in Josephine's eyes that she understood.

"Yeah, it really can be." Josephine gestured to the room. "When I started out, I was one of only a handful of Black people in these rooms. Now I'm one of maybe two handfuls." She sighed. "I really thought it would be better by now."

She felt so much more comfortable with Josephine than she did with Marta. If only . . . No, she couldn't think that way.

Josephine took another sip of wine. "Are you getting good work to do? Marta has some great authors over there."

Izzy nodded automatically. "Yeah, she does. But—" She swallowed. She needed to stop now. What was she doing, even thinking about confessing her feelings about Marta to anyone who wasn't Priya? This industry was way too small for that. "I'm learning a lot," she finished.

Josephine gave her a knowing look. "I'm sure you are," she said. "Learning how to juggle very well, I bet."

Izzy laughed. "Yes, absolutely." She needed to shift this conversation—she'd probably already said too much. "Anyway, I don't want to complain. I've had some really great opportunities."

"You don't have to pretend with me," Josephine said. "Look, the first few years especially can be really hard in this business, but—"

Someone touched Josephine on the shoulder.

"Josephine, there you are. Leah Jackson is here, she's looking for you."

Josephine's face lit up. "She made it! Fantastic!" She turned back to Izzy. "Isabelle, I have to run, but we'll continue this later, okay? If not here, let's get coffee or lunch when we're back in New York. I'll email you."

Izzy nodded. "I'd love that," she said.

She knew, though, that as much as Josephine might mean it in the moment, given how busy she was, the likelihood of her both remembering this conversation and then actually reaching out was slim to none. But then, Izzy wasn't sure she could deal with another pep talk about how you just had to stick it out a little while longer, how Marta would have never hired Izzy if she didn't see how talented and smart she was, how publishing could be a cruel business, but if you kept your head down and worked hard, you'd succeed.

Izzy turned away to go find Priya when she heard Marta's voice.

". . . the bane of my existence, you mean?"

Izzy stopped and took a sip of wine so she could pretend she wasn't listening. What—or who—could Marta be talking about? She turned slightly, to see who she was talking to. Hmm, that was Will Victor, another one of the big-deal editors at TAOAT. Izzy pulled out her phone to give herself cover for eavesdropping.

"I can't believe it's been a full year since you've heard anything from him," Will said.

Marta took a gulp of wine. "Well *over* a year! His agent gave me some bullshit about how hard he's working, but I haven't heard a peep from him, and haven't seen a page—haven't seen a word!—so I don't believe any of it."

Ahh. She must be talking about Beau Towers. The "bane of her existence" seemed strong—it wasn't like *Marta* sent emails to him every two weeks that got ignored. Though Marta was the one who had committed to a seven-figure book deal for him. To be fair, Marta probably didn't care about that—she'd just want the book.

"My poor assistant is probably tired of sending her little polite, cheerful emails to check in with him and his agent."

Izzy hid a grin when Marta said that. She definitely hadn't read any of Izzy's emails to Beau in a while.

"It's not even the blown deadline I care about," Marta continued. "Please, I expected that from him—for people like that, a deadline is more of a suggestion. But it seems like there's no path to ever actually getting a book out of him. I thought maybe being here in LA would mean I could beard him in his den, take him out for a drink and figure something out, but according to my assistant, he's not even in LA! He's holed up in some house in Santa Barbara! I don't want to cancel the deal—all that would do is make him pay the money back, and I don't care about the money. It's not *my* money. I want this book, Will! But I'm stumped on how to make it happen, and you know I'm rarely stumped."

Izzy had honestly never heard Marta admit defeat before. This was fascinating.

"At this point, you might have to threaten to cancel the deal to make anything happen," Will said. "Sometimes people like that only respond to threats. I don't understand why he's not just using a ghostwriter. Is it an ego thing? You've told him no one will know he didn't write it, right?"

Marta let out a sigh that was almost a hiss. "Of course I've told him that. So many times now. I did, my assistant did, his agent did. Do you know what he says to that? Nothing! I swear, I need someone to go to his house and pound on the door and ask him what's really going on with his book." Her eyes widened. "Actually, I'm brilliant. Yes, that's exactly what I need. The only way we're going to solve this is if someone goes straight to the source."

Izzy had no idea what made her do it. A burst of courage, a lightning bolt, a momentary lapse in judgment, the three sips of wine she'd had while she'd eavesdropped on this conversation. But suddenly, she turned around and took a step toward Marta.

"I'll do it," she said. "I'll go talk to Beau Towers."

CHAPTER THREE

"I don't know what got into me, Priya! Suddenly, I was talking with no control over my mouth, and when I stopped talking, I thought Marta was going to laugh at me, but instead she told me that it was a great idea and said she could always count on me?"

Izzy and Priya were back in their room at the end of the night, eating a pizza they'd had delivered to the hotel, and drinking vodka tonics. They'd busted into the mini bar, despite the astronomical prices. It was an emergency.

Priya shook her head. "Marta said she could always count on you? Did an alien take over her body?"

Izzy reached for her drink. She couldn't believe it either. "It seems unlikely to me, too, but I wouldn't have made it up even in my wildest dreams, so she must have said it. She even said I was the perfect person to do this!"

Priya's eyes opened wide. "Okay, now I'm concerned. Either an alien really did take over Marta's body, or this is some kind of a trap. Are you going to get out of this alive? Isn't Beau Towers a nightmare?"

Izzy grabbed another slice of pizza. "Of course he's a nightmare! Why do you think he got a book deal for his memoir, after all? He's basically your typical celebrity asshole—bar fights, car accidents, etc., different actress or model on his arm every other week, you know the type. The last major thing was when the press caught him on video screaming at his mom at his dad's funeral. Real classy. They had a messy divorce, but still."

Why, exactly, had she volunteered to do this again?

Priya reached for her phone. "Oh, that's right. Isn't his mom that gorgeous Black model?"

"Yeah, Nina Russell." Izzy knew far too much about Beau Towers at this point.

Priya took a sip of her drink as she looked through the results of her Google searches. "These pictures of his parents together are so weird. They didn't match at all. His dad was that director."

"Jim Towers, director and screenwriter." Izzy reached for her drink. "Anyway, the only response I've gotten to any of my dozens of emails was to the one I sent his agent asking for his mailing address so we could send him a basket of snacks at the holidays—that's the only reason we even know where he is."

Priya was still looking at her phone. "Oh my God. Isabelle Marlowe, I can't believe you told me all this nonsense about Beau Towers before you told me how hot he is! Well, that's if you like those big brawny guys, which I absolutely do. Who cares about a bar fight or two if he looks like that?"

Izzy laughed at Priya as she held her phone up. "You know me, Priya. I'm more into the skinny poet types."

Priya got up and went back to the mini bar. "Yes, unfortunately I do know that, and look where THAT has gotten you."

Priya had a point there. That skinny poet type Izzy had dated for a few months last summer spent most of his time playing video games and didn't seem to write much poetry . . . or spend much time with Izzy.

Priya grabbed two more tiny bottles of vodka and handed one to Izzy. "I can't believe you're actually doing this." She poured the liquor into her glass and added tonic. "You'll have to tell me how Santa Barbara is; I'll be there for my cousin's wedding next month." She shook her head. "I can't believe that on Wednesday, when we all fly back to New York, you're going to just drive up to Beau Towers's house and knock on his door."

Izzy laughed out loud. "It sounds ridiculous, doesn't it? The man hasn't answered a single one of the twenty-nine emails I've sent him—I counted—or any of the ones Marta sent, so why would he answer the door when I knock, if he's even there? But honestly, I don't even care. I get a whole extra day in California. Maybe I actually *will* get some time by the pool with a book."

And another day of not being in the office. Just the thought of it made her happy.

"Exactly," Priya said. "Plus, Marta might be just looking for some ammunition to make him finally get a ghostwriter. If he ignores—or even worse, yells at you—he'll look like a monster. Maybe that's just what she wants."

"Good point," Izzy said. "That sounds like the kind of thing Marta would do. I mean, obviously, I still want to surprise everyone and come back to New York waving a manuscript in my hand. You know, the one that Beau Towers has been hiding and decided to turn in only because I managed to talk him into it."

Priya laughed and raised her glass. "Cheers to that," she said.

So Wednesday morning, Izzy left the hotel to drive to Santa Barbara. At first, the journey was boring: freeways, traffic, etc. Whatever, she didn't mind; she had her favorite playlist to keep her company, and her rental car had a sunroof that she took full advantage of. But then all of a sudden, the freeway went around a turn, and the ocean was right *there*, in front of her. She looked out at the ocean, sparkling in the sun, and smiled. This was the California she'd hoped to see.

She got off the freeway and followed the slightly confusing GPS directions toward Beau Towers's address. There were palm trees everywhere, huge mountains in the distance, and all the buildings had terra-cotta tiled roofs, even the convenience stores. As she drove up into the hills, the houses got bigger, and had lots of cacti and other enormous succulents in their front yards. Later she should make sure to take pictures for Priya, who was obsessed with the three tiny succulents she'd kept alive on her desk for the past year.

Finally, her phone trilled, "You have arrived." She pulled up outside a big pink stucco house and threw her car into park.

She checked the address, just to make sure she was in the right place. Yes, this was it. It didn't look anything like she'd expected, though now she didn't know what she'd expected. Maybe something forbidding, a little scary, surrounded by, like, a creaky gate and dying bushes or something. But no, this seemed like all the houses she'd driven by on the way here: huge and sprawling, with a terra-cotta roof, a green vine with bright red flowers growing over the gate, palm trees and succulents out front. It was even kind of . . . charming?

And now she had to walk up to that house, knock on the door, and just . . . ask for Beau Towers? She was suddenly nervous about this. She'd been fine up until now.

She took a deep breath. Okay. She was going to do this.

She got out of the car and walked along the uphill path toward the house and the red tile front stairs to the big wooden front door and rang the doorbell. When the door opened, Izzy steeled herself for Beau Towers to yell at her.

But a woman opened the door. She had long dark hair, a smile on her face, and appeared to be around thirty or so. Was she Beau Towers's girlfriend or something? She looked too normal and friendly for that, especially given the models that Beau usually dated, but you never knew with guys like him.

"Hi," she said. She glanced at the street, then back to Izzy. "Is it a delivery?"

Izzy knew she had only a few seconds before the woman closed the door on her. She talked fast.

"Hi! No, not a delivery. My name is Isabelle Marlowe, I'm an editorial assistant at Tale as Old as Time publishing house, and I'm here to talk to Beau Towers." The woman's smile faded, but she took the business card Izzy handed her. Thank goodness she'd brought them along with her to the conference. "I work with Marta Wallace; she's the editor of his forthcoming memoir. He's a little . . . behind on it, and Marta asked me to come here to chat with Beau about his book, find out what's wrong, figure out how we can help."

The woman shook her head. "Hi, Isabelle. I'm so sorry you've come all this way, but I don't think Beau will talk to you."

Izzy had expected that. "If you could just check, see if there's a way I could chat with him for a few minutes? I just want to make sure he knows how much we care about getting this book out into the world, and that we're willing to assist him in any way he needs. We'll do anything we can to help him succeed."

The woman looked at her closely, a faint smile still on her face. Izzy couldn't figure out what she was thinking. For some reason, even though she'd thought of this whole mission as pointless, now that she was here, she wanted to win this thing. Granted, she didn't think she could deliver an actual manuscript, like she'd joked to Priya, but she still wanted *some* sort of win. She hadn't had a win in so long. She wanted to get into the house, talk to Beau, convince him to let them hire a ghostwriter so they could get the book done. If she could even just convince him to reply to one of her emails, it would be huge. And then she could go back to New York triumphant, and with *something* to show Marta.

Finally, the woman nodded. "Wait here," she said, before she turned and walked down the long hallway.

She hadn't closed the door all the way, which meant that less than a minute later, Izzy heard a loud "ABSOLUTELY NOT" from somewhere inside the house. Ahh, well, there was the mythical Beau Towers. As charming as she'd expected him to be.

The woman walked back to the front door a few seconds later. "I tried, but he says he doesn't want to talk to you," she said. "I'm so sorry."

Izzy smiled at her. Whoever this woman was, she seemed nice. If she was dating Beau Towers, Izzy felt sorry for her.

"Thanks so much for trying," she said. "I really appreciate it. And no need to apologize, it was a long shot, but worth a try. At least I got a mini vacation in Santa Barbara out of this."

The woman smiled back at her. "Oh, that's good. How long are you in town for?"

Izzy laughed. "When I said mini, I meant mini. I got here just now from a conference in LA and I have about four hours before I have to drive to LAX to fly back to New York. But I'm going to make the most of it. Maybe eat some tacos, go to the beach—it's about twenty-eight degrees in New York now, so I want to enjoy this weather while I can."

The woman's smile got wider. "I'll tell you just where to go. There's a great taqueria, not on the beach, but not too far away. Tell them Michaela sent you, they'll hook you up."

Izzy pulled out her phone to jot down the name of the taqueria Michaela gave her.

"Thanks, Michaela," she said. "I appreciate it." She took a deep breath. "And can you just tell Beau that I said he can email me anytime about the memoir? I'm not an expert, or anything, maybe he'd rather talk to Marta, but if he just needs some encouragement, or reassurance, or anything like that, I'm happy to help." Why had she said any of this? Oh well, it's not like she had anything to lose here.

Michaela gave her that look again. Like she could see right through her. "Sure, Isabelle," she said. "I'll let him know." She slipped on the sandals by the front door. Sandals in February, amazing. "Here, I'll walk you to your car. I need to check the mail anyway."

And she probably wanted to make sure Izzy actually left.

They walked down the sloping path together, and Michaela turned toward the mailbox at the bottom of the path. And then she slipped, or tripped over something, so fast that Izzy couldn't reach out a hand, and she fell, right at Izzy's feet.

"Oh no!" Izzy bent down. "Are you okay?"

Michaela looked up at her. "I think I twisted my ankle."

Izzy knelt down. "Can I help you up? Let's see how it feels."

Michaela held on to Izzy as she stood up, and then winced as she tried to put weight on her left ankle.

"Do you think you can walk up to the door?" Izzy asked.

Michaela tried to take a step, and stopped. "Can you help me inside?"

Izzy put her arm around Michaela as they turned to the door. "Of course. You need to get ice on that."

They moved, very slowly, back up to the front door.

"Thanks so much for your help," Michaela said. "I don't want to get in the way of your mini vacation."

"What was I going to do, leave you sitting on the ground?" Izzy said. "The tacos will be there."

When they finally got to the front steps Izzy helped Michaela up them and through the door.

"I hate to ask," Michaela said, "but can you help me into the kitchen?"

Izzy pushed the door open. "No problem."

They made their slow way down the long hallway. Izzy took the opportunity to glance around to see what Beau Towers's house was like. The floor was tile, the doors were all big and wooden—and mostly closed—and there was lots of art on the walls. Hmm, this wasn't the kind of house she'd expected Beau Towers to live in. It was a lot homier than she would have thought.

They finally got to the kitchen. It was sunny and warm, with fancy appliances and a cozy-looking breakfast nook with a round kitchen table under a big window. Izzy helped Michaela to a seat at the table.

"Here, sit down and put your ankle up. I'll get you some ice."

Izzy grabbed a dish towel off a hook on her way to the refrigerator. She pulled open the freezer and took out a bag of frozen peas. It was sort of comforting to see that even this rich guy had frozen peas in his freezer.

"Here." She wrapped the bag in the dish towel and handed it to Michaela. "Put this on your ankle, but give me a second—I'll fill up another bag with ice so you have more than one ice pack."

Michaela set the bag of peas on her ankle and let out a sigh before she looked up at Izzy. "I would say you don't have to do all of that, but I imagine that wouldn't do any good, would it?"

Izzy shook her head. "None at all, so I'm glad you didn't bother to say it. Now, do you have any of those gallon plastic bags? The ones that seal."

Michaela pointed. "That drawer, to the right of the dishwasher."

Izzy pulled a bag out and surveyed the ice maker on the fridge. "Oh wow, multiple kinds of ice. Perfect." She pushed a button and crushed ice flew out of the ice maker and straight into the plastic bag. "Now, put one underneath, and one on top. Wrap your ankle in the towel first, though, otherwise it might be a little too cold. And remember that these frozen peas have been used as an ice pack."

Michaela laughed. "I should label them somehow, just so I know."

Okay, Izzy *had* to ask.

"Do you live here? Are you and Beau . . . ?"

Michaela stared at her for a moment, then laughed very hard. "Oh, no, no. I'm his assistant." She gestured to the kitchen. "And also his cook. I do a little bit of everything around here. But no, I don't live here. And no. We aren't."

Ahh, okay. Though what Beau Towers needed an assistant for, in his long days of not responding to emails and not turning in his book, Izzy had no idea. But then, rich people lived very different lives than people like her.

"Got it." She was embarrassed now that she'd asked. "Sorry, I was just . . . wondering." She should probably get out of Beau Towers's house now and stop asking his assistant questions. "I should go. Oh, wait—you should take some ibuprofen. Do you have any?"

Michaela hesitated, then shook her head.

"Okay, hold on," Izzy said. "I think I have some in my bag." She turned to grab her bag from where she'd set it on the counter and rummaged through it for a minute. Finally, she found the bottle.

"Who the hell are you, and what are you doing in my house?"

She slowly looked up. And that's when she saw him. Leaning against the kitchen door and staring at her.

He was big; that was the first impression she got about Beau Towers. Tall, muscular, solid. How had she not heard him walking toward the kitchen?

He looked like an unkempt, unstyled, and very unhappy version of his publicity pictures. Light brown skin, curly hair, a very unruly beard. Gray sweatpants that looked like they'd seen better days, a black T-shirt, and a hoodie that probably cost more than Izzy's entire outfit.

And he looked furious. Angry and mean. Before she'd worked for Marta, she might have been scared of that look. But now she just smiled and walked over to him. What did it matter if this guy was mean to her? She might as well introduce herself to him, since she was here. And she'd better do it before he yelled at her.

"Hi, Mr. Towers, I'm Isabelle Marlowe, Marta Wallace's editorial assistant. I've sent you a few emails, you might recognize the name? I came here to—"

"I said I didn't want to talk to you. Did you break into my house to ask me about a book? You should leave." He raised his voice. "Now."

She'd expected him to yell at her, and now he had. She hoped Marta would be happy, at least.

"She didn't break in," Michaela said. "She helped me inside after I did this."

Beau looked over Izzy's head at Michaela, and his whole face changed. He rushed over to her.

"Oh no, Kettle, what happened? Are you okay?"

Michaela gestured to her ankle. "I'll be okay, but only because of Isabelle here—I went out to check the mail, and I slipped. Thank goodness she was there. She saw me fall, got me inside, and got me ice. Otherwise, I'd probably still be sitting out there shouting for someone to help me in."

Izzy waved that away. "I was happy to help."

"Have you taken anything?" Beau said to Michaela. "You should take some ibuprofen." He looked around, like it was going to appear in front of him somehow.

Izzy sighed. "I was just saying that. I have some right here."

Beau smiled at her for a half second, before he apparently remembered who she was and scowled again. "I'll get water," he said to Michaela, and stalked over to the cabinet.

When Izzy handed the bottle of pills to Michaela, Michaela gave her a very pointed look in Beau's direction. Was she trying to tell her to do what Izzy thought she was trying to tell her to do? Michaela nodded. She was apparently a mind reader. Izzy might as well try, right?

She turned around to face him. "Mr. Towers, I'd love to chat with you about your memoir. It's okay that you're behind on getting it to us, really. We just want to open the lines of communication and help you with it, in any way we can. We can set you up with a ghostwriter—that would be totally confidential, of course. Or Marta or I can talk through an outline, or pages, or a particular chapter with you, whatever the bottleneck is. And I'm great at pep talks, so I'm always available for those, if that's what you need—there's no shame in it!"

Beau set the glass of water down in front of Michaela, that furious look back on his face. "Now it's time for you to go."

Michaela caught Izzy's eye and motioned for her to keep going. So, for some reason, she did.

"Mr. Towers, we understand that it can be scary for authors to admit what the problem is, but we've seen it all, really. We're happy to help, in whatever way you need."

She'd given some version of this speech—either via email or on the phone—to various authors of Marta's, the ones who'd seemed stalled, or had fallen behind, or had sent her those emails where she could feel the panic between the lines. Marta never said anything like this to her authors—it was far too encouraging for her—but Izzy had started giving pep talks like this after she'd overheard other editors and their assistants on the phone with authors. It always seemed to help; this speech usually made people feel better, reassured. But Beau somehow looked angrier than when he'd walked into the kitchen. He let out a bark of laughter.

"You? You've seen it all? What are you, like twenty-two?"

Izzy forced herself not to roll her eyes. She had good genes, okay?

"I'm twenty-five." Not that it was any of his business. Plus, she happened to know he was exactly one year older than her. "But when I say 'we,' I'm not talking about just me; I'm talking about the collective knowledge of the team at TAOAT." He was still staring at her, with that superior, disbelieving look on his face, and she'd suddenly had it with him. Instead of being nice, she said exactly what was on her mind. "You may have realized that a memoir is too much for you to handle. That's okay, we understand that! Not everyone is cut out for this! We can easily connect you with a ghostwriter to do the heavy lifting. You won't have to worry about a thing."

Okay, yes, fine, that was kind of bitchy, but he'd asked for it. She might smile at him, the same smile she wore at work, but she refused to pretend it was okay for him to talk to her like she was dirt under his feet.

He looked at her with fury in his eyes. She just smiled wider.

"I don't need a ghostwriter," he almost spat at her. "You people think I'm stupid, don't you?"

Izzy made her voice as peppy as it could be. "Oh, of course not!" she said. "It's no judgment on you! We know how . . . busy your schedule is. It's just an offer—we want to explore all avenues here."

Beau bared his teeth at her, in what he possibly meant as a smile. "Fine. You want to help me in any way you can?" he asked, in a clear imitation of her voice. "You want to give me pep talks? How's this: I want you to give me a pep talk every day. How does that sound?"

Did this guy think he was going to trip her up somehow? After all of Marta's unreasonable requests?

"Whatever I can do to help, Mr. Towers. Would you like me to email you, or call you at a specific time, or . . . ?"

He laughed again. "No, you don't get it. You can stay here and give me your cheerful little pep talks in person." He threw out his arm and gestured toward the hallway. "We have plenty of room, as I'm sure you saw."

She knew this jerk was expecting her to back down, but she'd call his bluff. "I'd be happy to do that, Mr. Towers. My luggage is right out in my car."

He glared at her again. "Give me your car keys, I'll go get your luggage now," he said.

Wait, but . . . Okay, he couldn't actually mean this.

She couldn't be the one to chicken out, though. She dug in her tote bag and handed him the keys to the rental car. He didn't thank her.

"Michaela, it looks like I'll have a guest for dinner." He turned back to her. "Meet me at the stairs, I'll take you to your room. And stop calling me Mr. Towers. It's just Beau."

And then he turned around and stalked out of the kitchen as Izzy stared after him.

CHAPTER FOUR

How had she gotten herself into this?

Beau couldn't have been serious, could he?

"Any dietary restrictions?" Michaela smiled at her. "Food allergies I should know about? For dinner tonight, and for your stay here, I mean."

Izzy stared at her. Michaela didn't really think she was going to *stay*—for dinner or anything else—did she? But Michaela was looking at her expectantly. So after a few seconds, Izzy shook her head.

"Um, no. No food allergies."

She should be at the beach by now, reading a book and eating tacos! Why did Michaela have to fall down? Why had Izzy bothered to help her all the way into the house? Why had she lingered to provide her with ice, and ibuprofen, and sympathy? Why hadn't she fled this house as soon as possible?

"Okay, but is there anything you hate?" Michaela asked. "Mushrooms, eggplant, blue cheese? Are you a vegetarian? I do most of the cooking around here, so I want to make sure it's stuff you like."

She was supposed to be on a flight tonight out of LAX! An airport two hours away from here! Why was she talking about her food preferences with Beau Towers's assistant???

"Oh, um, I like all those things fine. And no, not a vegetarian. Mostly I just hate anything that jiggles."

Michaela gave her a strange look. "Anything that jiggles? What do you mean?"

People always thought this was weird about her.

"You know, custards, pudding, Jell-O—anything that if you poke it, it jiggles. It's a texture thing, I can't stand it."

Michaela laughed for a while. Izzy didn't think it was quite that funny. She also didn't know why she was talking about jiggly food when she'd just handed the keys to her rental car to Beau Towers so he could bring in her suitcase. What was going on?

"That won't be a problem, don't worry. And if you think of anything else, just let me know, okay?"

Izzy wanted to ask why someone as nice and competent as Michaela would work for someone like Beau, but she knew she couldn't ask that. But oh God, Beau must be furious at Michaela for letting her in the house.

"I'm sorry, Michaela. I put you in a bad situation there—letting me in after he'd told you not to."

Michaela waved that away. "Oh, it's fine. Beau's bark is a lot worse than his bite."

Izzy wasn't so sure about that. Her doubt must have showed on her face because Michaela laughed.

"No, really, don't worry. Beau and I have known each other for a long time." She nodded toward the door. "Speaking of, he's probably waiting to bring you to your room."

"Oh. Right." Izzy picked up her tote bag. "Okay. I'll go . . . meet him, then."

Michaela smiled at her. "Glad to have you here."

That made one person, at least.

Izzy walked out of the kitchen and down the long tile hallway. She couldn't believe she'd let Beau Towers get to her, and that she'd snapped back at him. She never did things like that—she got mad, sure, but she kept her anger buried, vented to Priya or another one of her friends later. But she'd antagonized Beau Towers on purpose. And the weird part was, she'd sort of enjoyed it. And now he was about to show her to a guest room in his house?

Marta would flip out as soon as Izzy told her about this, which she would have to do as soon as she got to the room. Pro: At least she had something more to tell Marta about Beau Towers. Con: absolutely everything else.

Izzy stopped in the entryway to wait and looked up at the enormous, curving staircase. It looked like something from a fancy magazine, with wide stairs and big gleaming banisters and a chandelier at the top. This wasn't a staircase a person would simply walk down, it was a staircase you would *descend*. Preferably, in a long, trailing gown.

A few seconds later, Beau opened the front door with a bang and shattered the moment. See, this was why people told her that she read too many books—all she had to do was see one staircase, and she'd inserted herself into a fairy tale.

"Follow me," he growled at her as he started up the staircase. She couldn't help but notice that he picked up her overstuffed suitcase like it was as light as a feather.

They walked up the staircase, then went down a long hallway. Izzy wondered what was behind all the doors they walked by. Did he really live alone in this huge place? Granted, what she'd seen of Santa Barbara was gorgeous, but she still wondered what he was doing here.

"Here." Beau threw open the door at the end of the hallway and set her suitcase down. "See you at dinner. It's at six. Don't be late."

And with that, he stalked away.

Izzy waited until he was all the way down the hall and then pulled her suitcase into the room and closed the door.

And then she leaned back against the door, closed her eyes, and finally laughed out loud. What else could she do? What was even her life right now? Was she in the midst of torpedoing her publishing career? Strangely, she didn't even care—Marta was never going to promote her anyway, she already knew that. At least she'd get a good story out of this: "Did I ever tell you about the time I broke into Beau Towers's house?"

Obviously, she'd have to embellish a little bit.

She didn't think there was any possibility she'd actually spend the night here—she'd have to figure out a way to leave by the time dinner was over—but she had to at least check out this room, for the sake of the future stories she'd tell. She hoped that Beau would carry her suitcase back down all those stairs on her way out.

Priya would *die* when she heard about this.

"Oh wow." Izzy walked toward the huge window at the far end of the room. It faced west, so she could see the sun, already making its way toward the horizon, the green downhill slope just beneath the house, the rest of the city below, and the ocean, off in the distance. She felt like she could look out this window forever. She wouldn't mind having to deal with Beau Towers if she got to have this view for a little while longer. He was a lot easier to deal with than most people in publishing; overt aggression almost felt refreshing after this past year. At least she knew where she stood with him.

Speaking of. She had to get this email to Marta over with.

She dropped down onto the bed and pulled her phone out of her bag.

To: Marta Wallace
From: Isabelle Marlowe
Re: Beau Towers

Hi, Marta—
I talked with Beau Towers a little while ago. He's still pretty resistant to discussing his memoir, but we're going to have dinner tonight here at his house and hopefully talk about it a bit more. I'm not sure if I'll

make that flight tonight, so I'll have the travel agent change it to tomorrow, if that works?

Isabelle

Izzy bit her lip and pressed send. Marta emailed her back almost immediately.

To: Isabelle Marlowe
From: Marta Wallace
Re: Beau Towers

I knew you were the right person to deal with him. Keep me posted.

For Marta, the message was almost effusive. Izzy shook her head and got up to check out the bathroom. She pushed open the door, and her mouth dropped open. This was the bathroom of her dreams.

The floor was blue tile, the walls were pale blue, and coupled with the big window over the bathtub that looked out over the world, it almost felt like she was outside, part of the sky and the water.

And that bathtub. Izzy stepped closer to it. It was a huge, deep, claw-foot tub, with little gold flecks on the feet. Had they originally been all gold? The window was just above the bathtub, so you could enjoy the view while you were in the bath. She couldn't wait until later that night, after dinner, when she sank into a hot bath with her book and . . .

Izzy tore herself away from her daydream. She'd forgotten. She wasn't going to be here after dinner. Part of her wanted to take a bath right now, just so she'd get to experience this incredible bathtub, but it felt weird to just take a bath in the middle of the afternoon in

Beau Towers's house. Plus, she didn't want to unpack her tightly packed suitcase to dig out her toiletries and shower cap and everything else.

She finally peed, washed her hands, admired the excellent lighting (due to that big window) in the mirror, checked out the shower—which was perfectly nice, but nothing in comparison to that bathtub—and went back into the bedroom. Before this dinner, she had to text Priya.

> Omg, Priya. I met Beau Towers. He's terrible. But. I'm currently in his house???? And I'm supposed to have dinner with him, here, tonight??? And give him a "pep talk"???
>
> Don't ask me how I got myself into this, I have no idea. Actually, no, I THINK I sort of dared him. I don't know what's gotten into me?!? Marta is delighted (for her, obvs). Will keep you posted.

Priya's response was more satisfying than Marta's had been.

> OMG what!!!
>
> I can't wait to hear EVERYTHING!!!!

A few hours later, Izzy walked down the big staircase on her way to dinner. She let her hand trail along the banister and sighed. She should have changed into that maxi dress that was in her suitcase. How many opportunities would she have to sweep down a staircase in a long dress? This was the first one in her lifetime, as a matter of fact. She should have taken advantage of it!

She laughed at herself as she walked down the hall toward the kitchen. She stopped in the doorway and saw Michaela taking plates out of a cabinet.

"Hi, Isabelle," she said. "Dinner is next door, in the dining room."

Izzy would rather stay here in the kitchen, with Michaela, than go into the dining room, with Beau.

"Okay, but can I take those plates from you? Shouldn't you be resting your ankle?"

Michaela waved her away. "Don't worry about me. I iced it for a while; Beau found me an ACE bandage; I'm feeling a lot better. Go sit down. Can I bring you some wine?"

Wine. That was exactly what Izzy needed after this incredibly strange day.

"I can see from your face that the answer is yes," Michaela said.

Izzy laughed. "Okay, yes, the answer is yes. Thank you very much."

She followed Michaela into the dining room and sat down. Michaela set the plates down on the table and then disappeared back into the kitchen.

Izzy was relieved she'd gotten down here before Beau. She'd thought about coming down late, just because he'd told her not to, but that felt childish. And yes, fine, she was a little apprehensive about this dinner—okay, *very* apprehensive about it—but she might as well be professional. Hopefully, she'd get to sip some wine and take a deep breath before she had to give Beau Towers some sort of pep talk. Part of her wanted to give him a snarky speech about perseverance, since the guy had blown off a two-million-dollar book deal, but she'd probably doled out enough snark for the day.

Michaela walked back in with two bottles of wine in her hands. "Red or white? There's also beer, if you want, and I can probably throw you together a margarita, if you'd like?"

Beau Towers just . . . lived like this, all the time. With someone offering to throw him together a margarita at 5:55 every evening. Incredible.

"White wine is great, thank you." Izzy sniffed. "Oh my goodness, what smells so good?"

Michaela grinned at her. "I thought that since I cheated you out of your tacos today, I'd make them for dinner." She poured Izzy a very full glass of wine. "Fish tacos, since that's what we had the ingredients for. I hope that's okay?"

Izzy suddenly realized that she hadn't eaten since that granola bar on the drive from LA. God, she was starving.

"More than okay, thank you so much."

Izzy took a sip of wine when Michaela went back to the kitchen. Either it was because she was in desperate need of wine or this wine was of far better quality than she usually got, but it tasted incredible.

"Tortillas, fish, slaw, rice, salsa," Michaela said as she set two big platters on the table. "I'll be in the kitchen for the next few minutes if you need anything, but I have to take off soon to go pick up my son."

Was Michaela really going to leave her here, alone in the house with Beau Towers? She'd kind of forgotten that Michaela didn't live here. Why did she suddenly want to cling to this woman she'd only met a few hours ago? She picked up her glass of wine and took another big sip.

"Um, thank you for dinner," Izzy said. "The food looks great."

Michaela smiled at her. "I hope you enjoy it. See you tomorrow, Isabelle."

Mmm, Izzy doubted that.

While she waited for Beau, Izzy sipped her wine and looked out the window. The sun had set, but now she could see the lights from the city, shining all the way down the hill, and the darkness of the ocean in the distance. She was suddenly glad she'd volunteered for this ridiculous thing and that she'd antagonized Beau Towers, if only to see this house, and this amazing view. And to drink this amazing wine.

"Aren't you going to eat?"

Izzy barely managed not to jump at the sound of Beau Towers's voice. Why didn't he make any noise as he walked through this house? Some warning would have been nice.

She turned to look at him standing by the door, scowling at her. Of course. "I was waiting for you," she said. "I didn't want to be rude."

Beau let out a huff at that and gestured to the food as he sat down across from her. "Be my guest."

Izzy supposed he meant that as an invitation to serve herself, so she did. She even poured herself some more wine. Why not? She took a bite of a taco and almost let out a moan. These might be the best tacos she'd ever had. Had Michaela made all this, just spontaneously? And with a sprained ankle? She tried the slaw and opened her eyes wide. Wow, rich people really did have great lives. She'd only given herself two tacos, but she was already looking forward to her third. Maybe even her fourth. She might as well take advantage of this while she could.

She took another sip of wine and glanced at Beau. Why was he looking at her like that? Like just the sight of her made him mad. He was the one who had invited her to dinner, or did he not remember that? Well, if that counted as an invitation.

He looked away for a second and then looked back at her. "Okay, go," he said.

Izzy tilted her head and looked at him. Wow, that tone in his voice infuriated her. "Excuse me?" Had no one ever taught this guy to say please or thank you? "Go?"

He nodded. "Yes, go. You said you gave great pep talks. Well? Show me what you can do."

Izzy stared at him for a moment over her glass of wine. Fine, okay. She would show him what she could do.

"Okay, you want to get right to it." She set her wineglass down on the table. "Great. Why don't you tell me what your struggles have been with the book so far? When I know what you're dealing with, I'll be better able to help and to give advice."

Beau picked up a taco. "No," he said, and took a bite.

Izzy took a deep breath. "No?"

He finished chewing. "No. I'm not going to tell you my 'struggles.'" That sarcastic tone in his voice made her want to throw her glass of wine in his face. She took a gulp of it, just to remind herself not to waste good wine. "I don't have to tell you anything. That wasn't part of the deal. The deal was that you give me a pep talk. So, like I said. Go."

He'd apparently invited her to dinner just to make her perform for him. Luckily, she *was* good at this. In college, she'd worked as a writing tutor, and while a lot of that work was on the page, even more of it was talking to writers, encouraging them, listening to their problems and helping them figure out solutions. It was one of the things that had made her good at this part of her job. Izzy took another long sip of wine and set her glass on the table.

"Okay. One thing I often tell writers is to just get words on the page. It's impossible to work with a blank page, but as long as you have a first draft—no matter how bad you think it is, or how much work you think it needs—that's a victory right there. I know it feels overwhelming to write a whole book—don't think about it like that. Just think about it step-by-step, page by page."

He was looking straight at her, and seemed to be . . . listening? Paying attention? She hadn't really expected that. She drained the wine from her glass and kept going.

"Just give yourself an hour a day to start with. You can even break it up into thirty minutes at a time, or even fifteen minutes, if you're feeling antsy. Just write as much as you can during that time, and don't let yourself edit or stress about it, just go."

Izzy was getting invested in this. Maybe, despite everything, she could actually get through to Beau Towers.

"You also don't have to write in chronological order! I know that trips people up a lot—they hit a difficult scene, or in a memoir, a difficult period in their life, and they just stall. Instead, you can jump around. Write your way into it. Start with favorite memories as a kid, or a pivotal moment in your life, a conversation you overheard once that you always think about, a time you stayed up all night, whatever stands out to—"

Beau burst out laughing. It was that mean laughter again. Directed at her.

No wonder this jerk lived alone in this house. He'd clearly been expelled from society.

"Is that all you've got?" he said, still with that mean look on his face. "Start with a pivotal moment in my life. Wow, what insight. Anything else?"

Izzy looked at him for one long moment. She forced herself to blink back the angry tears that had come to her eyes.

She was furious at herself for almost crying because of something Beau Towers, of all people, said to her. But she was even more furious at Beau Towers for saying it.

She didn't have to do this. She was already sick of her job, and she'd already done far more than she'd had to here. She neither wanted to, nor had to, smile at this asshole.

Or even sit there and eat with him.

She stood up and dropped her napkin on the table.

"Wait, where are you going?" he said as she walked to the door. "Aren't you going to eat?"

She turned around and looked him in the eye. "That wasn't part of the deal," she said. And walked out the door.

CHAPTER FIVE

Izzy ran up the staircase to her room. She couldn't believe she'd wasted an actual good pep talk on Beau Towers. She knew he was a jerk; she should have just given him some lackluster "we believe in you" nonsense, and then ignored him and eaten as many of Michaela's delicious fish tacos as she could handle before he told her to go away.

The worst part was that for a brief moment, while she'd been talking to him, she'd thought she'd seen a real person behind that beast sitting across the table from her. She'd thought, for a few seconds, that he was listening to her, wanted to hear what she had to say. It had felt, just for a little while, like this was the job she not only wanted to be doing but was meant to be doing. So she'd actually tried to help him. She'd tried to give him good advice.

She should have known it was all a trick.

She felt silly for being duped, but most of all, she felt silly for how disappointed she'd felt. Some part of her had thought she could really be the one to get through to Beau Towers. Well, that made her feel ridiculous.

But damn, had it felt good to walk out on him. She never let herself do things like that. She'd always just smiled, taken notes, done what she had to do, worked as hard as she could, and didn't let people see her mad. Often, she didn't even let herself really get mad. She knew being angry, let alone showing it, was dangerous for someone like her, working in the industry she wanted to work in. No matter how she felt, she just had to act cheerful, easygoing, not let anything get to her, and definitely never let anyone see her angry. But now she was furious and she'd let Beau Towers know it. And it felt great.

She walked into her room, ready to grab her tote bag and her suitcase and leave. She'd drive to LA, maybe see if she could still get on that original flight at LAX, maybe just stay at an airport hotel that night until her flight the next day, whatever. She just had to get the hell out of here.

She grabbed her suitcase, then stumbled. And then she sat down hard on the bed.

Oh no. The wine. She'd had two glasses of wine—two large glasses—in the past hour. Less than an hour really. And all she'd eaten today was breakfast at the hotel, a granola bar on the road, and three bites of a fish taco. And while she wasn't *exactly* drunk, she was certainly tipsy. She couldn't drive anywhere now, much less all the way back to Los Angeles. She could kick herself for asking Michaela for wine in the first place.

Now she just had to sit here, in this stupid, perfect room with the incredible view and comfortable bed and glorious bathtub, and wait until she was sober enough to drive.

She wished she could tiptoe downstairs and get some food. A few more tacos would certainly help absorb all of that wine. But Beau was probably sitting there in the dining room eating the entire platter of food like some lord of a manor; she couldn't ruin her dramatic exit by walking back in to pick up her plate.

She dug through her tote bag to see if she had any more snacks in there. Nothing.

She sat there fuming for ten minutes. She was mad at herself for not stocking her bag with more snacks . . . no, wait, she was mad at herself for eating all her snacks already, she was mad at Beau Towers for being such a jerk, and she was mad at California for being so stupid and big that she'd had to rent a car to drive to his house instead of just taking a rideshare like in a civilized place.

Was that a knock at the door?

Normal Izzy would have gone to the door, smiled at that jerk Beau Towers, and told him yes she knew he wanted her the hell out of his house, she was on her way. But angry, tipsy, out-of-character Izzy ignored the knock. Even though she thought for a second it might be Michaela, who maybe hadn't actually left, who maybe had come all the way up the stairs on her sprained ankle, she didn't move. No matter who was at her door right now, she didn't want to deal with them. Thank goodness whoever was there went away after just two knocks.

A few minutes later she got up. She definitely wasn't okay to drive yet, but she'd just go out to the car with her stuff anyway, sit there, and sober up, instead of here. Plus, she'd been sure she'd had a bag of potato chips; maybe it had fallen out of her bag in the car.

She slung her tote bag over her shoulder and grabbed her suitcase. She opened the door and stopped. There, sitting in front of her door, was a tray full of food. A plate of fish tacos—her half-eaten one, plus three more—a bowl full of slaw, and a stack of chocolate chip cookies. And another glass of wine.

Where had all this come from?

She poked her head out the door and looked from side to side. No one was out there. So she picked up the tray and brought it back inside the room and kicked the door closed on the way.

It must have been Michaela at the door, after all. Now Izzy felt bad that she hadn't answered it. Michaela had come all the way up those stairs with a sprained ankle, carrying all this food. Izzy hoped Beau paid her very well.

She should probably refuse to eat this, out of principle or something, but she was too hungry and still too tipsy to be worried about principles. She picked up her half-eaten taco and finished it. It was still just as good, even lukewarm.

It wasn't until she reached for her second taco that she saw the ripped piece of paper under the bowl of slaw. She pulled it out.

Sorry—B

Wait.

Was this note . . . from Beau Towers? Was the food from him, too? Did that mean that Beau Towers had filled a tray full of food and climbed up the stairs and left it at her door? Did that mean this was an *apology*? From him?

That seemed so unlikely as to be impossible. Granted, it was only a one-word apology, signed by just an initial, but still. He didn't seem like the type to apologize to anyone, let alone someone like her.

She was too hungry, and had already had too much wine, to figure this conundrum out. She picked up another taco.

After she finished all four of the tacos, she sat back and realized how tired she was.

She yawned. She'd woken up at six this morning for no good reason, she'd been running on adrenaline all day, she'd had two glasses of wine and a huge meal, and all she wanted to do was take a hot bath in that big, beautiful bathtub and then get in that enormous, fluffy bed over there and go to sleep.

No, no, she couldn't. She stood up and went into the bathroom to splash cold water on her face. She just had to pull herself together, that's all.

But when she walked into the bathroom, she saw the bathtub again.

And she could swear—she could *swear*—she heard a little voice say, "A bath is just what you need right now, don't you think?"

"Yes, I actually do think that!" Izzy said to the bathtub. "But . . ."

Wait. But what? Beau Towers hadn't actually told her to leave. Her new flight wasn't until tomorrow evening. She didn't have to go anywhere tonight. She could just lock the bedroom door, run a hot bath, eat one, or maybe all, of those incredible-looking chocolate chip cookies, read one of the mystery novels on her e-reader, and just . . . relax. Without her mom or dad knocking on the bathroom door to say, "You okay in there?" or to ask her to pick up groceries the next day, or tell her about what her aunt Georgia said on the phone that day. Oh God, that sounded amazing.

Before she could talk herself out of it, she turned on the bathwater.

There. She'd committed. For the rest of the night, she'd pretend Beau Towers didn't exist.

"Happy now?" she said to the bathtub.

She'd clearly lost it. She'd just had a whole conversation with a bathtub, and she was waiting for it to talk back to her. She obviously needed a real vacation. Not like she could afford one, but still. Maybe she *should* stay here in California. She could just hang out here and yell at Beau Towers from time to time and sit in the sun and take baths and drink wine and read and write and be far away from her parents and only have to deal with Marta from a distance. What an impossible dream.

She looked around the room and took a long deep breath. She still had those cookies. And that glass of wine on her tray. Now that she'd committed to staying for the night, she could drink it. Izzy unzipped her suitcase and took out her favorite pair of pajamas.

Once the water was high enough, she stepped into the tub and sank all the way down. It was the perfect temperature, almost—but not quite—too hot, and the water covered her all the way to her shoulders.

She could feel the tension seep out of her body, like she was a balloon with air slowly leaking out. And the tub was an old-fashioned one, with no extra drain to prevent flooding. That meant the water would stay right here, as long as she wanted it to. Incredible. She picked up her wineglass from the very convenient shelf right next to the bathtub and took a sip. Yes, her decision to stay had been absolutely correct.

Izzy woke up the next morning to the sound of her phone ringing. She squinted, bleary-eyed, at the room, at the very comfortable, totally unfamiliar bed.

Right. Beau Towers's house.

She rolled over and reached for her phone. Oh God. It was Marta. Why was Marta calling her at seven in the morning?

Okay, fine, it was ten in the morning in New York, but still. Marta knew that time zones existed.

Did Marta care that time zones existed? No, obviously not.

"Hello?"

"You have until Monday," Marta said, with no preamble.

Izzy sat up.

"Until Monday?" she repeated. Luckily, she'd worked with Marta long enough not to say "I have until Monday for what?" which was her first instinct.

"To get Beau Towers on track with this memoir. He emailed me last night and said you were very helpful to him at dinner and thanked me for sending you to him."

Beau Towers had *thanked* Marta? For what? Why? He didn't want her here! And he'd emailed Marta? She hadn't been sure he knew how to send an email.

"Wow, that's . . . surprising," Izzy said.

"Indeed," Marta said. "And I couldn't let this opportunity pass, so I informed him that you'll stay until Monday, to be even more helpful."

Izzy almost laughed out loud. "Even more helpful"—what was happening?

"Did he . . . agree to that?"

"He knew not to argue with me," Marta said. "Does this work for you, Isabelle?"

Izzy wanted to giggle. Did it work for her, to stay here in California until Monday, with this perfect weather and in this enormous house, with her beautiful bedroom and glorious bathtub and excellent food? Sure, she'd have to be with Beau Towers, but in New York, she'd have to be with Marta. And it was still February there.

It was ostensibly February in California, too, but not really.

"Sure, that works for me," she said. "Whatever gets the book done, right?"

"Exactly." Izzy noted that Marta—unlike Beau—didn't say thank you. "Work with him after hours, since obviously, you'll also have to do all your other work as well."

Obviously.

"What a great idea it was to send you to talk to Beau Towers," Marta said.

Was it even worth reminding Marta it had been *her* idea?

"Yes," Izzy said. "Great idea."

"I expect updates." Marta hung up abruptly, like she always did, and Izzy dropped the phone back onto the bed. She stared out the window at the bright blue sky, and the palm trees swaying in the breeze, and smiled.

She got to stay here until Monday. That meant four more days of California weather, and Michaela's cooking, and that bathtub, and not being anywhere near the office. All that and in return she just had to give Beau Towers a few pep talks?

Amazing.

This kind of opportunity would be a perfect writing retreat, actually.

She shook off that idea. She hadn't written a word in months. She'd given up on that.

She reached for her phone to text Priya.

> I get to stay here until Monday?!? To . . . help Beau Towers with his book? Yes, he's a jerk, but did I mention that the weather is perfect and he has a full-time cook and there's an incredible view from my bedroom??? I do NOT know what's going on, Priya, but I'm going to enjoy it while I can

Priya texted her back right away.

> I like the sound of most of that except that you have to stay with a jerk until Monday. Is it just the two of you? Are you ok there? Blink once for yes and twice for no

Izzy laughed and then thought about that. Despite how angry Beau Towers had made her yesterday, she'd felt perfectly safe around him. Even when she'd seen him in the kitchen for the first time, and he'd been so mad that she was there, she hadn't been scared of him. Maybe it was because of how comfortable Michaela was with him?

> Blink

She giggled to herself as she pictured Priya's reaction if she just left it at that.

Seriously, it's fine, don't worry. He's terrible but not like that. This is honestly as much of a vacation as I'm going to get for a long time, might as well enjoy it

She'd better text her parents, too. They thought she'd taken a red-eye the night before and had gone straight into the office.

Hey, guys! Looks like I'll be in California a few more days—my boss has me working with an author who lives here. Coming back Monday. Have a great weekend!

While she scrolled through her work email, her dad texted back.

Sounds like a great opportunity, honey! Have a great time.

She still didn't understand why Beau Towers had emailed Marta. Why would he do that? She wondered how furious he was that Marta had railroaded him into letting her stay here.

Well, there was only one way to find out.

She got in the shower—which wasn't as good as the bathtub, obviously, but was still excellent—got dressed, and went downstairs.

Michaela was at the kitchen table when she walked in. She set her teacup down and stood up.

"Good morning," Michaela said. "Coffee or tea? And how do you feel about a cookie for breakfast?"

Izzy grinned at her. "I feel great about a cookie for breakfast. And coffee, please, if you have it."

Michaela walked over to the coffeepot and poured coffee into a mug. "Milk? Sugar?"

"Just milk, thanks, but I can get it," Izzy said. "How's your ankle?"

Michaela glanced down. "Oh, it's a lot better today, thanks again." She put a cookie on a plate and handed it to Izzy. "So you'll be here until next week?"

Beau had told Michaela. This must actually be happening.

"That's what it looks like," Izzy said. "I hope that's not too much trouble for you?"

"Not at all," Michaela said. "Let me know if you have questions about anything; I know this house pretty well." She looked around the kitchen. "There's always something around here for breakfast; I make lunch and dinner. But feel free to come in the kitchen and forage for snacks or whatever anytime."

Izzy laughed. "Thank you, I'm kind of a snacker. I appreciate that."

Michaela grinned. "Beau is also kind of a snacker, so I've stocked up. Let me know if there's anything that you particularly want me to get you."

She threw open a big cabinet, and Izzy's mouth dropped open. The cabinet was like a snack wonderland. She immediately spotted a box of her favorite crackers, those fancy ones they had at work events with the fruit and nuts in them. There were also three kinds of cheese crackers, a few peppercorn flavored, some herb, some plain. Plus, an entire shelf full of potato chips, of many different flavors and brands, some of which she'd never even seen before. And then there was cereal, granola, popcorn, jerky, candy . . . Izzy had to turn away, she felt like she was getting woozy.

"Is this a magic house?" she asked.

Michaela just laughed. "Oh, and let me give you my number, in case there's anything you need and you can't find me."

Izzy pulled her phone out of her pocket and typed in Michaela's number. "Great, thanks. Also, I was wondering . . . did you knock on my door last night?"

Michaela shook her head. "Nope, I loaded the dishwasher and left."

So it really had been Beau.

Just then, Michaela looked past Izzy's shoulder. "Morning, Beau."

Izzy took a sip of coffee before she turned around.

"Morning," Beau mumbled as he walked into the kitchen. He didn't even glance in Izzy's direction.

"Beau, you should take Isabelle on a tour," Michaela said. "I'd do it, but I can't, because of my ankle." She limped over to the kitchen table and sat down.

"A tour?" Beau stared at Michaela. He looked just as horrified about the prospect of giving Izzy a tour as Izzy felt about going on one. Last night had been disastrous enough—this felt like a terrible idea.

"You know, take her around the house and the gardens, make sure she knows the lay of the land, etc."

Izzy almost laughed out loud. The house and the gardens? Was this a palace?

But then, a tour would force Beau Towers to talk to her, sort of. Maybe even about his memoir?

Would he let her actually help him with it? Unlikely. Would he even give her this tour? Almost certainly not.

"Fine," he said. "Let's go."

That was surprising.

"After you," he said, and gestured for her to precede him out of the kitchen. Oh, the tour was starting now? Okay.

Izzy downed the rest of her coffee before she walked by him and into the hallway. Good thing she'd put her work phone in her pocket before she'd come downstairs—if Marta sent an email that Izzy didn't respond to right away, she'd flip out.

Beau joined her in the hallway and pointed back the way they came. "Kitchen," he said. He pointed next to it. "Dining room."

Ah, this tour was just an excuse for him to be a jerk again. Got it.

He pointed back and to the left. "Michaela's office." He looked at her for the first time that morning. "The rest of this hallway is off-limits." Then he walked off in the other direction.

"Wow, a complete sentence," Izzy said under her breath.

She followed him down the hall. Was he going to bring up last night? Or tell her why he'd emailed Marta? Or even mention that she was going to be staying with him for the next four days?

He turned to the right when they got to the staircase, and pointed again. "Living room."

Apparently not.

Izzy followed Beau into the living room. It was a large, bright room, with a big fireplace, comfortable-looking couches, photographs on the walls, and the same gorgeous view as Izzy's bedroom. Huh. She'd assumed that Beau had bought this house a year ago, or that it was some kind of fancy rental, but this living room made it look like an actual home that real people had lived in. Now she was confused.

He turned and pointed to a half-open door a few steps down the hall. "TV room."

Did he watch TV in there? She could just picture him in there at night, watching wrestling or *Animal Kingdom* or whatever.

"Okay," she said.

He glanced over at her, then quickly away. Why had he looked away from her so fast? Did she have something in her teeth? Chocolate on her shirt? She looked down at herself: She was wearing jeans, a tank top, and a cardigan, since almost everything else she'd brought with her to California was either conference wear or pajamas. Thank goodness she'd brought those two sundresses in a fit of optimism. She'd certainly get wear out of them over the next few days.

They turned back toward the front entry, passing two big closed wooden doors that looked sort of like church doors. Beau didn't say anything as they walked by, but Izzy was curious about them. She shrugged to herself; she might as well ask.

"What's in there?" she asked.

Beau shook his head. "No." Oh great, there was that growl again. "Off-limits."

How many weird, cursed rooms were in this house?

"Okay." What else could she say?

He gestured to the staircase as they walked by. "Upstairs."

This time, she couldn't hold herself back.

"Yeah, I got that. Because of the stairs and all."

Was that a smile? It flashed on his face for a half second, but it was gone before Izzy could really be sure.

"Right." He glanced in her direction. "Upstairs is off-limits for me. While you're here, I mean. I don't want you to feel like . . . Anyway, upstairs is all yours. Go wherever you want, I don't care."

Was that . . . Was he trying to make her feel comfortable? It actually sort of worked, if that had been his intention. But now she had no choice but to bring up the night before.

"You, um, came upstairs last night, though," she said.

He looked away from her again. "I know. I . . . You hadn't had dinner." He looked back at her. "I won't do it again."

She nodded. "Okay. And thanks for bringing me dinner."

He shrugged. "It was the least I could do."

She started to respond, but he immediately turned toward the front door. Okay, then. She followed him outside.

He turned to the right when they got outside and went around the side of the house. "Vegetable garden." He pointed again. He'd managed to put actual complete sentences together for a while there inside, and now he was back to the stone-faced pointing.

She gazed at the vegetable garden. Vegetables growing outside in February. Incredible.

Beau turned and walked toward the back of the house, gesturing at the row of trees. "Orchard."

At that, Izzy laughed out loud. She couldn't help herself. "You have an actual *orchard* in your backyard?"

Beau looked at her sideways. "What's wrong with that?"

She rolled her eyes. "Nothing is *wrong* with it. It's just . . ." Rich people really lived in totally different worlds, didn't they? "Okay, what kinds of trees? What fruit?"

He looked at them. "Oranges, lemons, I think grapefruit maybe? Definitely figs. Oh, and of course avocado."

"Oh right, of course avocado," Izzy said. Yes, obviously, it made sense that there would be an avocado tree here. Izzy wasn't even sure if she'd known before this moment that avocados grew on trees.

There was that split-second smile again, so fast she wasn't sure if she'd imagined it. He turned back to the trees. "I should pick some of these for Michaela, actually. She always needs lemons." He reached up and plucked a few ripe yellow fruits off one of the trees.

Now she wanted to laugh out loud again, out of sheer amazement. She'd managed to finagle herself a "work trip" in this house that was so big and foreign to her it was basically a castle, where the gardens were so extensive she wouldn't be surprised if she walked over a moat, where she could just walk outside and pick lemons and oranges from the orchard, where she was a little too warm in a tank top and a cardigan in the middle of winter, and where someone was going to cook her all her meals? This was like those fairy tales about girls held captive by monsters. Except, opposite.

She glanced over at Beau. Well. Maybe not the monster part.

They walked through the orchard, turned, and came face-to-face with the moat.

"Pool," Beau said unnecessarily.

"Wow," Izzy said. She couldn't help herself, as she gazed at the huge blue tiled pool in front of them, sparkling in the sun. See, she knew she should have packed her swimsuit. She had to come back later so she could send Priya a picture; she was going to lose it.

"It's a great pool," Beau said. Another actual sentence. Izzy narrowed her eyes at him. Was this some sort of trick?

They walked past the pool, and Beau pointed again. "Rose garden." The rosebushes were scrawny, with no roses on them, and there were cacti growing around them.

Beau turned back to the house. "Back door." He pointed as he walked toward the door. A tiny smile danced around his lips. Was he enjoying this mockery of a tour? Probably. Well, now that they were going back inside, it must be over.

Her phone buzzed, and she glanced down at it. Email from Marta.

Send me an update on BT.

Right. She had to do this.

"Um. Can we . . ." She started over. "Since I'm here for the next few days to help you with your memoir, we should probably talk about it?" The smile fell from Beau's face, and his eyes clouded over again. She felt a slight moment of regret—just when they'd almost been getting along, she had to do this? But then she snapped out of it. Yes she did, this was what she was here for. "Yesterday you said you wanted me to give you pep talks—is that still what you want, or do you want to—"

"Whatever," he said. "That's fine. How about now?"

Oh no. Now? Why hadn't she had the foresight to think up another pep talk in the past twenty minutes? She had to do this spontaneously? She took a deep breath.

"So, um, I'm not quite sure what the problem is for you right now. . . ." He looked away when she said that. Okay, well, she just had to keep going. "If you ever want to talk about that—but honestly, there are so many reasons why writers struggle with their books, and

I promise you, they all do. There are tons of tips and tricks to getting through this, but—in my experience, at least—the only thing that works is just doing it. Sitting down every day and writing. Even every other day, or every few days. It's not about the number of hours, it's just the consistency. It's so hard at first, but it gets easier, a little bit, every time you sit down. And if you think you can't do it, I promise you, you can. Don't be discouraged if you think your work is bad; as long as you can get something on the page, that's a victory."

Beau's face was impassive the entire time she was talking. Was he listening to her, even? She thought so, but he wasn't quite looking at her, and she had no idea if anything she said was at all helpful to him.

"Okay," he said after she stopped talking. "Thanks."

And with that, he threw open the side door and walked inside the house.

Well. He didn't yell at her. That was a real success.

Izzy's phone buzzed again as she stared at the still-vibrating door.

Hi, this is Michaela with a few details you might need!

The Wi-Fi password is Lum1ere!

Lunch is Cobb salad and will be ready any time after 12:30, just come down to the kitchen.

Dinner is at 6:30 tonight. I'm making beef ragout. I was thinking a cheese soufflé to go along with it, but is soufflé too jiggly for you?

Izzy had to laugh.

Not too jiggly, thanks for checking! Looking forward to it.

Homemade cheese soufflé? She could deal with Beau Towers's glares for that.

CHAPTER SIX

It was one a.m. on Friday night—or rather, Saturday morning. Izzy turned over in bed. She couldn't sleep.

She'd been up since 5:45, dealing with Beau Towers and Marta and assorted other stressful people all day, and all she wanted was to sleep. Unfortunately, her brain hadn't gotten the message. She'd even taken a nice long bath in that beautiful bathtub while reading a soothing book, but it hadn't helped.

Things with Beau Towers had been more or less civil for the past two days. He'd given her that tour, he'd listened to two pep talks without making any snide comments, and they'd tacitly decided to eat all their meals separately. But she didn't think she'd actually made any progress with him. He hadn't told her anything about what he was struggling with, hadn't asked her any questions or for any advice; he hadn't said anything about his memoir at all, in fact. And that's what was frustrating her so much. She'd failed. Again.

For the past few hours, she'd mentally reread the messages she'd gotten from Gavin that day and had come up with at least four different—and better—ways she should have responded.

> Hey—how's it going out there? You okay?

Why would he think she wasn't okay? Had Marta said something to him about her and how this was going?

Going well, thanks! How's everything back in the office?

He responded right away.

Oh fine, normal. Don't feel bad if it's not going well out there. I knew Beau Towers would be a tough nut for you to crack. This one might take more experience than you've got, no offense.

No one ever ended a sentence with "no offense" unless they specifically meant to give offense. And look, it wasn't going GREAT with Beau Towers. But she'd done better with him than anyone else had in the past year.

Thanks for the concern, but everything's fine here! I think Beau is making some real progress, actually!

That was obviously a lie—she shouldn't have said it, but she'd suddenly been filled with an urge to prove wrong all the people who doubted her. Who thought that she wasn't smart enough, that she didn't work hard enough, that she couldn't accomplish anything, that she couldn't rise in her career.

Were they right about her? Maybe she wasn't cut out for this job, like all those people thought. Maybe she should quit and become a librarian, or a teacher, or, God forbid, go to law school or something. Publishing was so different than she'd thought it would be. It seemed like people only cared about status and profits and the bottom line, and not that feeling you got when you read a book that meant something to you, that wonder and hope and fullness in your chest, that feeling like there was a place for you in the world, and it was out there for you to find it.

Ugh. She sat up. Going over and over this in her mind wasn't helping.

A snack. She needed a snack. She'd been too shy so far to really investigate the snack cabinet, even though Michaela had told her she could. She was pretty sure Beau Towers didn't really want her here, even though this whole thing *had* been his own idea, sarcastic or not. But it was one in the morning, and she needed a snack, and she suddenly remembered those cheese-flavored potato chips she'd seen in the kitchen, and she knew she would absolutely not be able to fall asleep unless she had them. Cheese-flavored anything was the solution to every problem.

She got out of bed and pulled her big cardigan on over her pajamas. She'd already discovered that despite the sixty-five-degree weather outside, this house was freezing cold most of the day. Beau probably kept the heat down so he could be comfortable in his cave, or wherever he slept.

She walked through the long, dark hallway and tiptoed down the stairs to the kitchen. Why she tiptoed, she didn't know—she wasn't breaking in; Beau Towers was the only other person in this house, and he knew she was here. But she couldn't stop herself.

As soon as she got to the bottom of the stairs, she realized two things: 1) she should have put socks on, this tile floor was ice cold in the middle of the night; 2) she wasn't the only person awake. She came to a standstill as she heard faint murmuring and music coming from the direction of the TV room. It hadn't occurred to her that Beau Towers might be awake, too.

But she knew if she went back to bed she'd just lie there wide-awake, thinking of the cheese-flavored potato chips, so close yet so far away. Plus, Beau had probably just fallen asleep in front of the TV. She could sneak into the kitchen and grab the chips and then go back upstairs without him hearing a thing.

She crept down the hall toward the kitchen. As she walked, she kept one ear cocked toward the TV room but heard no other movement aside from the steady, quiet sounds of the TV.

She stopped by the kitchen door to turn the light on but realized she had no idea where the light switch in this room was. Well, it didn't matter; there was just enough light filtering in through the big window for her to be able to see.

She went straight to the snack cabinet, pulled out the third shelf, and grinned. There they were. She'd never seen so many flavors of chips before: jalapeño, ranch, pepperoncini . . . olive? Well, that might be taking it a little too far. Now to find the cheese . . .

"Wouldn't it be easier if you turned the lights on?"

Izzy spun around. He was standing there, a big, dark shape in the doorway.

"Yeah, probably," she said.

Beau flicked the light switch—ah, it was just outside the kitchen door, she hadn't even thought to look there—and Izzy blinked in the sudden burst of light.

He was in a different pair of fancy sweatpants—these were dark gray, the other ones had been light gray—and a white T-shirt. All the other times she'd seen Beau, he'd been wearing a hoodie. The T-shirt was snug on his biceps. And his chest.

She could hear Priya's voice in her ear.

If you like those big brawny guys, which I absolutely do.

Izzy looked away from him immediately. And suddenly realized that she was wearing shapeless pajama pants, a thin tank top, and no bra. Thank God she'd pulled that cardigan on before she'd come downstairs.

"What are you doing up?" he asked her.

She shrugged. "I couldn't sleep. So after a while, I thought maybe a snack might help." Izzy looked down at the three bags of chips in her hands and slowly put two bags down.

"It usually does," he said. "Plus, it is National Snack Food Month, after all."

Izzy's eyes snapped back to Beau. "How do you know that?" she asked him, probably too sharply. He didn't actually read her emails. Right? He couldn't. He'd showed no sign that he had any idea that Isabelle Marlowe existed, let alone that he knew who she was.

He looked confused. "Oh, um, I don't know." He shook his head. "I think it was on the back of a bag of chips or something."

That made sense. Beau seemed like more of a read-the-back-of-a-bag-of-chips kind of guy than a read-emails kind of guy. Or write-a-memoir kind of guy, for that matter.

"Oh. Okay. Um, sorry if I disturbed you. Or . . ." She put the chips down. "If you don't want me to . . ."

He shook his head and took a step toward her. "You didn't disturb me. And take the chips, I don't care. I mean, it's fine." He smiled at her. An actual, sustained smile, and not that quick, almost secret smile she'd seen the other day. "You have good instincts—those cheesy chips are my favorite. Perfect for a late-night snack."

She laughed. "That's what I thought. I saw them when Michaela showed me the snack cabinet, and I've been thinking about them ever since."

He was still smiling. "We all need snacks in the middle of the night sometimes."

She smiled back at him. "Yeah. We do. Especially after . . ." She stopped herself. Was she really so tired and frustrated that she'd been tempted to vent to Beau Towers of all people?

"Especially after what?" he asked.

She shook her head. "Nothing. Just a long day." He was still looking at her, like he was waiting for her to say something else, so she kept going. "I still have to do all my other work while I'm here, which means I have to be up and working by six a.m. Pacific time, and someone at work today said something that . . . I'm still annoyed by." She couldn't tell Beau what Gavin had said about him, obviously. "It was just . . . a frustrating day. That's all."

"Can I ask you a question?"

He still looked . . . pleasant, almost. He wasn't quite smiling, but he wasn't glaring at her either. Not the normal monstrous Beau Towers she'd gotten used to.

"Sure," she said.

"What's in it for you? This job, I mean. You deal with jerks at work, and from what I can tell of the rest of your job, it's just a lot of pointless drudgery. You act like you believe these little cheerful stories you tell me once a day, and you seem so committed to this whole pep talk routine, but you can't actually believe that 'a book changed my life' nonsense, right? What do you even do this for, anyway?"

His whole smiling and friendly thing had just been another way to make fun of her. How had she let him trick her like this? She was suddenly furious.

"I know this entire concept is foreign to you, but some people need to work for a living." The expression on his face changed when she said that. He looked angry. Good. She kept going. "But even beyond a paycheck, some of us actually care about our jobs. I work hard at my job because I love books. I love everything about them. I love the way you can fall into another world while you're reading, the way books can help you forget hard things in life, or help you deal with them. I love all the different shapes books come in, and the way they feel in your hand. I love seeing authors develop their idea from just a few sentences to a manuscript to an actual book that's on the shelves, and I love the face they make when they see their name on a book cover for the first time. I love when readers discover books that felt like they were meant just for them, and they're so happy and grateful and emotional that everyone in the room wants to cry, and sometimes they all do. Those books do change lives. I hope that answers your question."

Izzy stormed out of the kitchen past Beau and ran back upstairs. When she got back into her room, she tore open the bag of chips. Why had she believed that smile on his face? Why had she thought they were sort of bonding down there in the kitchen, about snacks and being up in the middle of the night and whatever else? Why did she feel almost disappointed in him now?

As she ate her chips, she replayed in her mind everything she'd said to him. She'd been frustrated with her job for so long and had been on the point of giving up on it. But she'd just given Beau Towers a full-throated defense of publishing. And the wild thing was, everything she'd said to him had been the truth.

Those things she loved—those were the things she'd held on to during the hard times, the times when Marta had said something casually cutting, the times when she'd tried to speak up about something important and everyone ignored her, the times when she'd lost hope about her own talents and abilities as a writer.

That's why she did all this. Because she wanted to shepherd the kinds of stories she truly believed in through the publishing process; she wanted to advocate for the kinds of authors who mattered to her; she wanted to really work with authors on their books and make them the best they absolutely could be.

Was she ready to give up on this dream? And was she ready to give up on the dream of being a writer herself? She hadn't truly asked herself that.

Was it all worth it?

She had no idea how to answer that question.

She stared down at the bag of (wildly delicious) chips. Thank goodness she'd at least grabbed them on her way upstairs.

CHAPTER SEVEN

Izzy woke up the next morning, groggy and covered in crumbs. She immediately turned and grabbed her phone. She always had work emails by, like, five a.m. here in California—how did people live like this all the time?

She sat up with a jolt when she saw it was ten a.m. How did she sleep so late? Why didn't she have any emails? Oh, right, today was Saturday. The good thing about publishing was that not even Marta sent emails before noon on Saturdays—or even, on most Saturdays, at all.

The house felt so still. So silent. It had been nice this week, to be away from her parents, from the office, where people were around her all day. But Michaela was the only person she'd really talked to all week; her short, weird interactions with Beau Towers barely counted. And now it was Saturday, and Michaela wouldn't be around today or tomorrow. That meant she'd be all alone, with Beau Towers. She had to live through two full weekend days in this house with him and with no work to keep her occupied and no Michaela to talk to.

How depressing was it that she was sad that Michaela wouldn't be there? As nice as Michaela was to her, she wasn't really her friend; she worked for Beau Towers, after all.

She suddenly missed her parents, Priya, home. All she'd wanted at home was to have space, and now that she had it, there was too much of it. She felt . . . lonely.

Coffee. She needed coffee. She really didn't want to go back down to the kitchen, but she also didn't think there was a way she could hide up here away from Beau Towers for the next few days, so she might as well get it over with now.

Though this time, she put a bra on first.

Thankfully, the kitchen was empty, though there were zucchini chocolate chip muffins on the counter. Michaela must have left them for the weekend. Izzy brought two back up to her room, along with two cups of coffee—she didn't want to go downstairs again until she had to.

When she got back to her room, she ate one of the muffins while she drank her first cup of coffee and scrolled through her phone. Priya texted right when she reached for the second muffin. Oh thank God.

Are you still alive?

If you text blink I'll fly out there and destroy you

Izzy laughed. She started to text back, but she was tired of texting. She'd been communicating almost solely via email and text all week.

"She's alive!" Priya said when she answered the phone.

Just hearing Priya's voice made her feel better.

"Yes, of course I'm alive," she said. "I texted you yesterday."

Priya scoffed. "I mean, barely. I need details. OTHER than about the bathtub and the pool."

Izzy laughed. She'd sent Priya many pictures of the bathtub, it was true.

"Unfortunately, the bathtub and the pool are all I've got." She sighed. "I don't think I've really accomplished anything here. Beau Towers doesn't listen to a word I say; he's absolutely never going to turn in this memoir."

Ugh, just thinking about the pitying look Gavin would give her when she got back to the office made her cringe.

"You already accomplished something!" Priya said. "You opened the lines of communication! He actually emailed Marta! That's far more than she had last week, and you know that. It's not like she thought you would come back to New York waving Beau Towers's manuscript around. Stop stressing about it! Enjoy the weather there while you can. But first, you haven't told me a single thing about what Beau Towers is like, other than he's very hot and he glares at you all the time. I want to know way more."

"I did *not* say he was hot!" Izzy said.

"You didn't have to," Priya said.

Izzy would just ignore that. "Okay, here are the pros to living in Beau Towers's house. First, it's enormous. It's so big that I have the entire second floor to myself. Second, his assistant is nice and at least she likes me, and she cooks fantastic food. Third, the view from my window, which I've sent you multiple pictures of. Fourth, and stop rolling your eyes, my bathtub: I think the two of us have bonded, I tell it about my day every night during my nightly bath, and I think it really sympathizes with me. Fifth, there's a snack cabinet, Priya. As in, a whole cabinet, as tall as me, devoted entirely to snacks. Sixth, there are gardens, plural. I go take a turn around them every afternoon like some Regency romance heroine. And I can do that, because seventh, the weather is incredible. It's overcast right now, but it often is in the mornings, and every afternoon is sunny and perfect."

She took a big sip of coffee. "Also—this probably should have been one with a bullet—it's so nice to be across the country from both Marta and my parents. That feels mean, to group my parents with Marta, and I don't mean it that way, but it's just so refreshing to be alone, not have someone ask me questions all the time or be in my space. That part is pretty relaxing, actually."

"You're sounding a little too happy," Priya said. "You'd better not stay there."

Izzy laughed out loud. "I haven't gotten to the cons yet. I'd be perfectly happy to stay here if I could be here with you and not Beau Towers! This weekend I'm stuck here alone with him, and he barely speaks to me, or even looks at me." She sighed. "I just realized that since I got here on Wednesday, I haven't talked to anyone in person other than him and Michaela. I work and stare at the walls and occasionally walk around outside in the gardens, I talk to inanimate objects like my teacup and the candlestick because Beau Towers doesn't talk to me, and I feel like at any moment the teacup and candlestick will start, like, singing and dancing for me."

"You have a candlestick?" Priya asked.

"You're missing the point!" Izzy said. "Since I've gotten here, I haven't taken a step off his property. Isn't that ridiculous?"

"Are you . . . locked in there?" Priya asked.

Izzy laughed. "Of course not. I'm sure I can leave whenever I want, but where would I go? Michaela returned my rental car, and plus, there isn't really any reason to leave—there's lots of food, I did laundry so I've got clean clothes, and plus—"

"Isabelle," Priya said in a stern voice. "Go for a walk. A real walk, not 'in the gardens,' whatever that means—go outside, into the real world. It's what, almost noon there now? Go to a bookstore, or a coffee shop, or I don't know, a grocery store and get some food that isn't made in that weird enchanted house. Just go be outside in the world away from the bathtub that you talk to far too much and the candlesticks that are singing to you so I stop being afraid for your sanity."

Huh. That hadn't occurred to her.

"That's a great idea," Izzy said. Being somewhere other than this place, even for a few hours, sounded amazing.

"Of course it's a great idea," Priya said. "Go. Now. Take a picture of the beach or weird California people or your latte art or whatever and text me to prove you did it."

Priya hung up. Izzy stared at her phone for a second, and then she jumped out of bed. She took a quick shower, threw on jeans and a sweater, dropped her phone and headphones and e-reader into her bag, and crept down the stairs.

She opened the front door and slid it closed behind her as quietly as she could. She didn't know why she was sneaking out of the house. It's not like she wasn't allowed to leave. Maybe it was just because she didn't want to run into Beau Towers and have another terrible interaction with him. Now that she'd decided to get out of here, even for a few hours, she just wanted to GO.

It wasn't until she started walking down the hill that she realized she had no idea where she was going. It had felt so urgent for her to get out of the house right away that she hadn't she googled a bookstore or coffee shop or any destination. She stopped a few houses down and pulled her phone out of her pocket. Perfect, there was a bookstore about a mile and a half away. She usually walked way more than that on just a regular day in New York. It was still overcast, but the sun would probably be out soon. And it would be good to stretch her legs and expand her view beyond what she could see from the bathtub.

Not to denigrate her bathtub, her only true friend in the house.

As Izzy set off down the hill, she realized something else: There was no sidewalk. She had to keep as close as possible to the high fences and gates and hedges of the other big houses to stay away from the cars that zipped by her going downhill. But once she put her headphones in and put on her favorite podcast, she sighed with relief. This felt normal, for the first time in days.

When she found the bookstore, she walked inside, then stopped and took a long, happy breath. God, she loved that moment when she walked inside a bookstore. Books were stacked everywhere, with friendly little signs directing you to local authors or signed copies or bestsellers.

A bookstore employee smiled at her. "Hi," she said. "Welcome. Looking for anything specific today?"

Izzy beamed at her as she looked around. "No, nothing specific. Just . . . browsing. This is a great bookstore."

Izzy wandered the aisles for over an hour. She peeked at the acknowledgments for one of Marta's books that had just come out to see her name and browsed the shelves for other books she'd worked on or read recently and loved. It felt good to see them there. It made her feel sort of at home, like she must have something in common with the people who lived here in this strange place on the other side of the country, if they bought and read and loved the same books she did.

At one point, she saw a book she was looking for, high up on a shelf, at least a foot or so out of her reach. But right next to it was a rolling ladder, one that could slide along the whole wall. She'd always wanted to climb up on one of those. She looked to the left and then to the right.

"I won't tell," the woman behind her said.

Izzy grinned at her and climbed up the ladder. She grabbed her book and then turned to look down at the bookstore from above. It was fun up there. She should have done that years ago.

When she finally left the bookstore, it was with two new books in her bag, a smile on her face, and warm, happy feeling in her chest.

One of the bookstore employees had recommended a nearby coffee shop, so she walked a few blocks until she found it. Izzy ordered a latte and a pastry and took them to a table outside. It was still overcast, but she didn't mind. She snapped a picture of her latte art and sent it to Priya as proof she'd left the house, and then sat there for a while, people watching and greeting the many dogs that walked by. Why didn't Beau Towers have a dog? Then at least she'd have a dog to hang out with this weekend.

He was probably too mean for a dog.

When she'd finished her coffee and pastry, she sighed and stood up. She didn't want to go, but she couldn't sit here forever. She already felt better than she had this morning. This walk had been a great idea.

She turned her podcast on as she walked back down the busy commercial street, laughing to herself at the Californians who were bundled up in this sixty-degree weather in puffy coats—but also still wore flip-flops. After a while, the businesses fell away, the sidewalks disappeared again, and she started up the hill toward the house. And up. And up.

Why, *why*, hadn't she realized, when she'd walked downhill all the way to the bookstore, that she'd have to walk uphill all the way back to the house? It wasn't like she was that out of shape—she walked a lot!—but walking up these hills did not feel the same as walking through New York City. And the hills just . . . kept going up.

When she first felt water on her face, she assumed it was just sweat, since by that point she was sweating profusely. But then it happened again. And again. Oh no. She looked up at the sky. California had betrayed her. It was no longer just overcast, but raining steadily.

She knew where her umbrella was: sitting in her suitcase, under her bed, in the house that was still a mile up the hill. And she was wearing jeans, a cotton T-shirt, a cardigan, and ballet flats. Fantastic.

She checked the rideshare apps on her phone to get a ride back to the house, but every car was at least twenty minutes away. She didn't want to wait for twenty minutes in the middle of the street, or loitering outside some random person's house, in the rain, because again, there was no sidewalk.

She sighed, looked at the road ahead of her, and kept walking. At first she hoped this would be a quick thunderstorm, and the rain would stop, but it just rained harder and harder. She trudged up the hill, half in the road, half on people's front lawns. She didn't step back fast enough as one car drove straight through a puddle, splashing water all over her. She wanted to cry, but she was too exhausted.

Finally, she saw the house up ahead. Oh, thank God. She couldn't wait to get inside, pull off her wet clothes, take a hot shower, and heat up whatever delicious meal Michaela had left her for dinner. It was early, but she didn't care; she was cold and wet and starving. And then, after she ate, she would take a very long, hot bath, with some of the fancy bath salts she'd found in that shop next to the bookstore.

She went around to the side door to pull it open. It didn't move.

The side door was locked? She'd gone in and out that door at least twice a day all week, and it had never been locked. She didn't have a key to the house—Michaela hadn't given her one, but it hadn't seemed necessary since she hadn't left it until today.

What was she supposed to do now? Tears of frustration pricked her eyes, but she forced them away.

She could call or text Michaela. But Michaela was probably home with her son, enjoying her two days off from dealing with Beau Towers. And, even if Izzy did text her, she'd have to sit out here in the rain for how long before Michaela arrived?

She sighed and closed her eyes for a long moment. Finally, she walked around to the front door and lifted her finger to the doorbell. As soon as she'd realized the side door was locked, she'd known what she would have to do. But she'd stood there in the rain for five extra minutes, putting off the inevitable, trying to think of something, anything else to do, because she didn't want Beau Towers to let her in, and know she'd gotten stuck outside in the rain, and see her all wet and bedraggled and shivering and still out of breath. But there was no way around it. She pressed her finger against the doorbell.

For a while, nothing happened. Should she ring the bell again? Or bang on the door? She couldn't do it. She just couldn't. She'd reached the limit of her abilities today. All she could do was stand here and hope that at some point he'd—

The door swung open with a jerk. Beau Towers stood there and stared at her, a blank look on his face. And then he slowly started to smile. And then he did something that made Izzy feel like she really was inside a nightmare.

He laughed.

At her.

If Izzy really could have shot laser beams from her eyes at that moment, she cheerfully would have at least severely maimed him. Lacking that skill, she just pushed past him into the house.

"What did you do, try to escape?" he said as she walked toward the stairs.

She swung around. "Escape? Am I a prisoner here? I went for a walk, am I not allowed to do that?"

He was still laughing as she stood there and dripped water all over the floor. "Of course you're not a prisoner, but where did you go? You look like you fell into the ocean."

Izzy took a deep breath so she wouldn't scream at him. "I walked to the bookstore. And, in case you hadn't noticed, it's raining outside. When rain falls from the sky, and you're outside, you get wet. So, if you'll excuse me—"

"You walked all the way down there? Why would you do that?"

All Izzy wanted to do was go upstairs and get out of her wet clothes and into a hot shower, but this jerk was still standing here laughing at her and asking her questions.

"Do I have to get permission from you to walk somewhere?"

He laughed at that, too. Great. "Of course not, but that's pretty far down the hill. That's why we have cars in California. We have umbrellas here, too, you know," he said, gesturing to the umbrella stand by the front door.

And that's when she lost it.

"Yes, I realize that things like 'cars' and 'umbrellas' exist, thanks for that. But I don't have a car here, remember? I also don't have a key to this house with no books in it, where I've been stuck all week with you, a person torturing me for sport, who mocks me and rolls his eyes at me when I try my fucking best to do my job, and is now laughing at me when I'm cold and wet and miserable. I've done a lot of weird things for this job so far, but babysitting a rich dude who has never had to work hard a day in his life is really high up there. I've spent almost a week trying to get through to you, a person in the midst of throwing away a multi-million-dollar book deal that landed in your lap without the slightest effort on your part. And I've been happy to give you your fucking pep talks, but I refuse to let a privileged, spoiled brat who doesn't give a damn about other people stand there and make fun of me because he has nothing else better to do. Now, if you'll excuse me, I'd like to take a hot shower and put some dry clothes on, since—as you so astutely observed—I look like I fell into the ocean."

She turned around and ran up the stairs before he could say anything else.

CHAPTER EIGHT

Izzy proceeded to take the best shower she'd ever taken in her entire life. It was long and hot and steam was coming off her body by the end. When she stepped out of the shower, she apologized to it for not embracing it as she'd embraced the bathtub.

God, it had felt great to yell at Beau Towers like that. She'd snapped back at him sort of that first day, and then again some when he'd made fun of her job, but this time she'd just lost it on him, and it had felt . . . incredible.

He was probably on the phone complaining to Marta about her right now. Any minute, Marta would call and yell at her, maybe even fire her for this. Fine. So be it. She'd spent all night obsessing about her job—here was her answer. Marta would fire her and she would go to law school or something, like her smarter friends had done. And then she wouldn't have to worry about publishing or Marta or Gavin or Beau Towers anymore.

She pulled her most comfortable leggings, her favorite T-shirt, and her warmest cardigan out of a drawer. Even though the shower had warmed her up, all she wanted were the coziest clothes possible right now. She didn't particularly want to go downstairs and risk running into Beau Towers again, but she was way too hungry to even care about him that much.

She didn't hear him in the TV room, and he wasn't in the kitchen, thank God. He was probably in one of the many "off-limits" rooms in this stupid house that was way too big for one man to live in alone.

There were two mason jars in the refrigerator neatly labeled BUTTERNUT SQUASH SOUP. Soup was just what she needed tonight. Had Michaela known it would rain today? Probably. She had magic powers like that. Or, you know, she'd checked the weather, unlike Izzy. Either way, Izzy was grateful. She poured some of the soup into a bowl, stuck it in the microwave, and checked the Post-it note Michaela had left on the jar.

Garlic bread in freezer; reheat in toaster oven—400 degrees for 5 min.

God bless that woman. How had someone as terrible as Beau Towers gotten someone as great as Michaela to come work for him? Izzy slid the foil-wrapped bread into the toaster oven and pressed start.

"You're right."

Izzy jumped and turned to see Beau Towers in the doorway. Again. Had he come to kick her out of his house finally?

"Sorry," he said. "I didn't mean to scare you. I guess I have a habit of doing that."

"I guess you do," she said. She turned back to the toaster oven. And then she turned back around. "I'm right about what?"

Beau took another step into the kitchen. "About me. You're right about me. That I'm spoiled and selfish and don't think enough about other people and all those other things you said."

She just stared. That had been the last thing she'd expected him to say to her.

He kept talking. "Well, except for that thing about torturing you for sport—I wasn't doing that on purpose. I'm sorry. I didn't mean to make fun of you today. Or last night. I think I've forgotten how to talk to people. It's been a while. I only laughed today because I didn't even know you'd left the house, and I opened the door expecting it to be UPS or something, and there you were, soaking wet, and you looked so . . . I just laughed because it was so unexpected. Anyway, that's not the point. The point is that you're right about me. Why do you think I'm having such a hard time writing this book?"

Izzy turned all the way around and looked straight at him. "I don't know," she said. "You wouldn't tell me."

He shrugged. "I know. Well, it's because of that. And, I guess, some other stuff, too. But how do you write a memoir about your life when you know your whole life was a lie and you're cursed to be a privileged asshole forever? What am I supposed to write? I have nothing good or uplifting or meaningful to say. I read those memoirs you recommended, and they all had some hopeful message at the end, and I just don't have one. But I tried—I listened to what you said the other day and I made myself sit down and write something and it all felt wrong and I don't know how to do it in a way that'll feel right."

He'd actually listened to one of her pep talks? And did what she'd suggested? She hadn't expected that at all.

Wait. Something else he'd said clicked.

"You read the memoirs I recommended? Snack Foods Month! You *did* read my emails!"

He grinned at her for a second. "Yeah, I read them all. They got kind of funny, you know. I almost started to look forward to them. I almost said that last night, but then . . ." He trailed off and shook his head. "Sorry that I never responded to them. I just . . . couldn't."

This conversation was quickly disproving most of what she thought she knew about Beau Towers.

"I know you all want me to use a ghostwriter," he said. "If I was smarter and less stubborn, I'd probably just do it and get the stupid book over with. But I want to do it myself and tell the truth about everything, and in order to do that I'd have to—" He stopped and looked down. "It would be really hard. And I'm stuck. That's . . . why there's no book."

There was so much pain in his voice when he talked about the book. He was genuinely upset. He really did want to write it. She'd had no idea.

The microwave dinged, but Izzy barely heard it.

She opened her mouth and then closed it.

Beau laughed. "Oh, come on. Just say whatever you were going to say."

Izzy smiled. "It's just . . . I was going to ask, but this is a kind of sensitive question. . . ." Beau made an impatient motion at her. "I was just wondering if maybe you're depressed? Because—"

Beau let out a bark of laughter so loud that Izzy took a step backward. "Of course I'm depressed! I've been in this house with no one to talk to—other than Michaela, I don't know how she puts up with me—for over a year! It would be a miracle if I wasn't depressed. But that doesn't make any of what I just said untrue." He stopped and looked at Izzy. "Wait, I'm sorry, I did it again. That sounded mean. See, I don't know how to talk to people anymore, if I ever did. I'm being an ass again."

This whole conversation was so unexpected.

"It's okay," Izzy said. "I. . . I didn't realize you really cared about the book, that's all."

He took another step into the kitchen. "I just don't know how to write it. I don't want to give up on it, but I might have to. I don't know what to do, and it feels so overwhelming, and I'm already so late on it that every time I think about it, it feels harder to do, and I freeze up."

He really did care about his book.

He really did need help.

The toaster oven timer went off. He went over to the cabinet, took a plate down, and slid the bread onto it.

"Anyway." He set the plate in front of her, then turned and walked toward the kitchen door. "You should eat. I just wanted to say that. And that I'm sorry. Again. I'll tell Marta that you tried as hard as you could with me, but there was nothing you could do."

He took a step into the hallway. Suddenly, she didn't want him to walk away.

"Beau."

He turned around. "Yeah?"

Izzy took a deep breath. "Will you let me help you? With the book. Really help you, I mean."

Beau looked at her. "Why would you do that for me? I've been terrible to you."

She didn't really know how to answer that question. She thought for a second. "You seem like you really want to write it. I didn't realize that before. I want you to get there. I can stay—if Marta lets me—and work with you on it, if you're willing to do the work. I'm not an expert at this, or anything. But . . . I'd like to help."

"Yeah," he finally said. "I'd like that."

He smiled at her. He looked a little nervous. Almost friendly. She suddenly . . . liked him?

She smiled back. "Can I ask you one more question?" she asked.

The smile faded from his face, but after a beat, he nodded. "Sure, okay."

"Can you please, please, tell me where the wine is in this house? I know it exists, there was some that first night, but I haven't seen any since, and after the day I've had, I desperately need some."

He laughed out loud. A real laugh.

"Wine is a great idea. And yes, there's plenty. Hang on, I'll grab something out of the cellar." He turned to leave the room, then stopped. "Actually . . . you don't have to say yes to this, if you want to have dinner yourself up in your room, I get it, you've had a long day. But . . . do you want to have dinner with me? I'll get the wine and we can watch a movie or something and I promise I won't make you give me a pep talk or talk to me about writing or your job or anything else. But it's okay if you don't—"

"Yeah," she said. "I'd like that."

CHAPTER NINE

Beau disappeared in the direction of "the cellar," wherever that was. This house had cellars and gardens and a moat and a seemingly magic kitchen and probably a dungeon she hadn't seen yet. She put the other chunk of garlic bread in the toaster oven for him, poured his mason jar full of soup into a bowl, and put it in the microwave to heat up. This had been the strangest day.

She couldn't believe she'd really volunteered stay here longer and work with Beau Towers on his book. Why had she done that?

Because of that look on his face. That look of shame, and longing, and pain when he'd talked about his book, and how hard it was for him, and how he didn't think he could do it. That look, and everything else he'd said, made her think he really cared about it and had something he wanted to say. And suddenly, she wanted to help him say it. When she'd first gotten here, she'd been so focused on escaping from the office and proving that she could do this job—to herself and to Marta—that she hadn't cared at all about the actual book. But now she did.

Well, she'd been looking for an answer to the question of what to do about her job, whether to stay and fight or give up and go. Beau Towers had just given her a way to figure that out, once and for all. If she really managed to do this—coach him through writing his book by the time she had to go back to New York—then she would stay at TAOAT and keep fighting for that dream. But if she couldn't do it, or gave up, or if he did, that was it: She was done with all this. Beau

Towers, and his book, would make this decision for her.

Beau returned to the kitchen, a bottle of wine in one hand and a set of keys in another.

"I got the wine." He handed her the keys. "And these are for you."

One looked like a house key, but the other . . . She looked up at him, not sure what this meant.

"The car's parked in the garage; use it whenever you want," he said. "I should have given you the keys on your first day here. I'm sorry you had to walk all the way up the hill in the rain, that's my fault."

She hadn't expected him to do this. "Thank you, but are you sure . . . ?"

He nodded. "Yes, of course. I don't use the car that much anyway. And I don't want you to feel like you're a prisoner here. If you're going to stay here and help me with this, I want you to feel free to come and go, and go to the beach and the coffee shop and wherever you went today—"

"The bookstore," she said.

"The bookstore, sure, there, too. I mean, if you're stuck in California babysitting me, you might as well get to enjoy being in California, you know?"

She looked up at him, an apology on her lips about that babysitting crack, but he had a grin on his face. It made him look different—younger, more relaxed, a little playful. And very attractive.

She pushed that last thought out of her mind.

"It's definitely been nice to be in sixty-three-degree and sunny weather all week when it was in the twenties in New York, that's for sure." She looked outside. "I guess that's why it didn't even occur to me that it could rain here."

He pulled out a tray from the side of the fridge and put their bowls of soup on it. "We do have weather in Southern California," he said. "It's just within a much smaller range of possibilities than you have in

New York." He picked up the tray and nodded at the wine bottle. "Can you get the wine and wineglasses?"

She took a corkscrew out of a drawer and grabbed the bottle and glasses. She followed him down the hall to the TV room, a room that she'd still never stepped inside. When Beau pushed open the door with his shoulder, Izzy stopped and stared.

The TV in this room was larger than any TV she'd ever seen in person. Maybe that's why she hadn't seen any other TVs in this house; there had originally been five or six, and this TV had just eaten them all.

Beau set the tray on the coffee table in front of the couch and then turned around to see Izzy still staring at the TV.

"I know, it's a little absurd." He looked embarrassed. "When I moved in here, it was kind of sudden. I'd only planned to come for a long weekend, to kind of . . . clear my head. And then I just stayed. It used to be my grandparents' house."

Oh. A few things made more sense now.

Izzy sat down on the couch and reached for her bowl of soup. It tasted as good as it smelled. She was glad there was more in the kitchen, since she had a feeling she'd eat this entire bowl and then some.

Beau picked up the corkscrew and reached for the bottle of wine.

"A lot of the furniture and stuff here is still theirs, but they had a really old TV, the picture was terrible, it barely got cable, and I knew I needed something else." He laughed. "I told Michaela I needed a new TV, and when she asked what I wanted, I said I didn't care, I just wanted the biggest TV they had. And so, well, that's what she got me."

Izzy laughed, partly at the story, but also at how chatty Beau suddenly was. It was like he'd been bottling up all his conversation for months and was letting it all out at once.

"Michaela seems very reliable that way." Izzy took the glass of wine that Beau handed her.

He laughed again. "She definitely is. That's also sort of how the snack cabinet came to be: She kept asking me what I wanted her to get for me at the store, and finally I just told her to get me every snack she could think of. And so she decided to take me literally."

Yes, that sounded like a thing Michaela would do.

"Well, I fell in love with the snack cabinet immediately, it's the love of my life, and we're getting married in a few weeks," Izzy said.

Beau tore off a hunk of bread and dipped it in his soup. "Sorry, no, I can't allow that, you're not taking my snack cabinet away from me."

They grinned at each other.

"I think Michaela really has fun with it," he said. "At first it was just chips and pretzels and crackers and beef jerky and stuff, but then she started stocking it with stuff from the Mexican grocery store, and then the different Asian grocery stores, and now there's so much good stuff in there. I'm obsessed with these spicy veggie straws, I don't even know what they're called or where they came from, but I love them."

Beau reached for the remote, but Izzy knew there was something she had to say before he turned the TV on.

"Um, I want to apologize, too," she said. He sat back and looked at her. "I kind of . . . I just assumed you were being a jerk last night and today. I think you just pushed my buttons, and I got mad. I'm sorry."

He shook his head. "Don't worry about it. I was an ass when you got here, of course you would take everything I said the wrong way." He picked up the remote. "Anything you're in the mood to watch?"

How should she answer? This always seemed like a test question, especially from guys—like you were supposed to answer something "smart" and tell them about the documentary you'd been dying to see, or the TV show about the angry man that you just love, or that superhero movie you couldn't wait to watch again. But it had been a long day. She might as well just be honest.

"Obviously, with the rain outside and with this bowl of very cozy soup, all I want to watch is some sort of luxurious period drama with lots of sweeping views of the countryside in England or Italy or somewhere like that, and people drinking tea and eating tiny sandwiches and scones. Do you know the kind of thing I mean?"

To her surprise, Beau nodded. "Good idea." He flipped through his many streaming services, and landed on something. "What about this one?"

"*This Provincial Life*," Izzy read on the screen. "I don't even need to read the description, the title is enough for me. Sold."

So for the rest of the night, they sat there, at opposite ends of the couch, eating soup and bread and drinking wine and watching a period drama. At one point, Izzy heated up more soup for both of them, another time, Beau made them popcorn, and right when Izzy was thinking about going to bed, Beau brought out a plate of warm chocolate chip cookies, so Izzy had no choice but to stay for one more episode.

They didn't talk much, but that was okay. Izzy was surprised by how comfortable it was to be here with Beau Towers. She didn't feel like she had to fill the silence with conversation. She didn't feel awkward, sitting here with him.

She still had no idea why he'd been shut away from the rest of the world for the past year, or why he was struggling so much with his book. He'd hinted at some realizations he'd made about himself, but she didn't want to ask about that, at least not yet. But if they were really going to work on his book together, she'd have to push him to write about those things, whether he actually shared any of it with her or not.

Could she really do this? She'd offered to help him, because the pain in his voice and the look on his face had made her want to reach out, want to do something to help. But did she know how to do this? Did she have enough knowledge, enough experience, to coach Beau through writing a memoir?

She had no idea. But she knew she had to try her best. If this was going to be her test to decide whether to stay in publishing, she was going to give it her all, and if her all wasn't good enough, then that would be her answer.

But, she realized, she wanted this for Beau's sake, too.

The episode ended, and Beau turned to her. "It's getting late. Do you want to pick this back up another night?"

Izzy nodded. "Yeah, sure," she said. "And also, about your book."

Beau sat back, midway through reaching for the plate of cookies. "Yeah?" He looked away. He did that when he was nervous, she realized.

"Maybe we should start working together on Monday? I have to do my other work from nine to six, New York time, so I'm done around three. How about we meet then, just to talk through some stuff. Nothing big yet, just ease into it, if that works for you?"

He bit his lip, then nodded. "Okay. That . . . that makes sense." He smiled at her. "Three sounds like snack time—we can meet in the kitchen and raid the snack cabinet and go from there?"

She laughed. "Perfect. See you at snack time on Monday. Good night." She turned to leave the room.

"Good night, Isabelle. And . . . thanks."

She turned back around and smiled at him. "You're welcome."

CHAPTER TEN

Izzy took a deep breath on Sunday before she picked up the phone.

"I can stay—if Marta lets me," she'd said to Beau on Saturday night, like it was no big deal, like it was a foregone conclusion that Marta would let her stay here longer and work with him on his book. And now she had to get Marta to let her.

She wanted—dear God, she wanted—to send an email about this. In an email, you could spend minutes, hours, laboring over each phrase, making sure you worded everything just right. In a phone call, who knows what you would say? But Marta did everything important over the phone. She dialed Marta's number.

"Isabelle."

Marta always answered the phone like that, with just the name of the person calling her. It had been so disconcerting at first.

"Hi, Marta," Izzy said. "Sorry to call you on a Sunday, but, um, I think I've been making some progress with Beau Towers. The tricky part is that he wants me to stay longer. For a while, I mean, to help him with his book. I think he's been having a really tough time, and it seems like it's helped him to talk it through with me." Ugh, she was babbling. She'd already said *help* twice. She should have written down a script.

Marta huffed. Was she running? Or skiing? Knowing Marta, she was probably, like, running in the snow.

"It might be time for us to cut our losses on this one," Marta said. "Throwing good money after bad isn't going to magically get a book out of this guy. I'm glad you've gotten him to respond to my emails, at least, but I don't want to force you to stay in some dinky little town in California for this. I'll tell him no."

Izzy thought fast. She had to get Marta to let her stay. She hadn't realized how much she cared about doing this until Marta was on the point of taking it away.

"Actually," she said, "I've been surprised at how committed he is to this book. You sending me here was just the push he needed." Yes, make Marta remember it was "her" idea to send Izzy here. "I don't think he ever would have made any progress on the book otherwise. I can't guarantee this will work, of course, but I'm pretty sure that if I *don't* stay, there will never be a book. And I've been able to get all my other work done remotely pretty well while I've been here—the isolation is good for reading manuscripts." As was the bathtub, and the sunshine, and the reduced stress from not having to walk into that building every day, but she didn't need to say that part.

"Hmm." There was a long silence on the phone, and Izzy forced herself not to fill it. A technique she'd learned from Marta herself. "Okay. You have a month. Don't let me down." And then Marta hung up the phone.

Izzy let out a deep breath. She'd done it. Now she had to do something almost as hard: tell her parents she was staying in California for a month. She hoped they didn't freak out, but even if they did, she was already on the other side of the country.

> Looks like I'm staying for a few more weeks, maybe longer! Getting some great experience and really good work done here, but I miss you guys!

Obviously, they didn't know she was living alone in a house with Beau Towers. Yes, she was an adult, but that didn't mean her dad wouldn't flip out about that. It wasn't like she'd lied to them, she'd just . . . implied it was more like corporate housing.

> Sounds great, honey! Glad they have so much faith in you! Can't talk now, but we'll call you later!

Well, that was uncharacteristically . . . chill for her dad. Okay, then. She really was staying here.

So at three on Monday afternoon, Izzy walked into the kitchen, the notebooks and pens that she'd picked up at the stationery store on Sunday afternoon in her hand, her phone in her pocket, and butterflies in her stomach. She hoped this worked.

Michaela was pouring hot water into a mug. "Hi, Izzy. Tea? I heard you'll be here for a while longer."

Michaela looked pleased about that. Good—Izzy had been worried that it would be more trouble for her.

"Yeah, it looks like it. And no thanks, for the tea, but maybe later, if you're still around when we're done?"

Michaela smiled at her on her way out of the kitchen. "Sounds good. See you later, then."

After a few more minutes, Izzy turned and looked at the clock on the oven: 3:05. Maybe he wasn't coming? Maybe he'd changed his mind? That "don't let me down" from Marta rang through her ears.

"No pressure," Izzy muttered.

"What was that?" Beau asked as he walked into the kitchen.

"Oh! It was nothing." Izzy forced herself to hold back her sigh of relief but apparently not well enough.

"Did you think I wasn't coming?"

Beau didn't quite look at her.

She shook her head, then nodded. What was the point of pretending? "I thought, just maybe, you'd changed your mind about this."

He walked over to the snack cabinet. "And blow off the snack cabinet? Never." He threw the doors open. "What are you thinking for today? Something cheesy, or something spicy?"

Izzy surveyed the options. "Why not both?"

His face relaxed into a smile. "A woman after my own heart." Before she could figure out how to react to that, he'd walked over to the fridge and grabbed that tray again. "I'll get us an assortment."

Izzy wondered where they were taking all these snacks. She'd assumed they'd work here in the kitchen. They were probably going to the TV room. That wouldn't be her choice for the best place to get work done—too many distractions, plus the coffee table was an awkward height for working on a laptop, but she'd let Beau have this one.

Beau piled the snacks on the tray, along with a stack of napkins and some drinks from the fridge.

"Do these drinks work for you?" he asked her. She glanced at the tray. He had two cans of seltzer, two Diet Cokes, and two bottles of that "green" juice stuff that was always in the fridge. It was really more of a greenish gray. She didn't know what was in it, and she didn't want to know.

"Okay, out with it," he said, before she could say anything. "Why are you making that face?"

Oops. She was usually better about masking her facial expressions.

"If both of those bottles of that juice are for you, that's fine, but please don't make me drink it."

Beau laughed. "Oh, come on, it's not that bad! Have you ever tried it?"

Izzy made a face. "No, and I don't plan to. It looks disgusting. I have teeth, I can chew my vegetables just fine."

Beau picked up the tray and walked to the door of the kitchen. "Sure you can, but you ate that soup the other night and liked it, didn't you? There was no chewing involved there."

"That was different," she said as she followed him. "First of all, it's soup! Everyone loves soup. It was a cold and rainy night, the soup was nice and warm. Secondly—"

"Okay, today is a bright sunny day, the juice is cool and refreshing," Beau said.

"*Secondly*," Izzy said, "the vegetables in the soup were cooked before they were all blended up. These vegetables are all just, what, put into a blender raw? That sounds very indigestible."

Beau turned back to look at her. "Did you ever read that book about the green eggs and ham when you were a kid? That's what you sound like right now. You're just talking about what you *think* the green juice is like, and not what it's actually like. Try it, try it, then you'll see."

Izzy scowled at him. "It's very cruel of you to quote one of my favorite children's books at me to try to get me to do something I don't want to do."

Beau laughed as he walked past the door to the TV room. Where were they going?

"Aren't we . . . ?" Izzy gestured back at the TV room.

Beau kept going. "Oh. No. I thought we'd have more room—and fewer distractions—in the library."

Of course. The library. Obviously a house that had gardens and cellars would also have a library.

Izzy followed Beau down the hall to those big wooden doors he'd told her were off-limits during the tour. He transferred the tray to one hand and threw the doors open. Izzy walked inside.

"Oh. The library" was all she could say.

She'd gone to the library with her parents, once a week, every week, when she was a little girl. It had felt like a magic place to her, full of books just waiting to be read—on shelves, in stacks, in every corner. She'd fantasized about having a place like that in her own imaginary future home, with shelves and shelves of books, wherever you looked.

This library was all her library dreams come true. It was a huge room, but it still managed to feel cozy and warm. There was a round table on the far side with chairs grouped around it, a plush love seat and two overstuffed armchairs in a little circle over by the fireplace, and cushioned window seats that looked like perfect reading nooks lining the walls. There was a long, dark wood table directly in front of her, and an old-fashioned desk in the corner. The room was well lit, with lamps everywhere and the sun streaming in the windows.

But what made this room so incredible was the books. Floor-to-ceiling bookshelves lined every wall, with those rolling ladders so you could reach each and every book.

Izzy slowly walked around the room, trailing her fingers over the spines and occasionally stopping to pick one up and flip through it. There was fiction, history, science, cookbooks, politics, and many shelves full of children's books. And the best thing about them was that these books looked read. She could tell. These weren't all brand-new books that some interior decorator had bought in bulk and arranged carefully on a shelf in some sort of order to make the room look good. As a matter of fact, many of them were in no order at all—she itched to organize them. But that also told her they were all books that had been reached for, and read, and maybe even reread. The spines were broken, the book jackets removed or a little torn, pages dog-eared. These books hadn't just been read, they'd been loved.

She wanted to touch each one, find out about them and where they came from, study the covers, sit on the floor with a pile on her lap and decide which one to dive into first.

She remembered that crack she'd made the other day to Beau, about how there were no books in this house. She winced. But also, she couldn't believe she'd been living here with these books all this time, totally unaware.

"Have these been here this whole time?" she said to one shelf, full of some of her favorites.

Beau laughed softly. She hadn't even realized she'd said that out loud.

"Did you think they just appeared by magic?" he asked.

If he'd said that, in that same tone, a few days ago, she would have bristled and stormed out of the room. Now she just smiled.

"I mean, sort of? This room feels a little bit like magic." She turned around in a circle and looked at it. "It's a great room. I've missed having books around me so much."

"Feel free to borrow any of these, if you want," Beau said.

That was so thoughtful of him.

"Oh. Thank you." Would she feel comfortable enough to do that? She wasn't sure.

He set the tray on the long wooden table, and smiled at her. "I'm glad I brought you in here, then. I love this room. I'm glad you like it, too."

She smiled at him. "It's incredible." She walked over to the table and inspected the snacks and picked up a bag of Takis. Then she hesitated.

"What's wrong?" Beau sat down across from her and opened one of his gross-looking juices.

"Oh." She was embarrassed. "Nothing. Nothing's wrong."

Beau grinned at her. "You're allowed to eat in this library, you know."

She laughed, surprised he'd read her mind like that. "Okay, but these are so messy! I don't want to get anything on the books!"

Beau picked up something else on the tray and tossed it to her. "Didn't you notice that Kettle keeps little packets of wipes by the messy snacks? She thinks of everything. I brought some in here, for exactly that reason."

Izzy laughed again and tore open the bag. "Okay, then we're in business."

In more ways than one. It was time to stop talking about the library and snacks and start talking about Beau's memoir. She had to get him to write enough of it in the next month in order to prove to Beau that he could write the whole thing, to prove to Marta that Izzy was good at this job, and to prove to herself that she wanted—or didn't want—to keep working in publishing.

No pressure.

Izzy flipped open her notebook and picked up a pen. "Okay." She looked at the list she'd made the day before. "How much do you have already? Let's start there."

He looked away from her. "Nothing."

"What?" She couldn't help her reaction. "What do you mean, nothing? You said you've been working on it for a while."

He looked down at the closed laptop in front of him on the table. "I have been. But I've deleted all of it."

"*All* of it?" she said. This was going to be a lot harder than she'd thought.

Beau stood up. "Yes, okay? Yes, I've deleted everything. None of it was working. This isn't going to work either, I don't know why I agreed to it."

Izzy took a breath and stayed where she was. "Beau."

He glared at her. "What?"

She looked straight at him. "Why don't we start over?"

He stared at her for a second, swallowed, and then sat back down. "Okay. Sorry. I'm just . . . on edge about this, that's all."

Izzy grinned at him. "Oh really? I couldn't tell."

He laughed, thank God. If he hadn't—if he'd taken offense to that, too—she'd be certain this partnership of theirs was doomed from the outset.

"I guess you're used to stress cases, dealing with writers all day," he said. "Or hotheads, as the case may be—I have no business calling myself a writer."

When he said that, he just looked sad instead of angry. Okay, now was the time for her best pep talk skills to come out.

"First of all," she said, "I am something of a hothead myself occasionally, I don't know if you've noticed that?" He laughed again. "Second: If you write, then you're a writer. You don't have to have written a book or even feel good about your writing to get that title. And you have been writing—you told me so. All that work you've already done? None of it was wasted. It's all building blocks; even if you can't see them, they're there. It will all inform the work you'll go on to do."

Now that she knew he'd been listening to her, that he was actually paying attention to her advice, talking to him about writing came easier. And maybe now it was easier because her heart was actually in it. She really cared if she helped him.

"Also," she continued, "lots of writers are just anxious as hell. Everyone deletes stuff in a panic sometimes. How about next time you feel like deleting something, just open a new document. Call it Deleted Scenes, or The Bad Words, or Stuff I Cut, or whatever, and cut and paste it over there. Hide it in a different folder, if you need to, so you don't have to see it. Email it to a friend, get them to promise not to read it, whatever. Just save it somehow."

He swallowed hard. "Okay," he said. "That's . . . that's a good idea."

She took a handful of Takis out of the bag to kill time while she thought fast. "Here's what you're going to do today." He opened the laptop, but she shook her head. "Not yet. Sometimes, if you have a block, or things aren't going well, it helps to switch from one way of writing to another. So here, this notebook is for you." She pushed one of the notebooks in front of her across the table to him, along with a pen.

"Write down ten scenes you have in your mind for this book. Don't think too hard, you don't have to say that much about them, just note them down, just a few sentences for each one. None of this is set in stone, don't worry." She picked up her phone and set the timer. "I'll give you five minutes. Go."

He looked at her. She could see the objection in his eyes. She didn't say anything else; she just looked back at him. After a few seconds, his eyes fell to the paper, and he reached for the pen.

When the timer went off, Beau kept scribbling for a few more seconds. He apparently did have something to say. He looked up at her after he put down his pen. "Okay," he said. "What now?"

Izzy tried to sound more authoritative than she felt. "Now: Pick one of those scenes, and for the next thirty minutes, write it. Right there in that notebook." She looked down at her phone and set the timer. "Starting now."

This time, he did object. "But I can't. That's the whole problem. I can't do that."

"You can," she said. "I know that you can. Just—"

He pushed the notebook across the table at her. "I told you I can't. I've tried before, it's always just bad, and wrong. I thought you were going to teach me how to do this, not just . . ." He stopped. He looked down at the table for a few seconds, then looked back at her. "Sorry. I interrupted you. Go on."

She'd been sure he would leave for real this time. "It's okay if it's bad," she said. "Just accept the badness now. For now, it doesn't matter if it's bad, it just has to be something. You can fix bad writing, you can't fix a blank page." Was she getting through to him? She had no idea. "It doesn't have to be perfect, it doesn't have to be just right, and you don't have to show it to me. I won't even ask. Just get something on paper. If you get stuck, if you don't know how to start, just write about me, and how annoyed you are that I'm making you do this, and then get back to it." She pushed the notebook back across the table to him. "I know you can do this, Beau. I wouldn't be here if I didn't know it."

He looked down at the notebook, then back at her. She held her breath.

Finally, he picked up a pen and flipped to a blank page. And started writing.

Izzy looked down at her phone so Beau wouldn't see the relief on her face.

For the next thirty minutes, Izzy read through work emails, ignored Priya's texts, and tried not to look at Beau. Despite that, though, she noticed when he sped up, when he stopped, when he put his pen down, when he took a deep breath and picked it back up. After the first ten minutes of stopping and starting, he wrote steadily, and she smiled every time she heard him turn a page and keep going.

Seeing him write like that made part of her itch to write herself. To turn a page in her own notebook, brainstorm that new idea that had come to her recently, unbidden, even after she'd told herself she didn't have the heart to write anymore, didn't have the strength for it. She looked down at her notebook and picked up her pen. Just then, the timer went off, and Beau dropped his pen with a sigh.

"Okay." He looked up at her. "What now?"

She smiled at him. "I think that's enough for our first day, don't you? Go clear your mind. Go for a walk, or a swim, or something."

He flipped the notebook closed and stood up. "*Thank* you."

She laughed. And then she stopped him as he turned to walk to the door.

"One more thing. Promise me you won't throw those pages away?" She gestured to the notebook. "Do I need to hold on to that notebook for you?"

She'd been joking, but he didn't laugh.

"I'm not . . . I'm not sure I can promise that. At least, not yet." He looked down at the notebook in his hand. "Can you promise *me* something? If I give you this, for safekeeping, promise that you won't read it?"

"I won't read it," she said. "I promise."

He held the notebook out to her, and she took it from him. "Thanks, Isabelle. I appreciate it."

She followed him to the door. When they walked out, they turned in opposite directions, until she turned back around.

"Just so you know. My friends call me Izzy."

She didn't even know why she'd said that. She didn't let anyone at work call her Izzy, except for Priya. Maybe she'd said it because Beau trusted her, and she wanted to let him know she trusted him, too.

He finally smiled. "Thanks, Izzy."

CHAPTER ELEVEN

On Friday, when she met Beau in the library, she handed his notebook back to him, like she'd done every day that week.

"I'm setting the timer, okay?" she said, and he nodded and flipped open the notebook, like he'd done every day that week.

Every day, as he sat there, writing in the notebook, she wondered what he was writing. Was this impulsive experiment of hers working? She had no idea. And what was it that was so hard for Beau to write about? She was so curious, but she'd promised not to ask him, so she didn't.

And every day, when she sat there with her own notebook, she felt the pull to write, herself. How could she not, when she was in this perfect library, with her favorite notebook in front of her and her favorite pen in her hand? But even thinking about it felt scary. She'd thrown her whole heart into her book, and she'd hurt so much and for so long after she'd gotten those notes from Gavin. She wasn't ready for that heartache again.

But as the days went on, she kept thinking about writing. Especially since she felt like such a hypocrite as she gave Beau all this encouragement and ignored every word that came out of her own mouth.

What was it she'd said to him yesterday? "The only way out is through. I know it's hard, really hard sometimes, but your options are to either give up, or push through the hard parts. And I know you don't want to give up."

She didn't want to give up either.

Fine. FINE. She would just work a little on that one idea. Just until the timer went off. She picked up her pen and flipped open her notebook.

When the waltz trilled from her phone, she stared down at her notebook for a few seconds. Okay. Okay, that was a start.

"Izzy?"

She turned the page of her notebook quickly so Beau wouldn't see what she'd been doing, and looked up at him. "Yeah. I was thinking." She gestured to the laptop at the end of the table. "Why don't you turn that on today?"

He looked at the laptop, and in that moment, she saw some of the fear and shame in his eyes that she hadn't seen since that day in the kitchen.

"Why? What's wrong with the notebook? I like the notebook."

She forced herself not to smile at that. "I know, I do, too. But I thought today, you could type up some of what you've written in it. Maybe what you wrote on our first day. You can just type it exactly how you wrote it, or you can make edits to it, expand it, whatever you want. But now's the time for you to look at it again, and for it to exist in a form that isn't just the notebook."

He was already shaking his head, but she kept going.

"I think—correct me if I'm wrong here—that you were almost scared of the laptop, after how hard it all was before. This might be one way to start using it again, and not be afraid of it anymore. Just fifteen minutes. What do you think?"

He narrowed his eyes at her. "Does it matter what I think? Or are you going to make me do this, no matter what?"

She started to respond, but then she saw he had a tiny smile on his face, and she smiled back. "How about this? It matters what you think, and also, I'm going to make you do it, no matter what."

He laughed out loud and pulled the laptop toward him. "Fine. I think this sucks, that's what I think and that you're mean for springing it on me with no warning on this bright and sunny Friday afternoon, just when I'd gotten used to the stupid notebook."

She pursed her lips. "I thought you said you liked the notebook, and now you're calling it stupid?" She had an idea. "Okay, how's this: If you do this, I'll drink one of those disgusting juices of yours."

His face lit up. "Seriously? Okay, fine, you have a deal. But you have to drink the whole thing—you can't just take one sip and make a face and act like you're done."

She took one of the bottles from the tray. "Fine." She unscrewed the top and suppressed a shudder. "I don't know why they call it green juice. Even this color is disgusting. More gray than anything else."

He flipped open the laptop. "A deal is a deal, Izzy."

She rolled her eyes and took a sip. Huh. This green stuff was actually . . . delicious? Not that she'd tell him that.

"It's as disgusting as I thought it would be, but I said I'd drink the whole thing, and I will. Now. Go."

He just looked at her. "You're a bad liar. You even sort of like it. Admit it."

She shook her head, but she couldn't help the smile she could feel on her lips. "I admit nothing. Don't you have work to do?"

He flipped pages of the notebook, still smiling, and started typing. Izzy kept smiling as she looked down at her phone. Her pep talks for Beau worked so much better now. Probably because they knew each other a lot better now. And also probably because she really meant them now.

Priya texted her right after she set the timer.

Ugh, I'm at happy hour with other people from the office and everyone is boring and/or annoying except for you. It feels like you've been in California forever. I can't believe you're going to be there for another three whole weeks!

Izzy forced herself not to laugh out loud.

I miss you, too! Omg but I just realized, I think I'll still be here when you come out for your cousin's wedding, I can see you then!

Priya wrote back immediately.

Oooh yesss I almost forgot about that! And you're going to introduce me to Beau Towers, yay! Holding you to that

Izzy would just ignore that. Should she go back to her notebook and her new project? Maybe just . . . look at it, to see if she had any other places to start brainstorming? But what if it was all bad, and she could tell immediately?

It's okay if it's bad, she'd said to Beau, just a few days before.

Okay, okay.

When the timer went off again, Izzy shut the notebook right away. She was terrified to be writing again, but she still liked this idea.

Beau started to close his laptop, but she stopped him. "Did you save it? Preferably in more than one location, so you have a backup?"

A panicked look washed over his face. "I . . . you're going to think this is stupid, but . . ."

"I bet I won't," she said.

He tried to smile but didn't quite make it. "I thought about that, saving it, but I didn't know what name to give it. It felt—it feels—too, I don't know, official, to call it a book, or even a chapter." He looked down. "I'm sorry, I'm being ridiculous."

She grinned at him. "How about this? Call it 'Isabelle made me do this.'"

He laughed. "Now, why didn't I think of that?" His hands flashed over the keys, and then he looked up at her. "Done."

Izzy picked up the green juice to take the last sip, but it was all gone. She looked across the table at Beau, who had a very smug expression on his face.

"Admit it," he said. "Admit the green juice is refreshing."

Izzy set her lips in a firm line so she wouldn't smile. "I will admit that it grew on me a little, in that same way mold does, but I admit nothing else."

Beau laughed and stood up. "If I didn't already know how stubborn you were, I would know for sure now." He flipped his notebook closed and handed it to her, like he did whenever they left the library. "Same time tomorrow?"

She smiled on the way out of the library. "I prefer the word *determined*, thank you very much. But tomorrow is Saturday—I'm not going to make you work over the weekend."

She expected to see relief on his face, but instead he looked disappointed for just a second, before that old angry look settled back on his face. "Oh. Okay. That makes sense."

Did he want to keep going?

"If you want, we can meet over the weekend, too," she said.

He shook his head, not looking at her. "I'm not going to make you work with me on the weekend, it's your time off."

She poked him with the notebook. He jumped and finally looked directly at her. "You're not making me do anything. I'm offering. Beau, do you want to meet here tomorrow to work on your book?"

He looked down for a moment and then met her eyes. "Yeah. Okay. Thanks."

She started to walk back to her room.

"Izzy."

She stopped and turned around.

"I was wondering," he said. "Maybe you've already watched some more episodes of *This Provincial Life* on your own, and if so, ignore me, it's fine. But if not, tonight, do you want to have dinner and watch one or two?"

She did, as a matter of fact.

"That sounds great," she said. "Meet you in the kitchen. What time?"

The tense look on his face relaxed. "How about seven? Kettle made lasagna. I'll tell her I can handle putting it in the oven. I'll grab us a bottle of wine." He paused. "I don't know if you want any, but . . . I don't know if you noticed, this week was a little stressful for me."

She burst out laughing. "You don't know if I noticed? Do you think this week was stressful just for you?"

He laughed, too. "Okay, good point."

When Izzy got down to the kitchen that night, Beau was already there, taking a big pan out of the oven.

"That smells amazing," she said.

He turned and grinned at her. "You have no idea. Kettle's lasagna is legendary. There's salad and garlic bread, too, but this is the star."

Beau dished out lasagna on two plates for them and set their plates on the tray, along with the garlic bread and bowls full of salad.

"Don't worry," he said. "I already brought the wine in there."

She laughed. "You read my mind."

Izzy followed him into the TV room and sat down on the couch.

"Is red okay?" he asked her as he picked up the corkscrew.

"I thought it would go best with the lasagna, but if you'd rather have white, I can—"

She took their plates off the tray. "Red is perfect. I'm not picky, especially not tonight."

He narrowed his eyes at her. "Are you trying to tell me that dealing with a stubborn, ungrateful, difficult student all week has made you really look forward to some wine?"

She glanced at him. He was smiling. She smiled back.

"Frankly, my work with my stubborn, ungrateful, difficult student has been the least stressful part of my week. It's probably been the best part of my week."

As soon as that was out of her mouth, Izzy felt embarrassed that she'd said it. It felt too honest, too earnest, to tell Beau how much she'd enjoyed working with him, to even hint at how strangely peaceful and happy she'd felt during their hours in the library together, how she'd started to look forward to it every morning when she woke up.

He pulled the cork out of the wine bottle and poured her a glass.

"Mine too," he said, quietly.

She looked up at him, and their eyes met. This time, she looked away.

"If I was the least stressful part of your week," he said, in a different voice, "your job is even harder than I thought. What else is stressing you out?" He sat down at the other end of the couch.

Izzy took a sip of her wine. She probably shouldn't complain to Beau about her job. He was one of Marta's authors, after all.

"You don't have to tell me, if you don't want to," he said, after a few moments of silence. "But you don't have to worry about me going back to your boss, or anything, about what you tell me." He waved his hand in a circle in the air. "This room is sacrosanct. Nothing gets out of it."

She smiled at him. "Oh, well, if that's the case." The smile dropped from her lips and she sighed. "Work hasn't been the easiest, this week. I've had to deal with a handful of Marta's most difficult authors—" Beau made a face when she said that, and she shook her head. "No, you're nowhere even close to the top of that ranking, trust me. You just didn't respond to emails, which, yes, was stressful, but all these people DO is email me. Three of them have books coming out in the fall, and it's just about six months before their releases, which somehow set off some sort of timer in them to start panicking and email me every day before I even log on to complain about anything possible. Their covers—which were all finalized months ago—their copy editors, the number of advance copies they'll get, why they've never gotten a *New York Times* review when their friend gets *New York Times* reviews for every book, even the number of pages their book is. That's an actual email I got this week. The book apparently ends in an unlucky number for her, and she wants it changed."

Izzy took another sip of wine. "And then"—she let out a sigh—"there's this guy I work with—"

Beau whistled, and she laughed.

"No, it's not like that at all. He used to have my job, and he got promoted. He's given me lots of advice in the past, which at first I was grateful for, but lately . . . it's been sort of getting on my nerves."

Beau poured more wine in her glass. "That sounds frustrating," he said.

She was glad he'd just listened, without interrupting her with questions, or offering her advice.

"It is frustrating," she said. She tried to shake that off. "Anyway. I'm glad for Friday, and wine, and Michaela's lasagna."

He lifted his glass to her. "I'll toast to all those things."

Speaking of the lasagna, why was she talking so much when it was sitting here in front of her, smelling so good? She took a bite and sighed in contentment.

"Ready for this?"

Izzy jumped. Beau was looking at her, the remote in his hand. Right, the show.

"Oh. Yeah, definitely."

They watched one episode, tucked into their opposite corners of the couch. When Izzy got toward the bottom of her wineglass, she picked up the bottle and raised an eyebrow at Beau.

"I can't even believe you have to ask," he said as he held out his glass.

"It was more of a rhetorical question," she said.

When the episode was over, Beau stood up and picked up the tray. Was he tired of this already? She'd sort of assumed they'd be watching more than one episode.

"I'm getting more lasagna, want some?" he asked.

She smiled, relieved. "I hope that was a rhetorical question," she said.

He picked up her plate. "Absolutely."

After the next episode, they both stood up. Izzy picked up her plate and wineglass, but Beau was empty-handed.

"I'm exhausted," she said. "I think I'm heading to bed."

He turned off the TV. "Yeah, me too."

But then why . . . She was clearly missing something.

"Why do you look so confused?" he asked as he walked toward the door.

She nodded toward his dishes, still on the coffee table. "Your dishes. Aren't you going put to them in the dishwasher? Or does the furniture in this house come to life and magically wash the dishes every night?"

He laughed. "Oh! No, don't worry about them, you can just leave your dishes there. The housekeeper comes on Monday morning, she'll take care of that."

She was suddenly wide-awake. "Let me get this straight. It's Friday night. And your plan is to let your dirty dishes sit there, all weekend, waiting for someone to clean them up for you, because you don't know how to wash dishes, or even load a dishwasher?"

He glared at her, the same way he had the day she'd gotten there, but it didn't bother her anymore.

"I know HOW to wash dishes. But why do it, when I pay someone else to do it?"

She pursed her lips. "Oh really? You know how to do it? When's the last time you washed a dish?"

He looked even madder. "That's not the point. The point is—"

Laughter exploded from her at the look on his face, the pure rage that he obviously had no memory of ever washing a dish. She laughed so hard she had to put her own dishes down on the sideboard so she wouldn't drop them.

"You're laughing at me," Beau said, after watching her for a while.

She nodded, still giggling. "I absolutely am. 'That's not the point.'" She let out another cackle. "Incredible. Just amazing." She pointed to the coffee table. "Get the dishes. I'm going to teach you how to load a dishwasher, Beau Towers."

He was still trying to glare at her, but she could see the smile peeking through.

"It's not that I don't know *how* to load a dishwasher." He walked over to the coffee table and piled his dishes on the tray, and then added her dishes on his way back. "I've seen people do it. Plenty of times. I've just never, exactly, done it myself."

"Great," she said on the way to the kitchen. "There's a first time for everything."

They stood in front of the dishwasher.

"Open that up," Izzy said.

Beau let out a long dramatic sigh, but he set the tray full of dishes down and opened the dishwasher. Then he picked up the dishes and tossed them all inside. "There. Done."

Izzy shook her head. "Bless your heart, but no, that's not how you do it." She gestured to the dishes inside the dishwasher. "First, you have to rinse the dishes."

He stared at her. "Rinse them?"

She almost laughed at him again. "Yes, rinse them. Put them under the faucet and run hot water on them."

"But why do I have to do that if the dishwasher is just going to clean them anyway?"

Izzy took a plate out of the dishwasher and held it up. "Look at all this cheese and tomato sauce caked on. Only the best dishwashers will get that food off, and this dishwasher, while fine, isn't top-of-the-line like your television. We see where your priorities were."

He growled something at her, but he took the dishes back out of the dishwasher and rinsed them while she watched.

"Second," she said. "There's an art to loading a dishwasher. This was my job at home for most of my life, so you're lucky to have someone like me to teach you how to do it."

"*Lucky* isn't exactly the word I would use right now," he said to the sink.

"Excuse me?" she asked him. "What was that?" She beamed at him. This was even more entertaining than the show had been. "Oh, nothing? That's what I thought. Now, the plates should go there—down in the bottom, you see, where there's plenty of room. The bowls should go *there.* The wineglasses you want to be careful with; they can easily break in dishwashers if you don't put them carefully in the top rack. And finally, the flatware all goes in that little container—no, no, no, don't just jam it all together like that! Separate the forks from the knives from the spoons! That way, when you unload it, you just have to grab a handful and put it in the right place in the drawer."

"When *I* unload it, she says," Beau said to a spoon. "Is she going to make me do that, too?"

Izzy ignored that. "Look, now we're all done! Isn't that better? Wasn't that fun?"

Beau looked at her as he dried his hands. "You think writing is fun, you think cleaning the kitchen is fun. . . . Isabelle Marlowe, I'm starting to think you need a new understanding of the word *fun*."

She just laughed at him as she left the kitchen.

CHAPTER TWELVE

Late Saturday morning, Izzy went out to the pool with coffee and some of the coffee cake that had been in the kitchen that morning—Michaela had obviously left them well stocked for the weekend. She'd wanted to go to the pool since the day she'd arrived—she'd even stopped and looked at it a few times on her stupid little walks around the gardens—but she hadn't quite felt comfortable enough to just sit there, on one of those tempting lounge chairs, and relax.

But today was Saturday, and the morning fog had cleared, so it was bright and warm and sunny. And she somehow felt more at home in this house than before. Like she was welcome here now. So she put on one of her cotton sundresses, grabbed her e-reader, and went outside.

She sat down in a lounge chair with her book, kicked her flats off, and closed her eyes. The sun was gloriously warm, she had a whole day and a half before she had to deal with Marta, she had three whole more weeks before she had to go back to New York, and she had a romance novel on her e-reader that she'd started in the bathtub last night. She should read a manuscript while she was out here, she knew she should. But she'd already read three of them this week, after working all day, then working with Beau in the afternoons, and she needed to read something that didn't feel like homework.

She checked the weather in New York—twenty-four degrees, cloudy—then texted Priya a picture of her bare feet in the sun with the pool in the background and laughed at Priya's expletive-laden response. She settled back in the lounge chair and started reading.

She was deep into the book when she heard a splash. And then another. She looked up. And saw Beau, in the pool. Swimming.

He was doing the butterfly, a stroke she'd never learned how to do but had always admired every four years when she watched the Olympics. It always seemed so hard, that big burst of energy as the swimmers almost leaped across the pool. All she could see were his back and shoulders. His incredibly powerful back and shoulders.

He probably hadn't even noticed her. Should she get up to leave? No, that would be silly. They were . . . friendly now, after all. After working together all week in the library, and dinner and everything last night. They could coexist, with her in a lounge chair, reading, and him swimming laps in the pool. With those arms. And . . . shoulders.

She just couldn't look at him doing it. That's all. She looked back down at her book.

But that was worse! She couldn't sit here, with him doing . . . that . . . and read a romance novel! This was the wrong book to be reading right now. That's probably why she was thinking about Beau like that! It was all the book's fault!

Suddenly, the splashing stopped, and she looked up again. To find Beau, at the shallow end of the pool, looking straight at her.

"Hi," he said.

"Hi," she said.

She could see more of him now, from the chest up. She could hear Priya's voice in her head. *Those big, brawny guys.* Yes, that described Beau well. He didn't look like a weight lifter or a model or anything like that, but he was big, solid. He looked bigger than he had in the old pictures she'd seen of him taken around Hollywood. It suited him.

Why did he look so good? He'd apparently been locked away

here for like a year; shouldn't he be, like, pale and pasty and awkward looking? Of course not. He'd been locked away in a mansion with gardens and a pool—that's why he was a nice even light brown, with that broad chest and wide shoulders and thank God she couldn't see anything else. She was *very* grateful she was wearing sunglasses, so he couldn't tell she was staring.

"Having a good day?" he asked.

She nodded. "Um, yeah. Just trying to get some . . . reading done. A manuscript. For work." She picked up her coffee cup. "And drinking coffee. It's, um, beautiful weather today."

He grinned at her. "Not like last Saturday."

She laughed. Could anyone blame her for being so outraged that it had rained then, when she was used to the weather being like this? "No, not like last Saturday."

He turned to take a sip out of his water bottle, and then lifted his arms and threw himself back into the water.

She watched him as he swam the whole length of the pool. She couldn't help herself. He flipped at the deep end and flew back toward the shallow end. She tore her eyes away from him right before he got there and turned back to her book.

Oh, the hell with it. Fine, she'd read a manuscript. Romance novels made you get too many ideas, everyone knew that. Made you think unreasonable, impossible, unlikely, totally implausible things. She needed to stop that, right away.

She read for twenty more minutes. If you could call it reading when she watched Beau swim the length of the pool and back and looked down whenever she thought he might catch her. She didn't absorb a single word of the manuscript.

Finally, she checked her phone. It was after noon! That meant she should go inside, get lunch. Excellent, great, that's what she would do. And then she'd go back to her room and watch something very G-rated on her laptop. Peaceful, relaxing, with no attractive men in it that would make her think . . . things.

She got up to leave just as Beau reached the shallow end of the pool again.

"Going inside?" he asked.

She slid her flats back on. "Yeah. I, um, I think I'm going to get lunch. More of that lasagna, I think. I didn't really eat breakfast, so I'm starving now."

He grinned at her. "Leave some for me."

Damn it, why did he have to smile at her like that? Now she understood why he'd been such a heartthrob as a teenager. And probably in his twenties, too. Even with that scraggly beard, his smile made him seem so alluring.

She turned toward the house.

"Can I ask you a question?"

She looked back at him. He wasn't smiling like that anymore. Now he almost looked nervous.

"Okay."

"I've been wondering something. That first night . . . after you left the dining room, I sort of expected you to leave right away, go back to New York. Why didn't you?"

She sat back down. "I'll answer that if you answer something for me. When you say you 'sort of expected' me to leave right away—is that what you intended?"

A week ago, she wouldn't have asked him that. But then, a lot had changed this week.

He looked embarrassed. "I don't think my thought process was particularly intentional. I was pretty angry. I kind of assumed that you were just here because you wanted to see the asshole Beau Towers in real life. And I was also kind of . . . ashamed, I guess, that I'd been ignoring your emails for so long. So yeah, on some level I was probably trying to drive you away." He reached for his water bottle but didn't take a sip. "Wow, does that sound shitty when I put it that way." He looked up at her. "I'm sorry."

She looked back at him. She could see, now that she knew him better, how much he really meant his apology.

"It's okay," she said. And then she bit her lip. "I'm afraid you're going to be disappointed with my answer now, about why I stayed."

He smiled at her. "Now I can't wait to hear this," he said.

She sighed. "I had too much wine! When I went back to my room, I *did* intend to grab my stuff and leave right away, but then I realized the wine had gone straight to my head. And then you brought the food, and then it felt too late to drive back to LA. And then Marta called in the morning, and, well . . ."

The smile on his face had widened as she talked, but it disappeared when she mentioned Marta. "Did she make you stay? That wasn't— When I emailed her, I was just trying to make it up to you, say something nice to your boss about you, so she wouldn't be mad at you because of me. I didn't mean to back you into a corner."

"No, you didn't at all," Izzy said. "Honestly, I really needed the break from the office, so when Marta called, and I was looking out my bedroom window at the bright blue sky, it felt like a gift to get to stay longer."

The furrow on his brow cleared. "Well, then." He put down his water bottle. "Thanks. For answering my question."

"No problem." She stood up. "I should . . . um, get lunch. See you in the library?"

He nodded. "Yeah. See you there."

As she walked back to the house, she thought she heard something else.

"I'm glad you stayed."

She turned around, but Beau was swimming. She must be hearing things again.

CHAPTER THIRTEEN

Monday midmorning, Izzy walked into the kitchen to refresh her coffee.

"Morning, Izzy," Michaela said.

Izzy reached for the knife to slice herself a piece of lemon pound cake. "Morning. I hope you had a good weekend."

Michaela dropped a tea bag into her mug. "I did, thank you. Oh, by the way, Izzy, it was so nice of you, but you don't have to wash the dishes here. You know there's a housekeeper who does all the cleaning, right?"

Izzy grinned at her. "Oh, I didn't wash the dishes. Beau did that."

Michaela stared. "Beau? Washed the dishes? Beau Towers?"

Izzy laughed as she turned to leave the kitchen. "Ask him."

She and Beau worked together in the library that afternoon, and every day that week. By Wednesday, she realized that she'd started to look forward to that hour—sometimes more—in the library with him. Unlike the rest of her job, the time with Beau was fun, challenging in a good way, interesting, and strangely, not at all stressful. She didn't write every time, but at least she thought about it.

"Can I ask you a question?" he said on Wednesday afternoon.

She looked up from her notebook. "Of course."

"What if I don't totally remember exact conversations? Like, I remember they happened, I know that, and I remember a few things perfectly, but the rest I remember in a sort of general way. You know what I mean? How do I . . . What do I do then?"

Beau hadn't asked her a real question about writing until now.

"I think the most important thing is to talk about how those conversations made you feel, what impact they had on you, both then and now. Like, you don't remember word for word exactly what you said, or what other people said, but you remember your emotions during those conversations, right? And if those emotions have changed as you've gotten older, or if you have different perspectives on them as the years have gone on, you know that. So lean into that, concentrate on that. This book is about you. So talk about you, and how you felt, and how you feel now."

He looked at her, and then down at the screen. "Okay. That makes sense." He tried to smile, though she could tell it was an effort. "That sounds really *hard*, but it makes sense."

She laughed, and after a moment, so did he.

Without even talking about it, they had dinner together every night that week. They met in the kitchen every night, loaded up their plates together, and then either ate at the kitchen table—if Izzy was tired, or if she had more work to do that night after dinner—or in the TV room. And now Beau always loaded the dishwasher after dinner.

Izzy didn't go back out to the pool, though. It was too dangerous out there. She and Beau were working together. She couldn't get her mind all full of Beau's bare arms and shoulders and back and dear God, his chest. At least he'd been in the pool the whole time and she hadn't been able to see the rest of his body. Better to stay inside, where there was no chance of that.

On Friday, when she walked into the library at three, Beau was already there, his laptop open, the tray of snacks on the table, and the bottle of green juice at Izzy's seat.

She sat down and twisted the cap off. "Okay, where were we?" She pushed Beau's notebook across the table to him. "You know what? It's Friday, you've worked hard all week, let's do something fun: Today, why don't you write down your favorite story about yourself. You know the one I mean, the funny one you tell at parties, some adventure you went on, something fun you did as a kid, whatever. Write as much as you can get to today; this weekend you can type it up and work on it. Starting . . . now."

Izzy set the timer. She looked down at her phone and sighed. She had more work to do, but she didn't have the heart for it today.

All of a sudden, Beau flipped closed his notebook and pushed it back across the table to her. She looked up from her phone. "What—"

"Today is a break day," he said. "I decree it."

Break day. What a concept.

"Oh, you decree it? Then it must be true." She took his notebook. "It's fine if you need a break, we all do sometimes." She started to get up. "Okay, well—"

"No," he said. "Not just me. We both need a break. It's Friday, and you've been working with me every day for almost two weeks. You need a break even more than I do." He stood up. "The thing I started writing was actually fun, but it reminded me that it's too beautiful a day to be inside. Get your stuff, we're going to the beach."

She stayed where she was and looked up at him. "Oh, I don't have . . . beach stuff here. I actually haven't been to the beach yet."

He looked at her, his mouth in a perfect O. "You haven't been to the beach?" She started to explain, but he kept going. "This is unacceptable. We have to teach you the true meaning of fun. There are plenty of places to buy everything you need. Be at the car in ten minutes."

He left the room before she could argue with him.

Izzy stood up slowly. The beach. It did feel sort of criminal that she'd been here for over two weeks and hadn't been to the beach yet. She looked out at the Pacific Ocean from her bedroom window every single day, but she'd never seen it up close. Beau was probably right; she should do something about that.

Okay. She smiled. The beach.

Izzy was down at the car in the prescribed ten minutes, after scrambling into a sundress, throwing her braids up into a big topknot, and grabbing the flip-flops she'd bought this week—she couldn't keep going everywhere in her ballet flats.

Beau shook his head at her as he unlocked the car. "I still can't believe you haven't been to the beach since you've been here," he said. "You've taken the car a few times, where have you gone?"

Izzy put her seat belt on. She hadn't realized Beau had paid such close attention to her comings and goings.

"Oh, just shopping. To the stationery store, to buy the notebooks and pens. And then also . . . when I packed to come to California a few weeks ago, I thought I was going to be here for four days for a work conference, not . . ."

"Not move in with a recluse for weeks on end and teach him how to write a book?" Beau grinned at her as he pulled out into the street.

Izzy laughed. "That's not exactly how I would have put it, but yes, as you can imagine, I needed to buy a few things." She couldn't believe she'd been here for so long already. She couldn't believe she only had two weeks left.

Once they were on the way down the hill, she turned to Beau. She'd been holding this in since they left the library.

"That thing you started writing was actually fun to write, huh?"

He sighed, but she could see the smile in his eyes. "I was hoping you hadn't heard me say that. Now you'll never let me hear the end of it."

She elbowed him. "That's not true! I'm just . . . glad. That's all."

He looked over at her for a second and then back to the road in front of him. "I'm glad, too," he said.

They got to the beach less than ten minutes later. She hadn't realized how close it was; a beach seemed like something you had to travel to get to, not like a trip to the grocery store.

They pulled into a parking space, and she started to follow Beau. But instead of walking down toward the beach, he turned and went in the other direction.

"Where are we going?"

He wiggled his eyebrows at her. "You'll see."

Beau walked into one of the shops, just off the beach.

"Hi, guys," he said to the people working there. "I need to rent a wet suit that will work for her." He pointed at Izzy. "And a surfboard for her, too."

Izzy took a step back and stared at him. "What are you talking about?"

He suddenly had a very wide grin on his face. "Now it's my turn to teach you something. Surprise: You're getting surfing lessons today, Izzy."

Her mouth dropped open. "Surfing lessons? But I don't . . . That sounds . . ."

He ignored her and turned back to the woman with a long blond ponytail working at the shop. "Oh, and she needs a swimsuit. She can change in the back, right?"

The blond woman was already beckoning to Izzy. "Oh totally, yeah. Come on back and try stuff on."

Izzy looked up at Beau. He was still smiling, but that challenging look from the first day was back in his eyes. And she reacted the same way she had then.

"Fine, I'll do this. But if I fall off the surfboard and drown, Marta is going to kill you, you realize that, right? It'll make so much extra work for her if she has to hire a new assistant."

He just laughed at her. "I'll make sure that doesn't happen."

Izzy walked into the back, wondering why she'd agreed to do this. She didn't even know if they had her size in this place, despite how certain the blond surfer had looked. This looked like the kind of place with lots of bikinis for people who were size 0, 2, maybe 4, not any kind of swimsuit for someone who was size 12. But no, she found a one-piece in the back that fit her, and it was bright pink, not boring black.

She pulled the wet suit on over the swimsuit and went out to meet Beau. She felt ridiculous, but she'd told Beau she'd do this, so now she had to.

He was also in a wet suit. Unfortunately, he did not look at all ridiculous in it. He looked strong, and powerful, and . . . She had to look away.

"Did you rent a wet suit for yourself, too?" she asked him.

He shook his head. "I brought mine along." He gestured at the bag at his feet. "My surfboard is a little big for you, though. I thought you should learn on something easier."

She narrowed her eyes at him. "You planned this from the beginning?" She'd thought he'd just had the idea when they got to the beach.

He laughed as he took the surfboard from the blond woman. "I am capable of planning ahead, you know."

She hadn't really expected that he'd plan ahead for her.

He turned down toward the beach. "And see, now you have a swimsuit," he said. "I still can't believe you made it two weeks here without one."

She gestured back at the shop. "Don't I need to pay for this?"

He waved a hand at her. "I got it. This was my idea, after all."

She started to argue with him, but she could tell from the look on his face there was no point. "Thanks," she said.

He ignored that and picked up the surfboard. "You ready for this?"

She looked out at the ocean and watched the waves crashing in to shore. They seemed . . . violent. She eyed the surfboard Beau was holding.

"Not exactly," she said. She was supposed to balance on that? On top of the ocean?

He put his hand on her shoulder. "Come on. It'll be fun."

"I'm going to hold you to that promise," she said.

He just grinned. It suddenly hit her, as the sun glinted in his hair, that there was such a difference in Beau between that first day and now. Then, when he'd laughed, there'd been no joy or fun in it. Or in him. But now . . . now as he walked down the beach with her, surfboard under his arm, his smile was real. She liked it. She liked him.

He dropped the surfboard down on the sand, not quite at the edge of the water. "Okay. Now stand on it," he said.

She glanced down at the surfboard, then back up at him. "Just . . . stand on it?"

He nodded. "Just stand on it, right in the middle. You're just getting comfortable on it now."

"Okay. Like this?" She stepped on the board. It sort of wobbled back and forth, and she had to catch herself. Now she knew why he'd wanted her to do this for the first time on the sand and not in the water. She absolutely would have fallen off right away.

Granted, she still probably would.

"See how it moves?" he asked. "It will do that even more in the water, that's why we started here. Now, here's how to stand on it when you're surfing."

He demonstrated the stance, one foot in front of the other, his body spread out in a bit of a crouch.

She tried to imitate him. He looked at her, a slight frown on his face.

"Good, that's good," he said. Hmm, she didn't believe him. "Except . . ." Ahh, see, she knew there would be an "except." "Not quite so tense in the upper body. Maybe try relaxing your shoulders a little?"

She tried to make her shoulders go down, but she could tell from his face it wasn't really working.

"I don't know if you've noticed this about me in the past few weeks," she said, "but I'm not that good at relaxing, okay?"

He just looked at her, and they both burst out laughing. "I have noticed that, actually," he said. "But then, we may have that in common."

She shook her head. "I thought we did, but you're apparently much better at it than I am."

He was still smiling. "Just on a surfboard, and that's only because I've been doing it for a long time. Come here." He motioned her over toward him. "Turn around."

She narrowed her eyes at him, and he laughed. "I'm not trying to trick you. Just turn around."

She turned and stood with her back to him. Two weeks ago—even a week ago—she wouldn't have done this. But everything felt different now than it had then.

She felt him step closer to her. "If you're tensed up like this, you won't be able to move with the waves."

She stared out at the ocean. "I'm not so sure that's possible."

They were so close that she could feel his laughter rumble through him.

"Here," he said. He put his hands on her shoulders and then almost immediately dropped them. "Is this okay? I mean, if you don't want me to—"

"It's okay," she said.

His hands dropped back down, each one gripping one of her shoulders firmly. "Okay. Here, let's see if this will help." He held on to her shoulders and shook her side to side, back and forth, until she couldn't stop giggling.

"What are you doing?" she managed to say.

He stopped and nudged her over to the board. "Try it again."

She got back up on the board and turned to face him, trying to stand the way he'd stood before. He smiled and nodded at her.

"There we go. That's better. Now, lie down on your stomach, with your feet really close together in back."

This at least felt more stable than standing on the board.

"Great, perfect," he said. "That's how you lie on the board to paddle out into the water. Now I'm going to show you how to stand up once you're out there." At Izzy's expression, he added, "Don't worry, I'm not going to make you stand up on the board in the water today, but I still want you to practice. I'll do it on your board so you can see."

He lay down on the surfboard like she'd been doing. "Start on your stomach, then you just arch up like this, and pull up and slide forward, until you get into that stance I showed you. See?"

He slid up, in one smooth movement, until he was standing.

"It looks so easy when you do it," she said.

He smiled at her. "You'll be able to do it, too. Keep practicing it now a bit, just so you get the hang of it."

It was a lot harder than it looked, but Beau smiled at her after she did it a few times.

"Now it's time to get in the water."

She looked at the ocean and bit her lip.

"Oh no. It happened again," he said.

She swung around to see him frowning at her. "What? What happened again?"

"Your shoulders are like, touching your ears," he said.

She had to laugh at that.

He bent down and picked up the surfboard. "Here, why don't you watch me so you can see how it all comes together?" He grinned at her. "Don't go anywhere."

She stood on the sand and watched him walk into the water with the surfboard, slide up on top of it, paddle out into the water, and then, once he was far out, pull himself to standing and surf back in to shore. She couldn't help but grin when he landed at her side, but she shook her head.

"I'm not doing that."

He laughed. "You can do it. I have faith in you, Izzy."

"Absolutely not." Wait. "Are you . . . Are you giving me a pep talk?"

He raised his eyebrows at her. "What does it sound like?"

He grabbed the board and paddled back out into the water before she could respond. She watched him ride the water toward shore again, a smile on her face.

"Now," he said, when he joined her on the sand again. "Let's get you in the water. Today, we're just going to get you comfortable on the board."

Wait a minute.

"You said *today*—does that mean you're going to make me do this again?"

He grinned at her. "I'm not *making* you do anything. Come on. I promise, you'll be fine."

She took a deep breath and followed him.

"Wait." He stopped when they were about knee-deep in the ocean. "You can swim, right?"

She rolled her eyes at him. "Of course I can swim! Do you think I would walk into the ocean with you if I couldn't swim?"

He shrugged. "You were staring at the ocean like it was going to swallow you up, how was I supposed to be sure?"

She elbowed him. Even though she knew she'd barely touched him, he stumbled dramatically. She rolled her eyes.

"I was *not* staring at the ocean like it was going to swallow me up. I was just . . . surveying the terrain, that's all."

He pursed his lips and nodded. "Mmm-hmm." He kept moving forward in the water, and Izzy followed him, until her feet didn't touch the bottom anymore and she had to swim next to him.

"Okay." He turned and set the board in front of her but kept one hand on it. "I just want you to practice getting on top of the board in the water a few times. For now, I'll hold on to it so it doesn't move anywhere. Don't worry about that."

"Mmm, I'm not worried about the board, I'm worried about me. Who's going to hold on to me?" she said under her breath.

Beau just laughed. "Are you ready?"

Not really. But she pulled herself up so she was lying on it like she had on the sand.

"Good job!" he said.

She glared at him. He just laughed again.

"Move your feet closer together. You want them flush together, both right at the edge of the board."

She did what he said, and he nodded.

"Perfect."

He watched her for a few seconds. She could tell from the look in his eyes he was about to suggest something she wouldn't want to do.

"How about I let go the next time a wave comes, and you can ride it in to shore?" He gave her an encouraging smile. It didn't fool her.

"Mmm. What if I just . . . stayed here, like this, with you holding on? This feels like enough, doesn't it?"

He narrowed his eyes at her. "Isabelle."

She looked back at him. "Beauregard."

He burst out laughing. "My name isn't Beauregard!"

She glared at him. "Then what is it? Why do you have a name like

Beau? Why am I lying on top of a floating board in the middle of the ocean? How did you convince me to do this?"

He was still giggling. His laughter was infectious. She had to work hard not to laugh with him.

"First of all, you aren't in the middle of the ocean, you're at the very edge of the ocean. Second, I have a name like Beau because of my father, may he not rest in peace. Third, I convinced you to do this because I asked nicely."

Beau had never mentioned his dad to her before. She'd table that for later.

"Because you asked nicely? That's not—exactly—how I remember . . ."

"FOURTH, I'll tell you what my real name is if you try to ride a wave into shore. You don't even have to do it, you just have to try."

She glared at him again. "Okay but that's not fair, because if I try and don't do it, that means I fell off into the water."

"That's true," he said, "but that's no problem, we all do it, and you know how to swim, you just told me that."

She shook her head. "I don't like you at all," she said. "I just want you to know that. Fine, I'll do it."

He grinned at her. "On the other hand, I like you very much." She didn't have time to react to that, because almost immediately, he looked behind her and nodded. "Okay. Here we go. Remember, relax, balance."

Then he released the board. Almost immediately a wave lifted the board—and her with it—up and propelled them both forward.

Oh, this wasn't that bad! It was even kind of . . . fun, just soaring along on the waves like this! She looked toward the shore and grinned.

She was almost all the way in to shore when another, bigger wave smacked against the board and lifted it up again. The board wobbled to one side and then the other, Izzy tensed up, and she slid right into the water.

Oh God, the water was freezing. Her entire body was only under for a few seconds, and she had the wet suit on, but still. Not even a wet suit could save her from the icy Pacific Ocean.

She stood up and shook herself, in an attempt to get water out of her ear. She turned, and Beau was right there next to her. A suspiciously solemn look on his face.

She pointed at him. "Were you laughing at me?" she asked.

"No! Absolutely not." One corner of his mouth poked up and then the other. "But you have to admit, it was a little funny. You were doing just fine, and you just . . . tipped to the side and went straight into the water."

"I admit nothing," she said, but let herself grin.

He put his hand on his hip. "You know. Like that song about a teapot? Just tip me over?" He tilted to the side, hand still on his hip.

Izzy did everything she could to hold her laughter in. "I've never heard that song; I don't know what you're talking about," she said.

He grinned at her, and finally, she grinned back.

"Come on, let's try again," he said. "This time, how about you paddle out first?"

She sighed, but didn't argue.

She fell off again the next time. But the third time, she sailed right into shore, not stopping until the board landed on the sand. She stayed there, a big smile on her face, until she felt Beau's shadow over her.

"I did it!" she said, smiling up at him.

"You did it!" He reached a hand down to her, a huge smile on his face. "Come on. Let's go celebrate."

CHAPTER FOURTEEN

After they dropped off the surfboard and Izzy's wet suit, she pulled her dress back on over her still-damp swimsuit. She knew she should go to the back and put her bra on, but her arms felt like Jell-O.

She glared at Beau on their way to the car. "You didn't tell me how sore this was going to make me. I can barely move my arms!"

"I forgot, I'm sorry," he said. Hmm, he didn't look sorry at all. "Just think of how much easier it'll be the next time."

Before she could tell him there wasn't going to be a next time, he grinned at her. "So, how would you like to celebrate your victory over the Pacific Ocean?" He opened the car door for her with a flourish, and she laughed.

"What are my options? I don't really know what there is around here. I've really only left the house, like, three times."

He pondered that as he started the car. "Good point. Okay, if you were at home, and you were celebrating something, what would you do?"

She smiled out the window as she considered this. "I'd probably make my friend Priya go out for happy hour with me." She suddenly missed Priya so much it hurt. "We'd eat a bunch of overpriced snacks, drink some cheap cocktails, talk ourselves into sharing dessert, and then talk ourselves into sharing two desserts."

Izzy turned back to Beau, but his smile had faded. It came back when he saw her looking at him.

"Sure, let's do that," he said.

Beau absolutely didn't want to do that. She could tell. There'd hardly been anyone around at the beach, but at a crowded happy hour people would recognize him. Right. She'd sort of forgotten he was famous.

"Or," she said, "we could get some really good takeout and an indulgent dessert to eat at home. Like, ice cream and hot fudge, or something. That might be better for now, since I would sort of like a hot shower, after being thrown into the ice-cold Pacific Ocean numerous times. I'm sure Michaela left a ton of food in the fridge for us for the weekend, but—"

Beau brushed that aside. "That'll just mean she'll have less food to cook for us next week. There's a great ice cream place in town; why don't we go pick some up and order dinner when we get home?"

That sounded fantastic, actually. And it sounded even better a few seconds later when Beau turned onto the main street, and she saw the rows of bars, packed with people. She wasn't exactly in the mood for a crowded happy hour either.

"Perfect," she said. "I'm thinking maybe Thai? Or sushi? But then, thinking about happy hour made me think about bar snacks, so now I'm obviously thinking about mozzarella sticks and buffalo wings."

Beau stopped at a light and turned to her with a grin. "How about all those things?"

One good thing about Beau was that she never felt self-conscious around him about how much she loved food. Maybe because he clearly loved it as much as she did.

"Are you just saying that because you're as hungry as I am right now?"

He nodded. "Probably. Being in the water does that to you. I looked up why once—something about your body temperature versus the cold water, blah, blah, blah. I was just satisfied that it wasn't only my imagination that I was so starving after swimming. Anyway, I hope that explains why I'm about to buy six pints of ice cream. Please don't tell me we already have some in the freezer; I know and don't care."

Like she would ever argue with someone about how much ice cream to buy.

"As long as one of the flavors is cookies and cream, I don't care what else you get."

He shook his head. "No, that's not fair, you can't make me make all the ice cream decisions on my own, you already know I'm indecisive and difficult; I'll hold up the line forever. You have to help."

Izzy rolled her eyes. "Fine, but I'm going to tell you right now, I'll vote against any ice cream with marshmallows in it."

Beau narrowed his eyes at her. "What's your problem with marshmallows? Start looking for a parking spot."

Izzy scanned the street around them. "They're only good melted: Rice Krispies Treats, great; put a stick in one, poke it in a fire, excellent. But that's it. I don't even like them in hot chocolate, they just dilute the chocolate flavor. And especially never in ice cream; they're just hard little frozen pucks." She pointed. "There! At the corner!"

Beau flipped on his blinker. "I have many points to argue with you on everything you just said, but you found us a parking space less than a block away, so I'll let you have this one. We will eliminate all ice creams with marshmallows in them from our decision matrix."

They walked toward the ice cream store, where there were already a bunch of people in line. She could feel Beau tense up next to her and turned to him, to say they could go somewhere else, but he just clenched his jaw and kept walking, so she followed him. At first when they got in line, Izzy felt self-conscious, standing there in a thin cotton dress over a damp bathing suit, especially standing there next to Beau.

Would people recognize him? And then wonder what he was doing there, with her, when he always dated people who were tall and willowy and mostly blond?

NOT that this was a date. But still.

As she looked at the people who walked by, she worried less. Lots of other people wore swimsuits under dresses, or just swimsuit tops over shorts, and no one in this entire city seemed to own shoes other than flip-flops, Birkenstocks, or sneakers. No one paid her, or Beau, the slightest attention.

Beau took a step closer to her and bent down to whisper in her ear. "Okay, Izzy. Can you do something for me?"

She could feel his breath against the hairs on the back of her neck. She shivered. She was probably just getting chilly, what with the wet swimsuit and the ocean air.

"Depends on what it is," she said.

He sighed. "I should have known you would answer like that. Okay. Don't make any sudden moves, but I need someone else to see this guy at the end of the line."

Izzy turned very slowly and looked at the back of the line. Her eyes widened, but she didn't say anything. She looked around for a few more seconds, trying to be casual, then turned to face Beau. His eyes were full of laughter.

"Okay," she said. "I could have handled the parrots on his shirt; this is California after all. Even the parrots on his shorts, they're a little matchy-matchy, but fine. But." She swallowed. "Um. I wasn't prepared for the live parrot on his shoulder. Is he going to bring that into the ice cream store with him?"

Beau's face crumpled. "I was trying to hold it together," he said. "But you just made me picture him standing there . . . asking for ice cream samples . . . with the parrot on his shoulder. And I just . . ."

Izzy started giggling, then Beau did, then they were both laughing helplessly in line. She turned away from him to look in the other direction, in the hope that it would make one or both of them recover, but they both just laughed harder.

She almost leaned back against him but stopped herself. That's not what this was.

Finally, they got to the front of the line. They decided on their ice cream flavors much more quickly than Izzy would have predicted. Caramel brownie, cookies and cream, coffee, triple chocolate, lemon and marionberry, and vanilla bean. Loaded down with ice cream, hot fudge, and raspberry sauce, they walked back to the car.

"Bye, parrot man," Izzy said as soon as they were out of earshot. "I'll never forget you."

Beau laughed so hard at that he could barely start the car.

On the way back to the house Izzy googled the name of the Thai restaurant Beau told her he liked.

"I've probably had half their menu. The only thing I don't like from that place is the desserts. When I put in a big order, they always send me this strange rice pudding thing, as like, a bonus or something. I'm weird about stuff like that, I hate any kind of pudding."

Izzy turned to stare at him. "So do I!" she said. "I hate all pudding. Anything with that jiggling texture, I just can't handle it." Ohhh. That's why Michaela had laughed on her first day.

"Really?" Beau laughed. "No one else ever understands this. They're always like, 'How do you like chocolate ice cream and not chocolate pudding, they're the same ingredients?' Just because they have the same ingredients doesn't mean they're the same thing!"

Izzy nodded. "People do that to me, too. They get all shocked that I don't like crème brûlée—once you get through the crunchy topping, it's just wobbly grossness in a spoon."

When they got back to the house, Izzy turned to go up the staircase.

"I'll put the ice cream away and order the food," Beau said. "Just come down to the TV room whenever you're ready."

She nodded and ran up the stairs, but Beau stopped her when she was halfway up.

"Wait, Izzy—we didn't decide what to order!"

She turned around. "I trust you. Order all the good stuff." She started back up the stairs, and then turned around again. "You were right. We needed a break today. *I* needed a break today. It was a tough work week and, well . . . thanks for suggesting it. And for the surfing lesson."

He looked up at her, a smile on his face. "You're welcome. And thank you. I hadn't gone surfing in . . . a while. It felt really good."

They smiled at each other, and then Izzy walked very slowly up the stairs. Her legs hurt, too? Why did her legs hurt this much?

After they were settled in the TV room, in comfortable clothes, with wine in front of them and with more Thai food than Izzy had ever seen in one place in her life, Beau nudged her.

"You said it was a tough work week—do you want to talk about it? You seemed kind of stressed in the library earlier."

Izzy took a sip of wine and thought about that. Surfing and being outside had definitely calmed her down from how upset she'd been earlier. But she was still angry.

"It's just . . . There's this guy, Gavin, who I work with," she said. "He's always been supportive of me, at least, I thought so. But yesterday after work, my friend Priya told me she'd overheard him talking to Marta. He said he was concerned about me being here, that I wasn't up for working with you, that she should have me come back."

"He WHAT?"

She turned to look at Beau, who had that rage in his face she remembered so clearly from her first week here.

"Yeah, that's what I said." She reached for a spring roll. "He told me that first week he thought someone with more experience should be here, and that Marta agreed, but I didn't realize he was still lobbying to get me sent back. I'm just so mad about it."

"Of course you're mad," Beau said. "I'm mad, too."

She was unreasonably pleased at how angry he was on her behalf. It actually made her less mad, seeing how mad Beau was.

"Like, I've had enough problems with Marta, I don't know why Gavin is undermining me like this. Especially when it feels like you and I are . . ."

"Making some progress?" he finished. "Yeah, we are. Don't let that asshole get to you. It sounds like he's trying to sabotage you with your boss."

She shook her head. "No, I'm sure that's not it. Gavin has always been . . ."

She thought about that. She didn't think Gavin was trying to sabotage her, exactly. But it did feel shitty that he would try to take this away from her and go behind her back to do it. Why would he do something like that?

"I'll email Marta," Beau said. "I'm not ready to send her anything I've written yet—just the thought of sending Marta anything terrifies me—but I'll tell her things are going well. Will that help?"

Oh no, she shouldn't have complained to Beau about this. Now he would think she'd done it to get him to advocate for her.

"You don't have to do that," she said. "I'm sorry, I sort of forgot that . . . Anyway, I didn't tell you that because I wanted your help."

Beau poured her more wine. "I know you didn't. I'm the one who asked, remember? I won't email Marta if you don't want me to. I just don't want that jerk to win." He sat up. "How's this—I'll only say something to Marta about you if she asks. Or if she tries to make you go back early. Does that work?"

It felt really nice that he had her back.

"Yeah. It does. Thanks."

It wasn't until they'd moved on to the ice cream that she said what she'd been waiting hours to say.

"So. About your name."

Beau put his bowl of ice cream down and glared at her. "I thought you forgot about that."

She let her grin spread across her face. "I was just biding my time. You promised to tell me."

He picked his bowl up with a huff, but she could tell he was smiling. "I guess I did." He took a scoop of ice cream. "Okay. My name is actually James Thomas, after my dad and my grandfather. My mom's father, Thomas Russell. This used to be his house, his and my grandmother's." Izzy had known his grandfather's name, but only because it was written in some of the books that she'd borrowed from the library and brought up to her room. But Beau had only ever talked about his family that one time. And this was definitely the first time he had ever even mentioned his mom. She was learning more about him today than she had in the entire time she'd been here.

"Anyway," he said. "My dad gave me the nickname Beau when I was a baby. He read it in a book, I guess, and it just sort of . . . stuck."

There was clearly a lot more behind what he'd said: about his dad, his mom, why he was here in his grandparents' house. Maybe even about why he'd struggled so much with his book. But Izzy didn't think now was the time to ask about any of those things.

"Well, I like Beau," she said. "It makes you sound like a soap opera hero, or a fairy-tale prince, or something."

He laughed and . . . was he blushing?

"Oh yeah, obviously two things I aspire to be, thanks for that."

At the end of the night, Izzy stood up. Very, very slowly.

"Ow. My entire body hurts. I'm going to get you back for this."

Beau chuckled as he piled their dishes on the tray. "I'm going to warn you right now, getting out of bed tomorrow morning will be rough."

She reached for the empty wine bottle and winced. She didn't even know her abs could hurt like this.

"Thanks for telling me this *now*. At least I don't have to get up before six a.m. like on a weekday."

They walked to the kitchen and loaded the dishwasher together, like they always did now. She took a step toward the fridge to grab a can of seltzer to take upstairs with her. But either because she was so sore her legs didn't quite work, or she was a little tipsy, or some combination, she tripped. Right into Beau, who caught her. And held on.

His chest was so broad, so warm. It was nice to rest her head here, just for a second. His arms were strong but gentle. It felt so good to have them around her, his hands resting there, on her back. She could feel them through her thin tank top.

She'd tried, all day, to ignore the way she reacted to him. But now the little moments from the day flooded back to her. When he'd put his hands on her shoulders on the beach; when he'd touched her hand, just for a second, in the water; when she'd felt his breath on her neck and the warmth from his body in line at the ice cream shop. Now she faced what she'd tried to look away from all day: She'd wanted those moments to last longer.

She could feel his heart beating against her ear. Or was it her own?

And then he dropped his arms.

"Izzy—"

No. That's not what this was, he wasn't interested in her like that. Of course he wasn't. She wasn't interested in him like that either. This was work, remember?

She didn't even like him, remember?

"Oof, I'm so sore I can barely stand up!" She took a step back, toward the kitchen door. "I should go to bed while I can still make it up the stairs."

She turned to leave the kitchen, like normal, like she always did at the end of the night. This was just a normal night, that's all.

"Good night, Izzy," Beau said, when she was at the kitchen door.

She looked back at him. He hadn't moved from that spot by the sink.

"Good night, Beau," she said.

CHAPTER FIFTEEN

Saturday morning, Izzy stayed in bed longer than usual. It wasn't that she'd slept all that late—she was wide-awake by eight. But at 9:30, she was still in bed, staring up at the ceiling. Because the thing was, when she went downstairs, she'd have to face Beau.

Maybe it hadn't been as bad as she'd thought. Maybe she hadn't *actually* rested her head on his chest. Maybe she hadn't enjoyed his arms around her quite so obviously. Maybe she hadn't wished . . .

Ugh. She pulled the covers over her face and then winced. Just that small motion made her arms hurt. Maybe that was her excuse to stay in bed forever?

Finally, she forced herself to get up. She had to go down to the kitchen, get coffee, pretend everything was normal. Except she and Beau had decided to work in the library this morning. Oh no.

She gave herself a stern talking-to once she got in the shower.

"Look, Isabelle. It's normal that you feel like you're getting close to Beau—you're living in the same house with him, you're working closely together, you even eat dinner together. But he's obviously not interested in you, you're not at all his type, you know that! He dates models and actresses, remember? He's not your type EITHER! You, unlike Priya, do not like big, brawny guys! It's just that he's the only man you've really interacted with in person for weeks, and your silly brain has latched on to him! You need to take a step back from all this! From him!"

"Are you sure about that, sweetheart?" she heard a tiny voice from the bathtub say as she turned off the shower.

"Yes, I'm sure!" she snapped. Oh no. She was talking to inanimate objects again. She had to stop that.

When she finally got down to the kitchen, Beau was there, sitting at the kitchen table with coffee and . . .

"Ooh, are those cinnamon rolls?" she asked.

He grinned at her and gestured to the top of the stove. "There are more over there. They might need more frosting, though."

She looked at the pan on top of the stove, at the buns slathered in frosting, and laughed. "I'm not sure if that's possible."

He looked at her, and their eyes met. They both smiled.

"I was a frosting fiend when I was a kid. My mom used to tell a story—I don't remember this, but it sounds like me—that one year for my birthday, she gave other people cake and just put a huge scoop of frosting on my plate."

Izzy felt so relieved, she couldn't hold back her smile. She was glad she had the excuse to put a cinnamon roll on a plate so she could turn away from Beau. She was just happy everything felt . . . normal between them.

"Want to take these to the library?" he asked. "If so, I'll grab another one."

She nodded.

"And I'll grab the wipes. We can't get frosting on the books, after all."

They worked together like normal that day, though Izzy tried her best to remember the lecture she'd given herself, and not let herself get too close to Beau. Or think about him too much.

On Sunday, their work time in the library started like it always did. Izzy pushed Beau's notebook across the table to him, he opened it, wrote for a while, then typed, and kept typing until the timer went off. Afterward, though, Beau did something different.

"Izzy," he started. And then stopped and looked down at the table.

"Yeah?" she asked. Was something wrong? He looked nervous.

"I. Um." He took a deep breath. "Can you . . . Would you like to read something? I mean, some of"—he gestured to his laptop—"this? If you don't want to, it's okay."

Izzy tried not to react. Beau was clearly stressed about asking her to read his work; she didn't want to make it into an even bigger deal. But inside, her mind was one big exclamation point.

"I'd be happy to," she said.

He nodded quickly. "How about, um, right now? Because if I don't show you right now, I might lose my courage here, so . . ."

Izzy tried to smile as encouragingly as possible. "Right now is great."

Beau brought her his laptop and then sat back down in his chair. "Okay. Um, just that part. The part that starts with 'This house.' It's rough, and it needs a lot more work, obviously, but I think it's time to see if I'm on the right track or not, and if not, what to do, or . . . something."

Izzy wanted to reassure him, but she knew that wasn't what he needed right now. He needed actual feedback.

"Sounds good," she said, and started to read.

> This house has always been a refuge for me.

Beau jumped up when she was only one sentence in.

"I can't sit here while you read that. I'm going outside, okay?"

He raced out of the library before she could say anything. Izzy looked after him for a few seconds. Then she turned back to the screen.

> This house has always been a refuge for me. When I was little, I would come here, sometimes with both of my parents, sometimes just with my mother, to visit my

grandparents. There was so much to explore in the house and the gardens, it was like I found something new to see, to experience, to play with, every time. New corners, hiding places, flowers, books. It always felt like there was a little bit of magic here.

The best times were when I got to spend weekends here with my grandparents alone. They would let me roam free, occasionally coming outside to bring me more snacks or call me in for meals, sometimes just yelling my name to make sure I answered. My grandmother was always in the kitchen, baking something delicious, so I would usually stumble inside, clothes torn and dirt on my face, and sit at the kitchen table, and she would set a stack of cookies in front of me with a smile.

My grandfather was always in the library. I spent hours there with him. He had shelves of children's books in the corner, just for me. He never told me when he'd added a new book to the shelves, but I would just check every time I came in, and there was almost always something new there, something I would grab, along with an old favorite or two, on my way into the room. My grandfather would nod at me, and I would nod back at him, and I would feel very grown up. I would curl up in the window seat and sit there in the corner for hours, as he sat at the long table, or in one of the chairs in front of the fireplace, working or reading.

As I got older, the house became a refuge for another reason: No one here seemed to know or care who I was, or who my parents were. At home, in

LA, everyone knew my whole family. Photographers would take pictures of us on the street. People would call out my name, or my mom's name, and I was supposed to be nice, polite, but I never wanted to be. In the neighborhood around my grandparents' house, people just knew me as their grandson; at the beaches here, no one paid attention to me at all. I loved that.

But I got busier, I worked more, and I had less time to come see them. My grandmother died, my grandfather got older and sicker. I would come here sometimes to see him, but they were quick visits, not the long, relaxed, peaceful times I had before. It got harder to come, after my parents' divorce, when things between my mom and me started to get strained, but that's just an excuse. I guess the truth is that it hurt to see him like that, hurt to have to answer the same question over and over, hurt to think of him as mortal. I think I thought I would have him forever. That's one of my many regrets.

When he died, it hurt to think of this house without him in it. Even after I knew he left it and all its contents to me, I didn't come here. I know, spoiled rich guy, saddled with a house he didn't know what to do with, boo-hoo. Trust me, you're not thinking anything I haven't already thought myself. But I felt like the house would feel empty without him, that I would feel his absence in every room. That it would hurt even more to be here.

But one day, after my whole world and everything I thought I knew changed, I had to get away. From my life, from everyone who knew me, from everything I knew. And without even thinking about it, I got in the car and drove straight to this house.

As soon as I got here, I realized how wrong I'd been to stay away. Instead of feeling my grandparents' absence here, I feel their presence. I feel him in the gardens, I feel her in the kitchen—talking to me, comforting me, and sometimes lecturing me, for all the many ways I've fucked up, and continue to fuck up. (Even though my grandmother would be horrified to hear me use that word.) But they would both lecture me in the kind, loving way they always did before, the way that made me want to be a better person, for them. (Not that I've been particularly good at that, but I keep trying.)

But I especially feel him in the library. Nodding at me, encouraging me, smiling at me. Helping me deal with everything I don't want to deal with. Helping me write this.

Izzy looked up. She glanced over at those chairs by the fireplace. They seemed old, worn, comfortable. She could feel approval emanating from those chairs. Like they were happy she was here.

She had to go find Beau.

She suddenly felt guilty for the way she'd been thinking about his book. When she'd first gotten here, she'd assumed there was no way someone like Beau could write a good book. She'd changed her opinion of him a lot in past few weeks, but she realized that perception of his book had lingered with her—that his writing wouldn't be good, that despite some of the things he'd said to her, he wouldn't think hard enough about his life, or the world around him.

She'd been wrong.

She found him over by the rose garden. The rosebushes were a lot fuller than they had been when she'd first gotten here, though there weren't any blooms on them yet. He turned around when he heard her coming.

"Okay, just say it," he said as she approached. "Tell me how bad it is, on, like, a scale of one to ten? With one being like, 'I'm embarrassed to be in a room with this guy' and ten being like, I don't know, I didn't think this scale through enough before I started talking, I don't know if ten is actually good or even more terrible than I could ever imagine, and now I'm just still talking so you won't say anything, aren't I?"

Izzy laughed out loud. "Beau, it's good." He looked at her with narrowed eyes, and she laughed again. "Don't look at me like that, I'm serious. Yeah, it's rough, yeah, there's stuff you need to tinker with, expand on, sure, of course. But it grabbed me right away, it drew me in, and it made me care about the story that you're telling, which is absolutely the most important thing you want it to do. I'm really—" She was going to say she was proud of him, but that felt condescending. Who was she, to be proud of him? "I'm really glad," she said instead.

He looked at her hard. "You know you don't have to say all this, right? If you don't know, I'm telling you right now: I know I seem all stressed, but I want you to tell me the truth. I want to know what you really think."

Izzy looked him in the eye. "I'm telling you what I really think. Haven't I done that, since I've been here?"

It was true, she realized. Most of the time—at work, even at home—she hid what she really thought behind the veneer of cheerful, everything's-fine-happy-to-help! Izzy. But she wasn't like that here, with Beau.

He nodded, but he still didn't look convinced.

"Okay," she said. "I can give you more detailed notes on it. I'll be happy to do that. But really, I thought it wouldn't be . . ." She bit her lip. "I wasn't sure what to expect from your writing. But, Beau, I'm telling you. It's good."

He took a step closer to her. "Wait. When you said, 'I thought it wouldn't be . . .' you thought it was going to be bad. Is that what you're trying to tell me? You're surprised that you like it. Aren't you?"

She sighed. "I was actually trying really hard not to tell you that, as a matter of fact. And it's not like I thought it was going to be *bad*! But the thing I *am* telling you, because it's true, is that it is good. You can do this. You are doing this. I'm excited to see what else you have in that notebook." She shrugged. "I don't have a lot of experience, obviously, and I don't know what Marta will think, so I don't want you to think that I—"

He brushed that aside. "I don't care what Marta thinks. I care what *you* think."

They grinned at each other.

He looked down, then back up at her. "I'd love it if you gave me those notes, actually. Tomorrow, maybe?"

Izzy nodded. "Tomorrow sounds great." She turned back to the house. "Come on, now it's your turn to celebrate a victory. There's a lot more ice cream in there and a whole lot of hot fudge."

Beau caught up to her. "Ice cream before dinner sounds like my kind of celebration."

CHAPTER SIXTEEN

On Wednesday morning, Priya texted.

Can't wait to see you this weekend!!!

That's right; this weekend was Priya's cousin's wedding in Santa Barbara. Izzy had totally forgotten. The past few weeks had gone so quickly.

Ahhhh when do you get here? Where are you staying?

She couldn't wait to see Priya. So much had happened in the past three weeks. And she couldn't believe she only had a little over a week left in California.

I get in tomorrow! Dinner tomorrow night? Do I get to see that house? And BEAU???

Izzy laughed at Priya's many punctuation marks and then bit her lip. She and Beau were in a good place now, with work and everything, but it still felt tricky to ask him if someone—anyone—could come to the house. She knew how special this house was to him. And she also knew how he felt about his privacy.

And Priya would want to go everywhere in the house and ask all sorts of questions.

> Dinner, yes! I can pick you up from the airport! But mmmm, not sure about coming to the house, or meeting Beau. I'll have to check

Priya's text came back in seconds.

> SO CHECK THEN!!! I have to see this place you've been living! And meet this GUY

Izzy rolled her eyes.

> He's not a GUY. But fine, I'll ask if I can bring you up here before we have dinner

Should she really ask him, though? She didn't want Beau to think that she was violating his privacy in any way. And she really didn't want to mess up the still somewhat fragile working relationship between the two of them, just to satisfy Priya's curiosity. She'd have to think about this.

Izzy still hadn't decided what to do when she got to the library that afternoon. After he finished writing, Beau pushed his laptop across the table to her. She read what he'd worked on, made a bunch of notes in the margins, and pushed the laptop back to him.

The first time they did this, he'd frowned at the screen when he read her notes. He had looked at her, but when he'd opened his mouth, she'd cut in before he could say anything.

"No—not yet. Don't answer my questions now. Answer them in your writing. But don't do that now either—wait until tomorrow, at least. Maybe even the next day, or sometime next week."

That angry frown she remembered from her first week had returned to his face.

"But you said—"

She'd shaken her head. "I know what I said, but you have to give yourself some time to think about it. Sure, maybe you think my idea for a change doesn't work—okay, that's fine, you're the one writing this, not me. But give yourself time to think about it, come up with a better idea. This is a marathon, not a sprint, Beau."

He'd looked at her for a minute, and suddenly his face relaxed. "But how am I going to argue with you about all this if I have to wait? The heat of the moment might be all gone!"

He was smiling. Good. She'd been worried for a minute there.

"I know," she'd said. "That's the worst part. You might even agree with me."

He'd laughed and given her the notebook.

After he read her notes on Wednesday, he looked up at her, his eyes narrowed.

"Okay, but what else?" he asked.

She stopped, midway through sliding her notebook into her tote bag. "What do you mean, what else?"

He set the laptop to the side. "You had this worried look on your face, the whole time you were reading. I thought there must be something really wrong with it, but nothing you said is that bad. Are you holding out on me? Giving me the easy notes at the beginning, so I can get used to it, and then bam, you'll come in and tell me to rewrite the whole thing?"

Izzy laughed. "No, and no. And I promise, I won't tell you to rewrite the whole thing."

He pushed his notebook across the table to her. "Then what is it? What's wrong? Something put that look on your face." He shook his head. "Wow, incredibly self-centered of me to assume it was my book, you do have other things in your life. Never mind."

Izzy rubbed her hand back and forth on top of his notebook. "Oh. Um. It kind of was about you, actually." Why was she so bad at hiding her emotions around Beau? She used to be so good at it. "It's just that . . . Okay, feel free to say no to this?"

She still wasn't sure if she should ask, but now she had no choice.

"I'm good at saying no." He looked amused. "As you're well aware. What is it?"

She swallowed. "Um, my friend Priya—I work with her, I've mentioned her, I think? She's going to be in Santa Barbara this weekend for a wedding, she has a million cousins. And she kind of wanted to know if she could come up here, and see the house, and everything?" She couldn't read Beau's face at all. He wasn't smiling anymore, but he didn't look mad, exactly. Just . . . blank. "It's okay, it's not a big deal, I'll just tell her—"

"Of course your friend can come here." He said it almost harshly, but then he smiled at her. "You're living here, aren't you?"

Did he mean it? Izzy couldn't tell.

"Are you sure? It's okay if—"

Beau stood up. "It's fine. Really." He still seemed . . . off, but she wasn't going to push it.

"Okay," she said. "I'll bring her by Thursday."

So on Thursday afternoon, right after she left the library, she drove down to the airport to pick up Priya. She'd left plenty of time to get through airport traffic and figure out where and how to meet her. When she pulled up to the tiny, adorable airport that didn't even have a single traffic light, she laughed out loud. She really hadn't needed all that time.

After a few minutes, her phone buzzed.

Just landed!!!

Izzy got out of the car to wait for Priya.

Yay! I'm here! See you soon!

She couldn't believe she was going to see Priya. Suddenly, the thought of seeing someone from New York, from her real life, almost overwhelmed her. She'd been in this tiny, almost dreamlike bubble in California, with Beau, for the past three weeks. It felt strange that someone else, even someone as great as Priya, would intrude on that.

She only had just over a week left in the month Marta had given her. Beau was on track, she thought, to finish his memoir, at least eventually. It wasn't as scary to him anymore, she didn't think. But . . . she hadn't quite told him the whole truth the day before. She *had* been holding out on him. Everything he'd written so far was good, but it was all missing something. If he'd written about whatever had made him leave LA and come to this house in Santa Barbara and disappear from the rest of the world, he hadn't shared it with her. In fact, she was pretty sure he hadn't put it down on paper yet. It was clear he was leading up to something big, but it was vague, only hinted at. Izzy had found herself getting impatient as the days went on, waiting for him to get there. She hadn't pushed him on it, not yet, but she knew she had to in the next week before she left. She wasn't looking forward to that.

"Izzy!!!!!"

She looked up, and Priya was running toward her, rolling suitcase in one hand and her long black hair flying behind her.

"Priya!"

Priya almost smothered Izzy with her hug, but Izzy didn't care.

"Ahhh, it's so good to see you," Priya said, when they finally let go of each other.

"It's so good to see you, too," Izzy said. "I feel like it's been forever."

She popped the trunk of the car and reached for Priya's suitcase.

"I can't believe you packed everything for the wedding in this suitcase."

Priya laughed. "I didn't. This is only like half of it. My mom has the rest." She held up a hand. "Wait: Where did this car come from? When you said you'd pick me up at the airport, I thought you meant you'd just take an Uber or something and meet me here."

"Oh." Izzy must not have told her this part. "This is Beau's car."

Priya's eyes widened. "This is HIS car? Okay, yet ANOTHER thing we're going to have to talk about."

Izzy rolled her eyes and went around to the driver side. "Oh, stop that. It's no big deal."

Izzy pulled Priya in for another hug as soon as they were both in the car. "I can't believe you're here. I've missed you so much!"

Priya nodded. "Yeah, yeah, I've missed you, too, etc., but you haven't told me yet if you're taking me to the HOUSE or not, and if I'm going to get to meet HIM. I'm dying here."

Izzy started the car. She was still nervous about this.

"Yes, I'm taking you to THE HOUSE," she said. "Beau said it was fine, but I don't know if you'll get to meet him; he may not be around." That was one way of saying that Izzy hadn't told Beau that Priya wanted to meet him. He'd seemed weird enough about the idea of Priya coming over. Izzy was pretty sure she'd been one of the only people, other than Michaela, who Beau had really interacted with in the past year—Priya might be too much for him. He'd probably be hiding away in one of the off-limits rooms while she gave Priya her tour. Her very brief tour.

Priya shrugged. "Oh well, I can't have everything. Though I can't believe he doesn't want to meet *me*."

Izzy laughed. "While you're obviously the center of the universe, Beau and I don't actually talk about you. We mostly talk about his memoir, since that's what I'm here for, remember?"

"Mmm, sure, his memoir. Oooh, look at the beach!" Priya stared out the passenger-side window, at the ocean right there along the side of the freeway. Izzy remembered when she'd driven this stretch of freeway on the way from LA to Beau's house, and how amazed she'd been at the ocean, and how nervous she'd been about her destination. It felt like a lifetime ago.

Only about fifteen minutes later, they drove up to the house, and Izzy pulled the car into the long driveway.

"We don't have a ton of time," she said, "because I managed to get us dinner reservations at a great place downtown, but we have to be there in less than an hour, and it'll take some time to find parking and stuff." She'd gotten the early reservation exactly so they wouldn't have a ton of time at the house. Not that she'd ever tell Priya that.

"I'm just excited to really be here," Priya said. "Oh wow, a real, actual palm tree, right in the front yard!"

Izzy laughed. "There are more in the backyard, too. You'll see." She lowered her voice. "I can't take you in all the rooms, though, okay? I'm just staying here, remember?"

Priya nodded, her eyes moving back and forth as she and Izzy walked up the path to the front door.

"Sure, whatever, but I'd better get to see the pool. Wow, look at that cactus; it's enormous!"

Izzy unlocked the front door and ushered Priya inside. They both slipped their shoes off by the door and started down the hall.

"Wowwww, that staircase! You didn't tell me about that!" Priya said.

Izzy laughed. "Isn't it great? I go up and down it multiple times a day—I always sort of want to slide down that banister, but the tile floor would hurt too much if I fell. My room's upstairs, let's go there now."

When Izzy opened the door to her room, Priya's mouth dropped open.

"Okay, the pictures you sent did *not* show how huge this bedroom is! This is, like, bigger than most New York City apartments! And you have your own bathroom?" She burst through the bathroom doors and turned in a circle. "This is, like, a five-star-hotel kind of bathroom! And it's the famous bathtub! Does Marta know you're living in luxury?"

Izzy shook her head. "Absolutely not, and I will murder you if you even so much as hint it to her. As far as Marta knows, Beau lives in some boring suburb, and I'm in the servants' quarters. I'd like to keep it that way, please."

Izzy led Priya back down the stairs and turned to take her to the kitchen.

"What's this room?" Priya said, standing outside the doors to the library.

"Oh. That's off-limits," Izzy said.

She hadn't sent Priya pictures of the library. She hadn't even told her about it. For some reason, it felt like the library was a private thing, between her and Beau.

Priya let out a dramatic sigh but thankfully didn't object. "Fine, fine, you're living in an enchanted house, with lots of mysterious doors, and some of them lead to magical wings or secret gardens or buried treasure, I get it."

They walked down the long hallway to the kitchen as Priya looked intently at the art on the walls.

"Where are we going now?" she asked. "To the pool?"

Izzy laughed. "The pool is after this, but first I'm taking you to the kitchen. There's usually something delicious in there, and I know you're probably hungry, so— Oh! Hi!" Beau and Michaela were both at the kitchen table, in front of Michaela's laptop.

"Hi," Beau said. He was wearing . . . jeans? She'd never seen him in anything but sweatpants before. Okay, or his swim trunks, that one time, but she tried not to remember that.

"Hi, Izzy," Michaela said. "Beau said you'd bring your friend by today."

Izzy turned to Priya, who didn't even disguise the triumph on her face.

"Michaela, Beau, this is my friend Priya. She's another editorial assistant at TAOAT, in town for a wedding. Priya, Michaela and Beau."

Michaela and Beau stood up.

"Nice to meet you, Priya," they both said.

Priya almost skipped across the room to shake their hands. "Nice to meet you! Thanks for taking care of our Izzy, so far away from home."

"It's been my pleasure." Beau smiled at Izzy, then turned to Priya. "Um. Where's the wedding?"

"The Four Seasons," Priya said. "It's apparently right by the beach? Though it seems like there's a lot of stuff right by the beach here, given what I saw on the drive from the airport. And the weather! It's incredible for March. There are so many flowers already blooming!"

Michaela smiled. "March in Southern California isn't like March in New York, that's for sure."

Beau looked over at Izzy, a glint in his eyes. "You should make sure to take Priya outside, show her the orchard."

"There's an ORCHARD?" Priya looked back and forth from Beau to Izzy.

Beau laughed. "That's what Izzy said, too. More or less."

Izzy laughed as she remembered the tour Beau had given her at the beginning. "More or less," she repeated, and they grinned at each other.

Michaela stepped over to the kitchen island. "Priya, would you like some chocolate cake?"

Priya beamed at her. "I would love some chocolate cake, actually! It's probably going to spoil our dinner, but I don't care. Where are we going, Izzy?"

Beau's eyes snapped to her. "Oh, you're going out to dinner tonight?"

Izzy nodded. He had that weird, blank look on his face again.

"Yeah, to a Mexican place downtown. Didn't I tell you?"

He shook his head. "It doesn't matter."

"Oh my God." Everyone in the room looked at Priya. "This cake. This cake is incredible. You told me about the pool, and the bathtub, but not the cake. Is there just cake like this here, all the time? You have to go back to New York in what, a week? How are you going to survive?"

Beau turned away and sat back down. Okay, maybe he'd had enough of Priya. Though, to be fair, he'd been a lot nicer to her than Izzy would have guessed. And a *lot* nicer than he'd been to Izzy when she'd gotten here.

"Speaking of the pool," she said. "Let's go outside. You can finish your cake as I show you the gardens and the pool. And the orchard." She smiled in Beau's direction, but he didn't look at her. She took Priya's arm and steered her firmly toward the kitchen door. "See you later, Beau, Michaela. Thanks for the cake."

Priya was subdued—for her—during the tour of the gardens and the pool. It wasn't until they got back to the car and were on their way down the hill that she exploded.

"OH MY GOD."

Izzy grinned. "Great house, isn't it?"

Priya let out a high-pitched noise. "House? The house? You think I'm talking about the house? Yes, yes, the house is lovely, that is not what that OH MY GOD was for. Isabelle Marlowe, WHEN are you going to jump that man? Or have you done it already? Tell me you've already done it, and you just haven't told me."

Well, at least Priya had waited to say this until they were out of Beau's hearing.

Though . . . her voice carried pretty far.

"No, I have not, and I will not," she said. "Beau and I are barely even friends!"

Priya threw her hands up. "If that man said, 'It's been my pleasure,' about me the way he said it about you, and then smiled at me like THAT? We would be a LOT more than friends by later that night."

"PRIYA."

"Well! I'm just saying! Did you see his shoulders?"

Izzy sighed. She should have known this would happen. This, she realized, was why she hadn't wanted Priya to meet Beau, because she *had* known this would happen.

"You can *just say* all you want, but nothing like that is happening. First of all, I'm here for work. Second of all, he dates models and actresses and people like that. Not people like me."

"Okay, well, FIRST of all, you're not working FOR him, you're working with him. People who work together date all the time. And SECOND, you're as incredible as ANY model," Priya said. "If Beau doesn't know that, he's not worth you!"

Izzy squeezed Priya's hand. See, this was why she'd missed her.

"You're the best," she said.

"BUT," Priya said. "I'm pretty sure he does know it."

CHAPTER SEVENTEEN

Izzy got home from dinner late that night and poked her head into the TV room to see if Beau was there, but it was empty. She usually ran into him in the kitchen during the day, either in the morning or at lunchtime, but on Friday she didn't see him at all until she met him in the library.

"Hi." She handed him his notebook when she sat down.

"Hi," he said, without quite looking at her. There was no real preamble that day; he just took the notebook, flipped it open, and started writing. A while later, he switched to his laptop—she'd stopped setting the timer; he didn't need it anymore—and she scribbled in her notebook. She was just . . . jotting down some more of that idea, that's all.

When he finished, he pushed the laptop across the table to Izzy.

> When I was sixteen, my dad finally won an Oscar. I say "finally" because that had been his goal for years. He'd been an acclaimed screenwriter since I was a kid. He'd written a ton of movies, and some of his movies had gone on to win Best Picture. Sometimes he was also nominated for the screenplay, but he would get so resentful when he wasn't.
>
> "Apparently, the movie just wrote itself," he would

grumble, every time.

My mom always looked at him when he said that, I remember that now. But she never responded.

The night he won, my parents left together for the ceremony, my dad a little frumpy, as usual, my mom glamorous, also as usual. She often tried to hide—or at least minimize—how much taller she was than my dad, but that night, she wore these super high heels. I overheard her on the phone with one of her friends that day, when she was getting dressed. "You're right," she said. "Flats just don't work with this dress. Fine, I'm going to do it."

When they got home that night, I expected them to be gleeful, celebratory, triumphant. But instead, they were quiet, angry, as they walked in the door.

"Stop putting words in my mouth," I heard my mom say in a low tone. I've always had much better hearing than my parents thought. "I didn't say that."

"You didn't say anything," my dad said. "Do you know how bad that made me look?"

They both stopped when they saw me, sitting there waiting for them. My mom smiled at me, but I could tell the smile was fake. I could feel the tension between them.

"Congratulations, Dad!" I said. I was thrilled for my dad; I knew how much he'd wanted to win.

He gave me a hug and grinned up at me.

"Thanks, Beau," he said. "You were watching?"

I nodded. "Of course I was watching! I made everyone shush at the party when your category came up. We all cheered for you."

He turned to look at my mom, who had kicked off her shoes and was taking the pins out of her hair. "Glad someone in this family is happy for me," he said.

My mom looked up at that, a weary expression on her face. "Don't" was all she said. She walked over to me, ran her hand over my hair, and kissed me on the forehead. I was just barely taller than her then. "Glad you were watching, Beau," she said. She smiled at me and then turned, not quite looking at my dad. "I'm going upstairs to get this dress off and take a hot bath." She kissed me again. "Good night."

I waited until I was sure she was all the way upstairs.

"What's wrong with Mom?" I asked my father.

He shrugged and dropped his bow tie on the table. "Your mother can be bitter. Jealous," he said. "I forgot to thank her, up there onstage. But I had to thank all of the industry people, everyone having to do with the movie—she knows that! And then they started playing me off and I just ran out of time. She should understand that. I thanked her after, in the press conference, and you too, of course. It's no big deal. She knows how important she is to me. But I don't think it's about that. I think it's just hard for her to see my success, especially since she failed at her own career. It's sad, really."

He'd said things like this to me before, so I nodded. But I wasn't sad for her, I was mad that she'd ruined this night for my dad for her own petty reasons.

He sat down on the couch next to me and sighed.

"That sucks, Dad. I'm sorry," I said. "I'm really excited for you, though! Let me see the statue!"

It was still in his hand, and he looked at it for a moment, before he passed it over to me.

"I've wanted this for so long." He traced his finger over his name, engraved on the bottom.

I was angry at my mom for weeks after that, for how deflated my dad was that night, for letting her own bitterness upstage his victory, for not being happy for him in the way I knew—or I thought I knew—she should be. To be honest, I was angry at her for years.

Now I'm just angry at myself.

When Izzy finished reading, she started again from the beginning, read it through once more, and thought for a while. Finally, she typed her notes into the document and pushed the laptop back to Beau.

Instead of looking at the screen, though, he looked at her.

"Why are you frowning like that? This time it is about what I wrote, I can tell. What's wrong with it?"

She shook her head. "'What's wrong with it?' is the wrong question. But you knew I was going to say that, didn't you?" She smiled at Beau, but he didn't smile back.

"Okay, pretend I asked the right question, whatever it is. I'm not in the mood to play guessing games right now. What's the problem?"

Izzy tried to stay calm. That was her job, remember? She gestured to the laptop. "I gave you my notes right there; it might make more sense for you to read them."

Beau pushed the laptop to the side. "I don't want to read them. I want you to tell me. What's wrong with it?"

Okay. She was finally going to have to do this.

"Fine. Like I said, it's not that there's something wrong with it, it's that you're skipping things. Why are you angry at yourself? What was behind the undercurrents that night? There's a lot missing here. Maybe it's a stylistic choice, maybe you're just building up to it." She didn't think that's what it was, though. "You sound like you're talking around something key—both to you, and to the story—but the reader doesn't know what it is, and it's confusing. We can tell your hero worship of your dad wasn't warranted. Why? Maybe you're planning to get there, but you keep dropping these hints, without actually saying it. Why don't you tell us what you're really trying to say?"

His face shuttered. He closed the laptop, picked it up along with his notebook—the one he always gave her before he left the library—and stood up.

"Thanks for your 'expertise.'"

He had that nasty tone in his voice again. Why had he pushed her to say all this if he was going to get mad? If he wasn't even going to listen to her?

She swung around in her chair and kept talking as he walked to the door. "If you're going to write a memoir, Beau, you need to either write the hard things, or ignore them completely—you can't just dance around them like you're doing. You could have written a very different book. I think you and I both know you intended to write a very different book." He stopped walking. He didn't turn around, but she kept going. "You could have taken the easy way out, but you didn't want to. So if you, Beau Towers, are going to write this book, you have to write about the stuff that hurts to write about. Look, I get that it's hard to write about all this, all of what you've shown me and all of what you haven't even tried to write. Believe me, I get that. But—"

He spun around to face her. "Do you? How, *exactly*, do you get that? How would you possibly get that? Because from where I'm sitting, you're just merrily tearing my work to shreds; ordering me to tell you all my hardest, worst, most difficult secrets; making cheerful little notes about how I need to tell more and be more honest; and then you smile and go back to your own boring little life where nothing bad or hard has ever happened to you. You're not even a writer! You don't know how this feels, and you certainly don't know how to do it yourself! So tell me, Izzy, how do you 'get' how hard this is, as you sit across a table from me, while I do some of the hardest work I've ever done, and you fuck around on your phone?"

Izzy stared at Beau as he spat those words out at her. Every word, every sentence was worse than the one before. After a few seconds of silence, while they stared at each other, she stood up.

"Have you ever stopped to think that you don't know a single thing about me?" she asked. "Of course you wouldn't. I was right about you. You *are* a spoiled, selfish asshole who doesn't think or care about anyone else."

And then she pushed past him and out the door. She ran up the stairs to her bedroom and then shook her head. She couldn't be here. She couldn't be in this house for one more second. She spun around in a circle to find her tote bag, grabbed it from the chair by the window, and dug inside it to make sure the keys were there. She ran back down the hall, down the stairs, and out the front door. Right before she shut the door, she heard Beau call out her name. It just made her run faster, to get away from him, from his house, from what he'd said, from her stupidity in trusting him, thinking they were friends.

She got in the car and drove away fast, before he could come outside and stop her. She turned down the hill and drove, without any destination in mind. All she wanted was to get away.

Eventually, she ended up at the beach. It was the only place she could think of to go. Luckily, on a gray, drizzly, depressing day like today, not a lot of people were there.

She walked along the water for a while and finally sat down, in a sheltered nook in the sand. She stared out at the horizon, where the gray sky met the gray water. Then she dropped her face into her hands.

She couldn't believe he'd said all that. She couldn't believe he would hit her exactly where it hurt, in just that way. She couldn't believe she'd let him in, let him get close enough to her to hurt her. If he'd done that three weeks ago, if he'd talked to her like that the first time in the kitchen, she wouldn't have cared. She would have smacked it away in her mind; it wouldn't have touched her at all. He didn't know her then. She didn't know him then. Then, she didn't care about him.

Why had she let him in? Why had she thought they were friends? Why had she let herself relax around him, care about him? Why had she given him the power to hurt her? And why, *why* had she let Priya's stupid little fantasies about Beau get in her head?

Over the past few weeks, she'd started to remember why she'd wanted to do all this in the first place. Publishing. Editing. Writing. She'd fallen in love with books again, stayed up late reading books she'd taken from the library, been inspired by her work with Beau. She'd almost decided to stay at TAOAT after she got back to New York, keep fighting for that promotion. Start writing again, for real. Writing, the dream she'd almost given up, had felt possible again.

And in just a handful of seconds, Beau had made all that hope, all those dreams, feel like ashes in her hands.

She obviously couldn't work with him anymore, not after today. She was sure he didn't want that either. Whatever, it didn't matter. She was supposed to go back to New York in a week anyway, she'd just move that up. She could go to Priya's hotel, crash with her for the rest of the weekend, and then fly back to New York with her after the wedding. Marta wouldn't care if she got back a few days early, as long as Beau eventually turned something in.

But would he? She had no idea. If he didn't, she was sure Marta would blame her for it—and Gavin would gloat—but there was nothing she could do about that. This was who Beau really was; she should have known that. She *had* known that.

Then why was she so sad about this? She'd thought . . . well, she'd thought lots of things, hadn't she? None of them had ended up being true.

She sat there for a while as the tears dropped from her eyes onto the sand. She'd told herself at the beginning that if she left California without something to show for her trip, that would be it for her publishing career and her dream of writing. This had been a test—if she failed it, she'd give up, go do something else with her life. This wasn't meant to be.

Okay. She'd failed. That was her sign: It was time to quit her job, figure out something else to do with her life, find a new dream.

She tried to accept that, to think about what was next. She'd thought she'd feel relieved when she finally made that decision. But instead, her whole body—her whole self—recoiled against it.

She wasn't ready to give up.

For the past few weeks, as she'd worked with Beau, as she'd worked on her own writing, she'd felt inspired, fulfilled, excited about the future. She didn't want to let Beau Towers, or Marta, or anyone else take that away from her. She'd almost decided to quit writing because of Gavin—she had to stop letting other people decide her life for her. Just because Marta made her miserable, just because Beau was a jerk, that didn't mean she had to leave publishing completely. There were lots of other publishing jobs out there.

What she'd wanted when she'd made this deal with herself three weeks ago was to know, one way or another, what she should do. And now she knew.

She wasn't going to stop fighting for her dreams, not yet.

CHAPTER EIGHTEEN

Izzy gave herself a pep talk as she drove up the hill to the house. She would go inside, pack, and text Priya from the Uber on her way to the hotel. She wouldn't even have to see Beau. And when she got back to New York, she'd take another look at her résumé and start applying for new jobs right away.

But Beau was sitting on the front steps when she drove up.

He stood up when he saw her, but she ignored him. She steeled herself as she turned off the car. All she had to do was get through this one encounter, and then she could get out of here and never have to see him again. She could do this.

He watched her as she walked toward him. She dangled the keys from her finger, and when she got close enough, she tossed them to him.

"I didn't steal it," she said. "Don't worry. I'll be gone soon."

He caught the keys but shook his head. "Izzy, I wasn't—"

"Don't call me that," she said. Suddenly, she couldn't hear her nickname on his lips anymore.

He stopped. Swallowed. "Isabelle. I'm sorry. For what I said in the library."

Sure he was.

"Great, thanks. Now, if you'll excuse me, I have to go pack."

He moved to the side so he wasn't in between her and the front door, but he kept talking as he followed her inside.

"I know you don't believe me. I don't blame you. What I said to you—that was awful, why would you believe me? I figured you'd want to leave now. But please know that I didn't mean it, I didn't mean any of it, that I'm so sorry for every word of it. You've done more for me in the past month than almost anyone in my life has, and you were right, of course you were right about everything you said about my writing, about me, about all of it. I learned that from my dad, to hit below the belt. That sounds like I'm blaming him, and I guess I am, but this is all my fault. I am so sorry. For everything."

Her steps slowed as she walked down the hall toward the stairs. She hadn't expected a real apology. She'd thought, if he apologized at all, it would be one of those sorry-if-you-were-offended kind of apologies. Or like one of those apologies toddlers gave when forced to do so, just to get it over with, the single word *Sorry* like he'd left on her tray that first night, so everything could go back to normal, be the same as before.

She knew she could never be the same as before.

She put her hand on the banister, ready to go upstairs.

He started talking again. "I want to explain, but I'm sure you don't want to hear it. You were right, I've been writing around all the hard stuff." She stopped walking. "For weeks, that's all I've been doing. It wasn't even that I didn't want to share it with you. I didn't want to put it on paper, to face it, to make myself deal with it. I tried to ignore that, to pretend I could keep just going on as I was, that eventually it would just, poof, by magic, show up in the book and I would keep not having to deal with it. But then you called me on it, and you were right, and the thought of having to write about all of that terrified me. And so I said those horrible things to you, things I never should have said. And I'm so sorry."

She turned around. "You hurt me," she said. "I trusted you, and you hurt me."

He didn't look away from her. "I know," he said. "I don't expect you to forgive me." He set the keys that she'd thrown to—at—him down on the table by the front door. "Take the car, go wherever you need to. Just let Michaela know where it is, someone will come get it whenever you don't need it anymore. I won't . . ." He swallowed. "If you were worried about this, I will only say great things to Marta about you and the work you did with me—great things that are all true. You're really good at this, I hope you know that. You struck a nerve, only because what you said was totally true, and you were right. I wish I'd . . . I don't know, talked to you, told you everything, asked you for advice on how to write about it. But instead, I just . . ." He shook his head. "Anyway. That's all I wanted to say." He started to walk away, then stopped. "Wait, no. I wanted to say one more thing. Thank you. For trying so hard with me. You didn't have to do that. It made a real difference to me, and I didn't say that enough. Or . . . ever, probably. Thank you."

He turned and walked toward the back of the house. After a moment, Izzy went upstairs. She sat on the bed and pulled her knees up to her chest.

She thought about what Beau said in the hallway. When she'd seen him sitting there waiting for her, she'd assumed he was either waiting to kick her out of the house or that he'd try to laugh it off, brush it aside, try to convince her to stay there. But instead he'd apologized, really apologized, for everything he'd said. And he hadn't tried to convince her of anything, other than how sorry he was, and how grateful he was to her.

She should pack. She should pull her suitcase out from under the bed right now, roll up the clothes that were in the dresser drawers and piled on the chair, stuff all her toiletries into plastic bags, shake all the sand out of this cardigan so she could wear it on the plane, text Priya.

But instead she just sat there and thought. About Beau's apology, about what she'd decided on the beach, about how the past three weeks had made her like Beau and trust him. She wanted to know, really know, if he'd been worthy of her trust.

Finally, she walked back downstairs and into the kitchen. Somehow, she knew she'd find Beau there. He was sitting at the table, his notebook in front of him, staring out the window. He turned when she walked in.

Was she doing the right thing here? She was about to find out.

"Isabelle. I thought you—"

"You said you wish you'd explained everything to me," she said. "Okay, then." She sat down across from him. "Explain."

He looked at her. "You don't have to let me explain."

She nodded. "I know I don't."

She was doing this for herself, not for Beau. She wanted to know if she'd been wrong to trust him, to care about him. She wanted to know if she'd been wrong to trust herself. And, selfishly, she wanted to leave Santa Barbara, and this house, with good memories—to remember this as the place where she'd started to write again, to believe in herself again.

He let out a breath. "Okay." He closed his eyes for a second. "Okay. About a year after that Oscar night, my parents split up. They'd had a lot of fights like that before that night, but then a lot more afterward. With my dad loud and pointed, my mom silent. I never thought they'd actually get a divorce, though—they'd been fighting like that for years, it just felt like that's how their relationship was. And then my dad took me out to dinner one night and told me they were splitting up. I should have expected it, but I didn't—it felt like it came out of nowhere. He said it was because my mom was bitter, angry at him for all his success. He told me she'd turned to another man, that he'd had to file for divorce because of that." He looked down at his folded hands. "And I believed all of it. She didn't . . . This sounds like I'm blaming her, I'm not, but she didn't say anything to me about it for a while. I'm pretty sure, now, that she didn't even know he'd told me. And then when she did talk to me about it, he'd already been telling me all those lies about her for a while. When she moved out, she just said that she loved me very much, and that she would always be there for me, no matter what."

He stared down at the table for a while before he started talking again.

"The divorce was really nasty," he said quietly. "They fought over money a lot, my dad ranted about my mom to me all the time, and I took his side. My mom and I had always been close, but somehow . . ." He sighed. "That's . . . When you said, in there, that I was originally going to write a very different kind of book, that's what I'd planned to write. What I'd started writing. A vindication of my dad, who, yes, I had hero worship for, parroting back all the stories he'd told me about my mom, defending him against all the people who criticized him and his work, all that. When he died, some of the stuff I read about him—some of the stuff I heard people say—made me furious. I wanted to tell the world what a great writer he was, what a great person he was."

He stood up. Izzy thought for a second he wasn't going to finish.

"Do you want some water?" he asked.

Izzy nodded. She wasn't particularly thirsty, but it seemed like he needed something to do.

He grabbed two glasses and poured them water from the tap. He started talking again almost as soon as he sat back down.

"Like I said—like I'm sure you know—he died two years ago. I kind of . . . lost it for a while when he died. You probably know that, too."

She nodded.

He looked down at his hands. "The worst thing I did—the thing I'll feel terrible about forever—is what I did, and said, to my mom, when she came to his funeral. She told me she came for me, and it infuriated me. I was just so . . . mad at the world then. And I was really mad at her. I blamed her, for him dying. I know it doesn't make sense, but I didn't make a lot of sense then. And so when she told me that, I said . . ." He stopped, and looked down for a few seconds. "I said such awful things to her. Like . . . like I did to you, in the library, except so much worse. I told her this was all her fault, that she was brainless, talentless, a leech on him. I repeated some of those things my dad said about her over the years." He was silent for a moment. "She . . . I'll never forget the look on her face when I said all of that. Sometimes when I can't sleep, I see it."

Izzy tried not to react to anything he said, to just listen.

"Not too long after that, an agent approached me about writing a book. I jumped at the idea. I haven't really had an acting career in years, and I wanted to write. I'd always sort of thought I'd turn to screenwriting eventually, like him, you know."

He laughed quietly, but there was a note in his laughter she didn't like. It was that same mean laugh from the first week.

"Don't," she said.

He looked at her.

"Don't laugh like that. That's not . . . I don't like it when you do that."

That sounded so silly, so pointless to say, but he nodded like he understood what she meant.

"I don't like it either. I don't like me, when I do that."

He folded his hands together. She could see his nails biting into his skin.

"A little over a year ago, I was going through some of his papers. Partly because it had been almost a year since he'd died, and it was time to clean out the house, and partly to do some research for the book. I found the boxes full of drafts of all the screenplays he'd written. I started to flip through them, just, you know, to see how his work had changed from draft to draft. And that's when I realized that my mom had done the bulk of the writing of them. All of them."

She looked up at him, but he was still staring at his hands.

"How did you—"

"Her handwriting," he said. "It was all over them. He would draft something, and on the sides, or the back—often both—she'd make extensive, lengthy, huge changes. Not just little edits, but entire scenes, story lines, character motivations. And then I'd flip to the next draft, and there it would all be, neatly typed up, with his name on the title page. It was like that for everything. I have no idea why he kept them all, other than he had such a big ego he never thought anyone would know that the handwriting wasn't his. But I knew. I went through them all, in one long, terrible night, read them all, just to see, to make sure, to confirm that it was all true. That one that won the Oscar, God, that one was basically completely hers. And he didn't even fucking thank her. And then I said . . ."

No wonder he felt so terrible.

No wonder this book was so hard for him to write. She thought back to how when she'd first gotten here, she'd demanded he tell her what his struggles had been with the book, and winced. Of course he couldn't have told her any of this then.

He got up again, opened the tin on the counter, took out two lemon bars, and put them on plates. He came back to the table and pushed one across the table to her.

"Iz—Isabelle, I can't describe to you how I felt that night. That night, and most days since then. I guess . . . if I'm really going to write this book, I guess I'm going to have to describe it, at some point, but as you saw, I've done my best to avoid doing that." He laughed, but she didn't think he really found any of this funny. "I hated myself. So much. I still do, I guess. At first, I thought there was no way I could write a book, knowing what I know now. Knowing who he is, and who I am. The same kind of monster he was."

"Beau, you're not—"

He held up a hand to stop her. "And then I decided I did want to write this book. That I wanted to tell the world what kind of person my dad really was. And what kind of person my mom really is. Admit how wrong I was, about everything. I thought I could do it. But it's really . . ." He swallowed. "It's really hard. It's a lot harder than I thought it would be."

He stared down at the lemon bar on the table. Izzy didn't know what to say to him, but she wanted to say something, to do something so he knew she saw what he was going through, that she appreciated him telling her. That she cared.

She slid her hand across the table and put it on top of his. He looked at her and smiled, just a little bit. He turned his hand over and squeezed hers, and then let go.

He got up again, looked at the table, and then sat back down.

"That was the night—or rather, the morning—I left LA and came here. I had to get out of there. I packed a weekend bag, of just whatever I could throw into it, and drove straight here. I meant to just stay for a weekend, and well, that was well over a year ago."

She had a lot of questions she wanted to ask him, but one main one.

"What did your mom say, when you talked to her?"

He turned away, but then, with clear effort, turned back to her.

"I didn't . . . I haven't talked to her."

She started to say something, but he shook his head.

"I know. There's nothing you can say to me that I haven't already thought, trust me. I was going to call her, right away. I read all that stuff late at night, I drove here at the crack of dawn, I was going to call her later that day, apologize, talk to her about it all. But what was I going to say to her? What could I say to her? 'Sorry for what I said at the funeral?' That sounds so . . . inadequate." He sighed. "I felt—I feel—so guilty about believing him, abandoning her. About what I said to her. I just wish I could tell him how mad I am at him. For doing this to her, and to me. But I can't. But I also can't blame him, forever, for what an asshole I am."

He looked out the window, and she just waited. Finally, he turned back to her.

"Every day I meant to call her, and every day I told myself I'd do it the next day. Once I hired Michaela, and we started making plans for a foundation, to do some good with the money I inherited from him, I told myself I'd call her when that was done."

A foundation. That's what Michaela was doing here. That made sense now.

He went on. "Then, after you got here, I decided I'd call her once I had a draft. Maybe I'm just procrastinating. I mean, I know I am. It's just . . . I don't know how to do this."

She looked up at him. "Are you, um—I know we've talked about this stuff a little, but . . . have you thought about therapy?"

He looked away from her. "I had someone in LA who I went to, on and off for years. After that car accident, and then the divorce, and stuff. I keep thinking about calling him, but it felt . . . easier not to."

She waited until he looked at her.

"I know," he said. "You're right. You don't have to say it."

He broke off a piece of lemon bar but didn't pick it up.

"Anyway. That's what I left out. Most of it, anyway. I haven't really told this to anyone. I can't believe I thought I could write about this. It was so hard just to tell you, and I like you! How did I ever think I could tell the whole world?"

The notebook was still in the middle of the table. She pushed it toward him.

"You can. You will." He shook his head, but she kept talking. "Write down everything you just told me. It's going to be rough, but you can do this. We can work on it together, after you've gotten it all down."

He put his hand on top of the notebook and looked at her. "We? Does this mean you're staying?"

"Yeah," she said. "I guess it does."

She hadn't known she'd made the decision to stay until this moment.

"Isabelle, you don't—"

She cut him off. "I know I don't have to."

He let out a breath. "Thank you. I . . . I'm really glad." He picked up the notebook and tucked it under his arm. "And—I know I've already said this, but—I'm sorry, again, about what I said earlier about you. That's not how I really feel, at all. I'm so sorry I hurt you."

Despite everything, she believed him.

"Okay," she said. "I accept your apology. You don't have to say it again." She stood up and looked him in the eye. "But, Beau: Don't ever do that to me again."

He looked back at her. "I won't," he said. "I promise."

CHAPTER NINETEEN

When Izzy came downstairs the next morning to get coffee, Beau was in the kitchen.

"Oh, hi," she said. She felt awkward with him again, like she had at first. Was he going to regret all those revelations of the night before?

"Good morning." He smiled at her, a little tentatively. He held up her key ring, with the keys to the house and car on it. "These are still yours. If you want them."

She held out a hand, and he walked over and dropped the keys in it.

"Also." He took the milk out of the fridge and handed it to her. "You didn't tell me when that homework assignment you gave me was due. But I couldn't sleep last night, so I wrote it all up. And then I typed it up this morning. You don't have to look at it now. I just wanted you to know."

"No time like the present," she said. "Where's your laptop?"

"Oh." He looked terrified. "I didn't expect— You don't have to do it now. I just wanted you to know I was taking it seriously. What you said."

She took a gulp of coffee. "You keep telling me I don't have to do things—Beau, do you think I don't know that? You've lived with me for almost a month now. Is there a lot that I've done here that it seemed like I didn't want to do?"

She hadn't been like that before she'd gotten here. She'd done so much that she didn't want to do for Marta, at work in general, even with guys she'd dated. She'd thought she had to—to advance in her job, for them to like her, keep dating her. All the terrible movies she'd seen, boring lectures she'd sat through, gross beers she'd sipped. She'd smiled the whole time, but now she realized how unhappy she'd been.

"Now that you mention it, I can't think of a single thing that you've done here that it seemed like you didn't want to do," he said. "Well, other than those pep talks that first week."

She laughed. "You've got me there."

They smiled at each other, for real this time.

"I think I keep saying that," he said, "because I don't want to be like my dad. And sometimes I am like him. I was, in the library yesterday. So I want to make sure that . . . you're sure."

She picked up a cinnamon roll from the pan next to him on top of the stove. They were still warm. She looked up at him as she thought about how to respond to what he'd said. He looked at her intently as he waited.

"Yesterday you promised me you'd never treat me like that again." He started to say something, but she held up a hand to stop him. "I'm still here because I believed you. And if I ever feel like you're doing anything—even unintentionally—to break that promise, I'll tell you. Okay?"

He suddenly looked lighter. "Okay," he said. "Thank you."

She smiled at him. "You're welcome."

He smiled back. He picked up a cinnamon roll and pulled off a piece of it. He popped the bite into his mouth and then licked the frosting off his finger. She suddenly realized they were standing very close. Closer than they'd been since . . .

He took a step closer to her. "Isabelle."

She liked when he said her name like that, all low voiced and sleepy and a little growly. When did she start liking that? She hadn't liked it before, had she? Had she liked it when he'd done that at the very beginning?

She had. Of course she had.

She took a step back. "So, um, where's your laptop?"

He dropped his hand. "In the library."

She reached for the coffeepot and filled up her mug. "Let's go to the library, then."

Izzy had worried that the library would be tainted for her after their fight in here yesterday, but as soon as she walked in, it felt like the room welcomed her back in, like a friend who had been gone too long. It felt like the walls, the shelves, the chairs had known she would be back, had been cheering for her the whole time, were cheering for Beau now. She sat down in the chair she always sat in, and felt the way they settled in together. It felt like a hug.

She laughed at herself. Was she anthropomorphizing furniture again? *It's not actually hugging you, Izzy!*

Beau set his laptop in front of her, and she scooted the chair in closer to the table.

"That's it, that's everything I told you last night, and a little bit more. Maybe this is weird, but, um, I just wrote it like I was writing it to you. I didn't change that as I typed it up, I was too worried that I'd trash it. It's . . . It was easier to write it like that, somehow."

She looked across the table at him, not sure what to say.

"I'm really glad that made it easier. But also." She gestured to the notebook on the table. "I don't think I can trust you alone with this overnight again, can I?"

He shook his head. "Absolutely not."

They grinned at each other.

Then Izzy turned to the laptop screen.

Beau jumped up, like he hadn't done since the first time she'd read his work. "I'm not going to go outside again, I'm just going to, um, go over there." He pointed to the far side of the library. "I'll look at some books, otherwise I might, like, stare at you too much."

Izzy laughed. "Okay. I'll let you know when I'm done."

Once Beau was at the other end of the room, Izzy concentrated on what he'd written. It was rough, more so than other parts of the book he'd shown her, but it also felt more honest. More like him. She made a few notes, asked a few questions, but she held on to her biggest question.

"I'm done, you can come back now," she said.

Beau came back so quickly she knew the book in his hands hadn't distracted him at all.

"I was just reading some . . ." He looked down at the book he was holding. "Russian literature."

She tried not to smile. "Russian literature?"

He nodded very quickly. "Oh yeah, totally, all the greats, you learn so much from them about writing, and life, and um, vodka."

They both burst out laughing. Beau put the book down at the end of the table and sat down across from Izzy.

She pushed the laptop across to him. This was where they usually just sat in silence while he read her notes, but this time she started talking.

"I only had a few notes that I put in there—like you said, it was mostly what you told me last night. I'm glad you wrote it when it was fresh in your mind, it made it have that same urgency, that same honesty that it did when you told me. There's a lot you can expand on, of course, and this is going to bleed out into a lot more of the book, but I'm sure you know that." He nodded as he listened to her. "But I had one big question that I didn't put in there, and I wanted to ask you."

He let out a big breath. "Okay. Ask."

Would he get mad if she asked him this? She didn't think so, but she supposed if he did, it was good to know that now.

"You said last night that you haven't talked to your mom about all this."

He nodded. "Yeah."

"But yesterday," she said, "you sat outside and waited for me to come back so you could apologize to me. How long did you sit there, anyway?"

He looked down. "I don't know, an hour? I wasn't sure what to do—I don't have your number, it's not like I've ever had to text you, we live in the same house. I knew Michaela had it, and I almost texted her. I decided I would have, if it got dark before you got home, and it was getting there when you drove up." He sighed. "But that wasn't your point. What you meant was, I sat there and waited for you so I could apologize to you right away—why have I waited all this time to talk to my mom? Wasn't it?"

She nodded. "Sort of, but I wasn't going to say it quite like that. I mean, I get it, you've barely known me a month, it's not a big deal; your mom is a different story."

He looked right at her. "It *was* a big deal, Isabelle. You're a big deal to me."

She met his eyes and then looked away. "I . . . But—" She didn't know what to say. This conversation was suddenly a lot more than she'd bargained for.

"But yes, I get what you mean," he said. "It's different. But I think part of why I sat there and waited for you—part of why I knew I had to talk to you—was because I know how bad it feels not to do it right away, I know how bad it feels to wait until it's too late. I knew that if I didn't get to tell you how sorry I was as soon as I could, I'd regret it forever."

She looked at him, and she could see the sincerity in his eyes.

"Then don't you think you've waited long enough, to talk to your mom?" she asked him. "Just think how much better you'll feel afterward."

He swallowed hard. "You're right. Of course you are. But also. Does it have to be today? I can only deal with like, one hard conversation a month, and that's pushing it, and so far there have been four in less than twenty-four hours. I'm sort of reaching a breaking point here."

She laughed, and he did, too, even though she was pretty sure they both knew he wasn't kidding.

"How about this?" she said. "How about you text her and ask if you can find a time to come see her. That way, you've done the hardest thing, and you'll have a plan, and you won't have to think about it for a while."

He looked down at the table. "That's a good idea," he finally said. He pulled his phone out of his pocket. "I usually don't even have this with me." He unlocked the phone and scrolled through it. "I don't know what to say to her, though."

Izzy smiled at him. "Yes you do."

He looked at her, then down at his phone. "Yeah. I guess I do." He typed quickly with his thumbs. "There." He lifted his head, a terrified look on his face. "It's done."

She smiled at him. "Good. Also, you should probably have my number, just in case."

He pushed his phone across the table to her. "Good idea."

She added her number to his phone and pushed the phone back to him. He stared at his phone for a second, and his eyes widened.

"What if she doesn't text me back?"

The age-old question.

"I think we need to fill the next few hours with something that makes it impossible for you to check your phone compulsively." She stood up. "Do you want to teach me to surf some more?"

His face relaxed. "Absolutely."

CHAPTER TWENTY

As they drove toward the beach, she looked out at the horizon. It was still overcast and drizzly and windier than the day before. It didn't feel like the best day for surfing. Especially when she remembered how hard it had been the last time, when the weather was much calmer.

"Maybe we should just . . . sit on the beach, instead of surfing?"

Beau laughed. "Oh, you're not getting out of this so easily. You said surfing, we're going to surf today." He put his hand on her shoulder, and his voice got more serious. "The surf isn't too high for you today; I checked. And I'll be right there. But if you really don't want to go, we don't have to. Whatever you want to do."

Did she still trust him, after the past few days? She shouldn't. She still felt wary of him, she knew that. And it shouldn't reassure her when he said he'd be right there. But it did.

"It's okay," she said. "We can try it, at least."

They got down to the beach and went back to the surf shop. The same blond woman was there from last time, and she greeted them both.

"Beau and Izzy, hey!"

How did she remember their names?

Beau smiled at her. "Hi, Dottie. Can we get that same surfboard and wet suit, or similar, for Isabelle again today?"

She nodded. "Sure thing."

She turned to go through the wet suits, and Izzy nudged Beau.

"It's okay for you to call me Izzy," she said.

He turned and looked down at her. "Thank you. I will." He smiled. "But I like Isabelle, you know. I like the sound of it."

He was so close to her they were almost touching.

"I do, too," she said.

"Okay, great!" Izzy jumped at the sound of Dottie's voice. "Here's your wetsuit, Iz." Sure, okay, that seemed like a very beach town surf shop kind of nickname. She could live with it. "You know where the changing room is."

They went down to the water, Beau carrying the surfboard again. He dropped it down onto the sand.

"Okay," he said. "Let's have you lie down on it, like before, and then practice sliding yourself up into that same stance I taught you last time. Do you remember how to do that?"

Oh no. Why had she suggested surfing?

"Yes, I remember. My body hurts just at the memory."

Beau made Izzy practice lying down on the surfboard and then sliding into a standing position over and over again on the sand. Finally, he said she was ready to go into the water. At first, he had her pull herself up so she was kneeling on the board. Once she'd done that successfully a few times—which took a while—he told her to try to stand.

As soon as she tried, she fell off.

And then again.

And again.

The fourth time, though, she finally got herself into a standing position for a few seconds, before a wave came and she lost her balance and fell off again. When she surfaced, though, they were both grinning.

"That was great!" Beau said. "Now let's do it again."

They stayed in the water for a long time. After she managed to stand up two more times, they walked together onto the beach. Izzy collapsed onto the sand, and Beau sat down next to her. The sky and the water were still just as gray as they'd been the day before, but now Izzy could see all the gradations of color: the paler, brighter gray where the sun was trying to poke out, the darker gray where there was more cloud cover, the bright white of the surf, the soft beige of the sand. It no longer looked sad and depressing, but peaceful.

"I came here yesterday," she said. Beau turned to look at her, but she kept looking forward. "I sat here for a while. It helped."

"I'm glad," he said.

She was glad he didn't apologize again—they'd already had that conversation, that wasn't why she'd said it. She just wanted him to know.

He nudged her. She could feel the warmth of his body through her wet suit. She wanted to lean into it but resisted.

"Thanks," he said. "For making me send that text today."

She smiled at him. "You're welcome."

They were silent for a while. It felt nice. To be there with him, to be comfortable with him, to be at peace with him again.

"Can I ask you a question?" he said.

She looked at him. He had a tiny triangle of freckles on his right cheek that she'd never noticed before. She usually wasn't this close to him.

"Okay," she said.

He hesitated a moment. "I've been wondering this for a while. Why aren't you a writer? You read so much, you have such good instincts about writing, you're such a good editor. Haven't you ever wanted to write, too?"

She looked down at the sand. Maybe he knew her better than she'd thought. "I have. I did. I used to be a writer."

Now he turned his whole body to face her. "What do you mean, you used to be? Do you write? Then you're a writer. Aren't you the one who told me that?"

She looked at him sideways. "I hate you so much, do you know that?"

He laughed out loud. "I know. But . . ."

She sighed. "You're right. I wanted to be a writer since I was little. I was a writer for a long time. For years. I wrote a novel."

She closed her eyes for a second. She'd never told anyone—really told anyone—about this. She'd been too ashamed. But after the past few days, it felt like all the barriers had come down between her and Beau. She felt like she could say anything to him.

"I was really hopeful about it. And then a while ago, someone I work with, one of the assistant editors, read it. He was very kind about it, said it was a very sweet first effort and he didn't want to discourage me at all, but that it felt very juvenile. He didn't want me to embarrass myself by passing it along to anyone else." She looked out at the water. "I felt like all my dreams died, right in that moment."

"Let me guess," Beau said. "That guy Gavin."

She turned to look at him. He looked furious, more angry than she'd ever seen him.

"Yeah," she said. "It was Gavin."

Beau shook his head. "You can't listen to that guy! I told you, he's trying to sabotage you. He's scared of you and how good you are. He wanted to make you feel like you're not talented, not accomplished, not good enough. He probably didn't even read the whole thing—just pulled out enough from it to say things that he knew would sting, so you wouldn't talk to anyone else about this."

She was scared to believe that. Scared to hope.

"If that was his goal, it worked. It was a real hit to my confidence. There were a lot of those over the past year, actually. I was on the point of giving up on all this. Writing, publishing, the whole thing."

He rested his hand next to hers on the sand. "You said *was*. Have you changed your mind?"

She nodded slowly. "I think so." Then she let herself smile. "I want to say that a different way. Yes, I've changed my mind. I'm still scared about it, but all the pep talks I gave you . . . I guess they got to me, too. Since I've been here, I've started writing again. Just a little. I had this idea that wouldn't get out of my head, so I started writing little bits of it, and . . . it's making me really happy."

He smiled at her. "That's great, Izzy. I'm glad."

She smiled back at him. "Me too. And even my job has felt different. Don't get me wrong, the problems are all still there. Maybe it's partly the distance—I have a better perspective on work, now that I'm not in that building every day. But it's also been my work with you. I've felt excited about my work, hopeful about what this job could be. It's made me want to bring my old dreams back to life. So thank you, for that."

"You're welcome, but I didn't do any of that. You did it all." A grin slowly spread across his face. "I have an idea. What if there's a new rule for the writing time in the library: We both have to write, not just me?"

She pulled her knees up to her chest. "You're not going to take no for an answer on this one, are you?" she asked.

He shook his head. "Absolutely not. But then, you wouldn't have told me about this if you wanted that from me."

He was probably right about that.

He put his hand on her back. She wanted to lean into it, reach out for him, but she didn't.

"Come on," he said. "Let's go home. We have lots of snacks waiting for us."

She jumped up. "You're right. I bet the snack cabinet misses us. It's probably making up little songs, just to be ready for us to come back."

When they got back to the car, Beau tossed her a hoodie from the backseat. "Here. You look cold."

She *was* cold—she should have worn something other than a sleeveless dress to the beach in this weather. As she slipped it on, he cleared his throat.

"I know you said not to apologize again. But I just need to say this. I can be a real asshole, but if I'd known that, about you and writing, I never would have said what I said yesterday. I really hate that I hurt you like that."

She touched his arm. "I know."

They were mostly quiet on the way home. Izzy was glad she'd suggested surfing. Things felt better between them. Not back to how it had been before—that was impossible. Good in a different way, though.

Izzy checked her phone when she got back to the house.

> Met a hot medical student last night, friend of my cousin. Keep your fingers crossed he asks me out!

Izzy laughed. Priya always managed to find hot guys wherever she went.

> Fingers and toes are crossed!

When Izzy got back downstairs after a shower, she wandered to the kitchen. When she got there, she stopped and stared.

Beau stood at the kitchen island, his hands—and part of his T-shirt—dusted in flour, rolling out dough.

"What . . . What are you doing?"

He looked up from the dough to her. "Making croissants. I started them last night, after you went to bed. They take forever, but now it's time to laminate the dough."

"Laminate the dough . . . What are you talking about?" Then it suddenly hit her. "Wait. *You* make the baked goods?"

He laughed. "Yes, of course I make them, where did you think they came from?"

She walked over to the island to look at what he was doing. "I don't know, I thought maybe the mixer and the oven became sentient and just popped them out on their own after we went to bed." She grinned at him. "That, or Michaela."

He went back to rolling the dough. "Michaela does do everything important around here, but no, it was me." He shrugged. "When I got here, I had nothing to do other than just sit around and feel bad about everything. And I did that for a while, and then one night when I was up late—I haven't slept all that well in . . . a while—I watched some cooking show. One of the old ones, where no one looked camera-ready and they were all kind of boring and pedantic, but I sort of got into it. And so I dug out some of my grandmother's old cookbooks from the library and tried to make biscuits." He shook his head. "They were terrible, that first time. Heavy and dense. But it just made me want to try to get them right. And once I did, I kept trying, with other stuff." He looked down at the dough, and then turned to open the refrigerator. "I tried croissants once before, and they were good, but I knew I could do better. It's been a while, though, so we'll see how they turn out. But I figured I'd wait until I really needed to, and last night felt like the right time."

He took a flat square of something out of the fridge and peeled the plastic wrap from around it.

"What do you mean, wait until you really needed to?" she asked.

He set the square in the center of the dough.

"It's—this is going to sound stupid—a good distraction for me, when things are . . . difficult. And the more complicated the recipe is, the better it is at taking my mind off things. I mean, it's fun, too, don't get me wrong, I've gotten very dorky about different kinds of flours, and I now have a favorite brand of vanilla, please don't ever tell anyone I said that. But having to do a million steps means I can't think about anything else. And croissants take a lot of concentration."

He folded the dough around the square and pinched the corners together. She couldn't take it any longer.

"Is that butter? Because if so, that's a LOT of butter."

He laughed, definitely at her, this time. "It is butter. That's why croissants taste so good."

He picked up the rolling pin again and rolled the dough-encased butter gently, from the middle outward. Izzy came closer to the island to watch.

"You have to let the butter soften and then sort of press and squish it into a square shape, and then roll it out so it's flat enough, and then refrigerate it again." He picked up the dough and turned it sideways. "And then you fold it up like this, in your dough, and roll it all out. And once you've done that, you fold the dough in thirds, like this. Then roll it out again. That's called laminating—it's how you get all those flaky layers." He made a face. "Well, if you do it right. I didn't last time; I was too impatient."

She looked down at the dough. "I didn't realize it was that complicated."

He held up the rolling pin. "Do you want to try?"

She walked around the island to stand next to him, and he handed her the rolling pin. She put it down at the edge and started to press down, when he stopped her.

"No, not like that—have you never rolled out dough before?"

His voice was teasing but not mocking. She could tell the difference now. She shook her head. "My grandmother makes biscuits, too, but she never lets anyone else help." She thought back to those times and laughed. "Plus, I was always busy reading."

He put his hands on hers, still holding the rolling pin, and moved them to the center of the dough, and then took a step back.

"You roll from the middle outward. That way, it makes the dough more even in the end."

She pressed down and felt the dough move as she rolled the pin in one direction and then in the other.

"Like this?" she asked.

He nodded, but she could tell something was wrong.

"What is it? Am I ruining your dough?"

One corner of his lips tipped up. "Not ruining it . . . exactly. It's just that . . ."

She laughed. "I knew there was something. Show me."

He moved behind her and put his hands on top of hers. "You need a little more power here, that's all." They rolled the dough together, first in one direction, and then in the other. "It's easier for me, because I'm so much taller."

It felt nice, with him standing behind her like that. Surrounding her with his warmth. With his strong hands on top of hers, with his arms around hers. She wanted to lean into him. Into all this.

It felt far too nice.

She dropped her hands, and so did he.

"I'll let you finish this part, then." She stepped back, and he moved away. "I can, um, get dinner warmed up? Because I don't know about you, but I'm starving."

She had forgiven Beau, but that didn't mean that she had to let herself go back down that particular path. It would be too easy, and it would hurt too much. Especially since she was going back to New York in a week.

He nodded, without looking at her. "Good idea. I'm starving, too."

She turned to the fridge, then stopped. "Wait. So you're telling me that up to a few weeks ago, you did all this baking, and then just . . . left the kitchen like this for someone else to clean up? With lots of dishes and flour everywhere?"

He looked around at the kitchen, then back at her. "When you put it like that, it makes me sound like an unmitigated jackass."

She cracked up, and so did he.

"I didn't say it, you did."

By the time dinner was ready, he'd chilled, rolled, and folded the dough again. They decided to eat in the kitchen so Beau could keep working on the croissants. When he brought silverware over to the kitchen table, he picked up his phone, and then stilled, his back to her.

"Beau?"

After a few seconds, he turned around. "She, um, texted me back. My mom. She asked if I could come to LA next weekend, to see her."

Izzy looked at Beau to try to gauge his reaction to that, but she couldn't tell from the tone in his voice or the look on his face.

"How do you feel about that?" she asked. She shook her head. "Sorry, I sound like I'm trying to be your therapist or something, that's not what I mean, but—"

He looked at the kitchen island, still dusted with flour. "I don't know," he said. He walked over to the toaster oven and scooped pigs in a blanket on their plates. They were going full-on frozen snack foods for dinner tonight. "Do you want honey mustard or barbecue sauce? We have a number of different kinds of each, of course."

Well, that was a clear change of subject.

"Both, obviously," she said, "but I'm not picky on what kind."

After they sat down at the table, Beau looked over at her. "Sorry. I'm just a little talked out, if that's okay."

Izzy reached for a pig in a blanket. "That's totally okay." And then she stopped. "Also—if you want to be alone now, that's okay, too. I can just—"

He shook his head. "I don't. I was actually kind of . . . looking forward to this."

She looked at him for a second, then down at her plate. "Me too."

They didn't talk about anything else hard, for the rest of the night. They just ate dinner, and finished the croissant dough, and made cookies, and watched TV. But somehow, she felt closer to him at the end of the night than she had at the beginning.

CHAPTER TWENTY-ONE

On Monday afternoon, Izzy met Beau in the library. He raised his eyebrows at her as she sat down.

"Are you still up for our deal?" Beau asked. "About us both writing, I mean."

Izzy gestured to the notebooks she'd brought with her. One was Beau's, the one they passed back and forth every time. The other was her own.

"I'm not one to back out of a deal," she said. "Haven't you learned that about me yet?"

There was a certain amount of bravado in her voice, bravery she didn't exactly feel. Yes, she'd been tinkering with an idea for the past few weeks, jotting down notes, tiny scenes, here and there. But she was scared to really commit to writing again.

She was glad, in a way, that this deal with Beau would force her to write. But another part of her was terrified. That she'd discover Gavin was right, this was too hard for her, she was no good at this. Or, even worse, that her experiences with writing and publishing over the past few years had taken away all her joy in writing, that joy she used to have when she was a teenager, sitting on her bed with her notebook for hours, deep into a world she'd created.

But it scared her even more to never try again, to leave that part of her life, of her dreams, behind.

She pushed Beau's notebook across the table to him and took out her phone to set the timer. This time it was for her, not for him.

She took a deep breath as she opened her own notebook.

"Hey," Beau said from across the table.

She looked up at him.

He was smiling softly at her. "You're gonna be great. You know that, right?"

She could tell from the look on his face that he wasn't fooled by her. He knew she was nervous about writing again.

She swallowed. "Thanks." She wanted to say more, to say it helped for him to say that, it helped to have him there, sitting across the table from her, it helped to know he believed in her, but she couldn't get anything else out. But she thought he might already know all of that.

She picked up her phone again. "Okay." She pressed start. "Go."

And then she looked at her notes from the past few weeks. The ones she'd barely admitted to herself that she had envisioned as a book. Okay. She could do this.

She flipped to a blank page in her notebook.

When the timer went off, she sat up with a jolt. It had been slow going, at first. She'd hesitated over names, places, transitions. She'd wanted to reach for her phone more than once, to look something up, to distract herself from the hard parts, to see if Priya had texted her. But instead, she'd made herself keep going, partly because of the timer, mostly because Beau was sitting across from her. And eventually, after a while, she'd forgotten to worry about whether that name was right, or if that place was really spelled like that, or if Priya had gone out yet with that hot medical student she'd met at the wedding. She'd even forgotten Beau was there. She'd just fallen headfirst into her own words, her own story, her own imagination.

And it felt great.

Beau's smile was wide this time as he looked at her.

"It was good?" he asked.

She nodded. "Yeah," she said. "It was good."

When it was time to leave the library, he started to say something, then shook his head and stood up.

She stayed in her seat. "What?"

He sat back down. "Sorry. It's just . . . I wanted to ask you something, but I think it's probably . . ." He looked at her face and laughed. "Okay." He sighed. "This is your last week here."

The smile fell from her face. "Yeah. It is."

He nodded. "I'd sort of managed to ignore that, until your friend said something, and . . . maybe that's why I was so on edge the other day." He sort of smiled. "I mean, one of the reasons I was so on edge."

He thought maybe he was on edge because . . . he was upset about her leaving? Was that what he meant? She didn't have a chance to linger on that question.

"Anyway, what I was going to ask was, do you think maybe you could stay? For a little while longer? Until I feel—" He stopped and then smiled at her. "Until I feel like I can actually do this without you is I guess the only honest way I can end that sentence."

"Yes," she said. "I can stay."

She didn't have to stop to think. She knew she wanted to stay.

"But this time," she finished, "*you* have to ask Marta."

His face fell at her last words. "Right. That makes sense." He sighed. "Have I mentioned that she scares me?"

Izzy laughed. "Oh, don't worry about that—she scares everybody."

"Well, at least it's not just me," he said.

He pulled his computer toward him, but Izzy shook her head.

"You can't email her about this. You have to call her."

He looked at her, wide-eyed. "Call her? On the PHONE?"

Izzy nodded. "I know. Trust me, I know. But Marta does everything important on the phone. If you email her, she'll do one of three things: She'll ignore it; she'll say no right away; or she'll call you. Wouldn't you rather be the one to call? Plus, Marta respects that."

He pulled his phone out of his pocket. "I have to do this right now. Don't I?"

Izzy didn't say anything.

"Fine," he said. "But you have to stay here, okay?"

Like she would miss this.

"I'll be right here," she said. "Do you have her number? She'll probably still be in the office right now, but if not, I can give you her cell. Here."

She pulled out her phone and texted him Marta's numbers. He stared at her as he called.

"Hi, Marta, this is Beau Towers," he said when she answered the phone. His voice got deeper, which made Izzy have to hold back a giggle. He shook his finger at her.

"Yes, yes, everything is going well with Isabelle, I'm making a lot of progress on the memoir. That's actually why I called. I was wondering if I could borrow her for a while longer. She's been a great asset to me, you know."

A great asset? Izzy pressed her lips together so she wouldn't laugh out loud, and Beau grinned at her.

He nodded. "Yes, I've talked to Isabelle about this, but of course you'll need to talk to her as well to make sure she'd like to stay longer."

She could hear Marta's voice, but she couldn't hear what she was saying.

But she suddenly knew. Oh no, she should have prepped Beau better before he made this call.

She says how long? he mouthed to her.

She ripped out a piece of paper from her notebook and started writing.

"Um, I was thinking . . . a month?" he said. He made a panicked face at Izzy, and she almost laughed. "After the week we already have remaining, of course."

Marta was still talking, but Izzy knew exactly what she was saying. She held up her note so he could see it.

NEGOTIATE!!!

His eyes widened, and he nodded at her. "I don't think an additional two weeks is enough time," he said, in a much more assured voice. "Especially given where I am in the book. But an extra three weeks might do it."

He listened for a second, and then grinned at her. "Excellent," he said. "I'll let her know."

Izzy grinned back at him, but his attention went back to the phone. Beau's smile faded.

"Okay," he said after a while. "Of course."

Izzy raised her eyebrows at him, but he shook his head. What did Marta say? Did she change her mind?

"Okay. Thanks, Marta. I appreciate it." He hung up the phone and stood up. "We did it!"

Izzy jumped up. "We did it!"

He came around the table and enveloped her in a hug. She hugged him back.

"She's even scarier than I remembered," he said. "Thank God you were there for that. I never would have made it out alive on my own."

She leaned into the hug. She'd forgotten how good this felt. For him to hold her like this. It had only happened one time before, that accidental time in the kitchen, but this time it was on purpose, for both of them. He was so big, and strong, and it just felt so . . . right, to have his arms around her like this. She didn't want him to ever let go.

As soon as she thought that—as soon as she realized that she'd thought that—she made herself drop her arms and take a step back. He was smiling down at her, with a look on his face that . . . She swallowed and looked away.

"I, um, I should have prepped you better for it, though," she said. "I forgot to warn you that with Marta, everything is a negotiation." She looked back up at him. "What did she say to you, at the end there?"

He turned to the door. "Oh, just that she'd confirm this with you, to make sure you want to stay. And that she's looking forward to the book."

That all made sense, but Izzy had thought there had been something else. Maybe she'd just imagined that anxious look on Beau's face.

Beau stopped, just after they'd gotten out of the library. "I should teach you to bake a cake tonight so we can celebrate."

She put a confused look on her face. "A cake? But I didn't see any cake mix in the pantry?"

He looked horrified. "Mix? You think I'd make you cake out of a mix?"

She laughed out loud. She knew that would get him. He glared at her, but she could see the smile underneath.

"Oh, that was a joke, was it? You think I'm just that easy to antagonize?"

She laughed again as she turned to go upstairs.

CHAPTER TWENTY-TWO

When she walked into the library on Friday afternoon, she could tell something was wrong with Beau. He had that tense look on his face that she now knew meant he was stressed, not angry.

"Everything okay?" she asked him when she sat down.

"Everything's fine, why wouldn't it be?" He took the notebook that she pushed across the table to him. They were well past the point when either of them was worried that he'd delete a part of his book—at least, she was pretty sure they were—but they still exchanged the notebook every day.

"No reason. You just seem out of sorts, that's all," she said.

"I'm fine," he said, without looking at her.

Okay, then.

She opened her own notebook and pulled out her phone to start the timer. They wrote in silence for a minute or two.

"I'm nervous," he said.

She stopped the timer and looked at him. He was staring down at his notebook.

"I'm seeing my mom tomorrow," he said. "Every day this week, I've typed out a text to cancel. So far, I haven't sent one, but who knows what will happen later today, or tomorrow morning, or tomorrow if I actually make it in the car to drive to LA."

She'd been so intent on her own work that week that she'd almost forgotten that Beau would be seeing his mom this weekend, and how hard that would be for him.

"Do you want to talk about it?" she asked. "About what you're nervous about?"

He let out a short laugh.

"What am I not nervous about? Seeing her again, telling her how sorry I am in person, finding out how mad she is at me, hell, I'm not sure whether she'll even let me in her house, given what I said to her, how I acted. And not just at the funeral, but . . . Her text was nice, but she has every right to be furious."

He tried to smile at her, but it wasn't that successful.

Izzy thought for a moment. "Do you want me to come with you? Not to see your mom, but just, like, in the car to keep you company so you don't turn around and come back here?"

Until recently, she would have hesitated to ask him something like that. And then hedged it more, with "You don't have to say yes to this" or "My feelings won't be hurt if you say no." But they didn't have to be careful around each other anymore.

His eyes widened. "Would you really do that for me? Yes. Of course I want you to come. But it's a lot to ask."

She tried to ignore how good it felt for him to say "of course" like that.

"You didn't ask. I offered. I can't solve any of those other problems for you, but I can sit in the car with you and go to a coffee shop or something and write or read for however long you're with your mom. And I can hold on to your phone on the way so you don't cancel."

He looked down at the notebook. "Okay," he said after a moment. "Thanks."

She started the timer. "You're welcome."

So Saturday, late morning, they walked to the car together. Izzy offered to drive, but Beau shook his head.

"No, I can do it," he said as they walked to the car. "I want to do it."

He'd trimmed his beard, she noticed. He still seemed on edge, like the slightest thing would cause him to jump.

"Oh." He reached into his pocket at the first stoplight they hit and handed her his phone. "You said you'd take this?"

She slid it into the pocket of her denim jacket without a word.

They'd been on the freeway for about thirty minutes before he said anything else.

"Remind me," he said. "Before we leave LA, I want to stop at this one tea place. They have Michaela's favorite tea, and it's hard to find. I thought, since we won't be that far away, we should get her some."

That was nice of him, to think about Michaela like that.

"What's it called?" she asked. "I can go pick it up while you're with your mom."

"Oh. That's a good idea. It's that brand in the kitchen with the black boxes and gold letters. The tea place is called Off to the Cupboard."

She nodded. "Sounds good."

They drove on for another thirty minutes until suddenly, Beau pulled off the freeway and into a gas station right off the exit. She expected him to get out of the car to get gas, but instead he turned to her.

"I'm not sure if I can do this," he said.

She turned to him and grabbed his hand. "You and I both know you can do this, that's not in question. The question I want you to think about is whether it will feel worse for you to push through this hard, scary feeling now, and do it, or if it'll feel worse to turn around, walk back in the house, and wake up tomorrow, and every day after this, knowing you didn't do this."

He looked down at their hands, his large hand holding tight to her smaller one, his pale brown skin against her darker brown skin, and didn't say anything for a while.

Finally, he let go.

"Okay." He started the car again and pulled out of the gas station and back onto the freeway going south. "Okay, fine."

Would it help him to talk? She couldn't tell, but she knew he'd make it clear if he didn't want to.

"The foundation," she said. "The one you and Michaela are working on. What's it for?"

Beau seemed relieved at the change of subject. "It's to support libraries that don't have big sources of funding. Schools, community centers, places like that."

Izzy almost laughed. What a wonderful idea. And not what she would have expected from Beau when she first met him. She smiled at him.

"Oh wow, that sounds great," she said.

His hands were a little less tight on the steering wheel.

"Yeah. At first I wanted to build whole new libraries, do that kind of thing. But I got some advice from a friend who runs a foundation, and she said the goal is to find the people who are already doing good work and give them more money to do it with, so that's what we're going to do. Eventually, the goal is to fund writing tutors, scholarships, stuff like that, too. Getting a foundation all organized is a lot more complicated than I thought. At least Michaela knows what the hell she's doing because I definitely do not."

She laughed at that, and so did he.

He got quiet for a few minutes.

"Naming it after my grandparents," he said.

She put her hand on his for a second. "I'm sure they'd like that."

A few miles later, she turned to him. "I didn't mean it. What I said that day about you. Being spoiled and everything."

He glanced over at her, a small smile on his face. "Yes you did."

She had to smile at that. He knew her too well. "Okay, then, I don't mean it anymore," she said. "I don't believe it anymore."

The smile hovered around the corners of his lips. "Thank you for saying that," he said.

"I wouldn't say it if I didn't mean it," she said.

"I know," he said.

After another hour or so of driving, they pulled up in front of a modest bungalow on a quiet side street. Granted, the quiet side street was just past the WELCOME TO BEVERLY HILLS sign, so it was only modest in comparison to some of the other houses on the block.

He turned off the car and handed her the keys and then some cash from his wallet. "For the tea."

She tucked the cash into her wallet. "Okay." She took his phone out of her bag. "I think it's safe to give this back to you now. Just text me when you want me to come back, okay? I have my notebook, my laptop, lots of books, so I'll be fine for however long."

He took the phone from her. "Okay." He looked down at his phone. She could tell he was stalling—they were a few minutes early.

"If you get stressed," she said, "just think about watching *This Provincial Life* later tonight."

That made him smile. "I'll also think about what snacks we're going to eat during *This Provincial Life*."

Izzy took off her seat belt. "Michaela restocked the cabinet, did you notice? We have *lots* of options."

His eyes brightened. He took off his seat belt and reached for the door handle.

They both got out of the car. Izzy came around to the driver side to take the keys from him. Beau looked at her, then at the house. She could see his shoulders tense up.

"Do you want a hug?" she asked him, without thinking about

it, then immediately wished she hadn't. That last hug had been way too dangerous.

But then he took a step toward her.

"I absolutely do," he said. He wrapped his arms around her, and she pulled him in close. Her head was nestled into his chest, his arms were hard against her back, and he bent his head so it rested on top of hers. They stayed like that for a while, holding on tight, not saying anything. Finally, he took a step back.

"Thanks. I really needed that."

She backed up, too. "Glad I could help."

They looked at each other for a few more seconds, and then he turned to the house again.

"Okay. I guess I'd better . . ."

She nodded, and opened the car door. "Just text me. I'll be close by."

She watched him walk up to the house and waited until he was at the front door before she drove away.

Izzy found Off to the Cupboard relatively easily, though she had to pay an arm and a leg for parking. She saw the boxes of Michaela's tea and got her four boxes with the money Beau had given her. They cost more than she'd ever expected tea to cost, but then, she'd always been more of a coffee person. There was an empty table by the window, so she ordered herself some tea and a slice of chocolate cake, and sat down.

Then she stared at her laptop. All week, she'd been trying to make herself open the file for her old novel again, read it, and try to decide, now that she'd had time and space away, if she wanted to keep working on it. After this month with Beau, she no longer believed that Gavin was right about her talent and potential. Now she knew that she wanted this enough to work hard, to fight through setbacks, and to conquer the Gavins of the world.

But she was still scared to open this manuscript.

She set her jaw. If Beau could text his mom, could drive back to LA to see her, could walk into her house to apologize to her, despite how hard all of that was for him, she could at least open this damn document.

She had to search for the file. She'd hidden it away from herself, so she wouldn't have to see it every time she opened her laptop and wouldn't be tempted to delete it. Huh, maybe she and Beau had more in common than she'd thought. She finally found it, tucked away in a folder called Misc, in another folder called Taxes, and another folder called Spreadsheets. Izzy took a sip of tea and a bite of cake. And then she opened it.

She spent the next hour reading, skimming, then reading again. She found a lot she wanted to fix: paragraphs, whole pages that dragged, characters that she needed to tweak, plot points that didn't make sense. But sometimes, she stopped thinking about what she had to fix, or cut, or add, and just got swept away in the story. Her story.

Finally, she sat back in her chair and gulped the last of her now cold tea. Her book wasn't perfect, and she had a lot of work to do. But she knew it was good. She knew it, to her core. She knew it, the same way she knew that it meant something, something that she wasn't quite ready to interrogate, that she could still feel the imprint of Beau's hands on her back from their hug, hear the way he'd breathed her in, smell that scent of salt water and fresh air that always lingered around him.

She shook that off. She flipped to the beginning of the manuscript again, opened her notebook to a page in the back, and started to make notes of all the things she wanted to fix, chapter by chapter.

She was through the first half of the book when her phone buzzed.

You can come whenever you're ready

She'd lost track of time, but now she realized that Beau had been with his mom for almost three hours. But the curtness of his text made her worried.

She texted him back right away.

Fifteen minutes

His response came quickly.

Ok. Let me know when you're outside

And then, a few seconds later.

I'm glad I came

CHAPTER TWENTY-THREE

When Beau came out of the house to meet Izzy, he wasn't alone. A tall, elegant Black woman was with him. Beau looked a lot like his mom, Izzy realized.

They both walked toward the car. As they got closer, Izzy could see from Beau's facial expression, from his body language, that it had gone well. He looked calmer, more at peace. Happy.

Izzy got out of the car as they approached, and Beau smiled at her.

"Izzy, I'd like to introduce you to my mom, Nina Russell. Mom, this is Isabelle Marlowe."

Izzy held out her hand, and Beau's mom took it in both of hers.

"It's very nice to meet you, Isabelle," she said. "Beau has told me so much about you. Thank you, for everything you've done for him."

Izzy blushed as Beau's mom smiled down at her.

"Nice to meet you, too, Ms. Russell," Izzy said. "And it wasn't . . . I didn't . . ."

Beau's mom laughed. "Nina, please." She patted Izzy's hand and released it. "I won't keep you two, but I hope I'll be able to get to know you better soon."

Izzy smiled at her. "I'd like that, too," she said. She turned to get into the passenger side of the car; she wanted to let Beau and his mom say goodbye without her standing there. "It was really nice to meet you."

Beau turned to his mom and gave her a short, but very tight, hug and then said something to her that made her laugh and hug him again. He got in the car, rolled his window down, and waved.

"Bye, Mom," he said. "See you soon."

Beau didn't say anything as they drove away, navigated to the freeway, and merged into traffic. Music was on, the same hip-hop playlist they'd listened to on their way there. Izzy took her cue from him and didn't ask any questions.

He didn't have to tell her what happened with his mom, obviously. Even though she was dying to know.

When he pulled into a gas station again, he turned off the car and finally looked at her.

"Sorry," he said. "I didn't want to talk about this while I was driving."

Then he didn't say anything for a moment.

"It was great to meet her," Izzy said, to help him along. "You both seemed happy."

He ran his hand through his hair and smiled. He looked embarrassed but pleased. It was nice to see him like that.

"Yeah," he said. "I think so. But at first . . . I didn't know what to say, or how to start. For a while, we just made awkward conversation about the weather and her house and the Santa Barbara house. I wanted to apologize for real, but it was so hard. So finally I pulled up one of the chapters on my phone, one I've been working on this week, about what I discovered that night, and how awful I felt, and feel, about what I said to her, and what he did, and everything else. I handed my phone to her and asked her to read it. And then she started crying and I hugged her and she hugged me and then we talked hard for the next two hours about everything." He laughed. "Well, maybe not everything. We have a lot more to talk about, years to catch up on, but we talked about a lot. It was really . . . hard. But good."

Izzy touched his hand. "I'm so glad" was all she said. She wanted to say more, about how happy and relieved she was for him, but from the way Beau squeezed her hand and smiled at her, she could tell he understood what she meant.

"Me too." He let go of her hand. "Anyway, I just wanted to tell you that. And to thank you, for helping me do this. I wouldn't have done it without you."

She almost said, "Oh, I didn't do anything," or "Yes, you would have" but she stopped herself. It was true. He wouldn't have done it without her.

"You're welcome," she said instead.

He turned back to the steering wheel and then stopped. "Wait. We actually do need gas this time."

They both laughed as he got out of the car.

They didn't talk a lot on the drive back to Santa Barbara, but the silence didn't seem tense. She didn't occupy herself with her phone, scrolling through social media and sending meaningless texts to Priya like she had done on the way to LA. Instead, she just sat there in the passenger seat and daydreamed.

When they pulled up to the house, Beau stopped the car but didn't get out.

"You have your keys, right? I think I want to go down to the beach for a little while," he said.

She dug through her bag and found the keys. She opened the car door, but then she turned to him. "Do you want company?"

He smiled at her. "Only if the company is you."

Izzy looked away so he wouldn't see her smiling. Her cheeks felt warm—was she blushing? If she was, at least Beau wouldn't be able to tell.

They got to the beach just as the sun was starting to set. Beau spread an old blanket from the trunk onto the sand, and they sat down. For a while, they both just stared in silence at the pink-and-orange horizon.

"I could use another one of those hugs, if that's still on offer," Beau said.

Izzy immediately turned to him. He wrapped his arms around her and rested his hands right in the small of her back, where they'd been before. She tucked her face into that little divot in his shoulder. He dropped his head down onto her shoulder and let out a long sigh.

After a little while, his fingers moved gently up and down her back. It made her whole body tingle. She didn't want it to stop. She didn't want this to stop. She didn't want to let go of him. She just wanted to sit here, with him, so close there was no space between them, feeling his touch, breathing in and out together, listening to the waves crashing into shore.

But after a little while, she could feel him start to pull away, so she forced herself to let go of him, sit back. He moved away slowly and stopped to face her, when they were still so close, when her hands were still touching his shoulders, when his palms were on her upper arms.

"When I told my mom about you," he said, "about these last few weeks, everything you've done for me, she said something else. She said she was so glad I had you. She said how lucky I was, to have someone like you."

Izzy tried to say something, but for once, she had no idea what to say.

He brushed her hair out of her face, and his fingertips lingered on her cheek. "I told her that she's right. That I'm very glad to have you. That it was the luckiest day of my life when you knocked on my door."

Izzy stared at him for a long moment. She noticed the flecks of green inside his golden-brown eyes. He was looking straight at her, in a way he never had before. It made her so happy, and so scared, all at once. She knew she should pull away, get up, break this moment between them.

But she'd been wanting this for so long. And from the look on his face, she thought he did, too. She let her hands move up his shoulders. And then, slowly, she leaned forward and kissed him.

He kissed her back, at first softly, gently. And then the kiss changed, became urgent, insistent. She could tell, from his kiss, from the way he pulled her closer, that he wanted this as much as she did.

They kissed for a long time as the sun set in front of them, until finally, Beau rested his forehead against hers.

"Do you know how long I've been wanting to do that?" Beau asked. "The answer is, a very, very long time."

She pulled back and looked into his eyes.

"I didn't know that, no," she said. "I kind of thought I was all alone in wanting to do that. I didn't even really let myself think about it, because I thought . . ."

He laughed and dropped a kiss in her hair. "I'm not sure whether to be glad I hid my feelings so well from you or to be furious we wasted so much time when we could have been doing this." He brushed his fingertip over her bottom lip. "But mostly, I'm just happy to be here with you right now."

Izzy leaned forward and kissed him again. "I'm really happy to be here with you right now."

They sat there for a while longer, holding each other, kissing, talking about nothing, kissing more. Finally, Beau stood up and reached for her hand.

"Those snacks aren't going to eat themselves, you know," he said.

She laughed and grabbed his hand as she stood up.

They held hands on the way back to the car. Izzy smiled as she put on her seat belt.

"What is it?" Beau asked.

She shook her head. "I'm just happy. That's all."

He put his hand on her cheek. "Me too," he said.

Beau put on his seat belt and started the car. Izzy felt like she was tempting fate, she was so happy. She tried to temper herself, push down her smile, just in case. And then she thought to hell with that, and she smiled so big out the window that strangers smiled back at her.

CHAPTER TWENTY-FOUR

When they walked in the house, Beau reached for Izzy and pulled her close.

"I just needed to be able to do this again, when we were all alone," he said, his voice muffled against her hair.

His words, his touch, went straight to Izzy's heart. She couldn't believe this had actually happened, that she'd kissed Beau on the beach and he'd kissed her back, that he'd said those things to her about how long he'd wanted to kiss her, that they were back here in the house together, like this. She rested her head against his firm, broad chest and felt his arms around her, and it felt so good. But then, suddenly, it wasn't enough, and she lifted her face and pulled him down to her, and they were kissing again, and it was immediately more than it had been on the beach. Faster, closer, more intimate. His big, warm hands moved up her back, and the way he held her, kissed her, touched her, made her feel like the whole world had just sparkled from black-and-white into color.

Finally, he pulled away. She was glad he was breathing as hard as she was.

"We have to pace ourselves, Izzy," he said. "We only made it just inside the door."

She pulled him back down to her and kissed him softly on the lips before she took a step back. "I prefer to think of it as making up for lost time, don't you?"

He gave her a slow, very sexy smile. “Mmm, that’s a very good way to put it.”

She smiled at him. “But also, I’m starving.”

He laughed and moved toward the kitchen. “Me too.”

She turned to go with him, but he shook his head and steered her toward the staircase. “I’ll get the food ready, you go up and change,” he said.

She raised an eyebrow at him. “You don’t like my dress?”

He narrowed his eyes at her. “Oh no, I’m not going to get caught in that trap. Number one: Your dress is great, but this is only the second time I’ve seen you wear it, and I don’t want to be the jerk who spills one of the assorted dipping sauces we’re going to have with dinner on it. If you’re thinking, ‘Does that mean Beau has been paying that close attention to what I’ve been wearing?’ the answer is yes. Which leads us to number two: You always change before we have dinner.”

This *was* only the second time she’d worn this dress, and she did always change before dinner.

Beau grinned at the look on her face. “See? Also, both of those things lead to number three: I was hoping you might wear one of those little tank tops tonight that have been driving me wild for weeks.”

Well, when he put it that way.

She lifted her chin and smiled at him. “Mmm, I’ll see what I can do. Meet you in the TV room in twenty minutes?”

His smile widened. “Absolutely.”

Izzy ran up the stairs, conscious the whole time that he stayed at the bottom of the staircase and watched her. When she got to her room, she just stopped for a moment and smiled. She had no idea where this was going, she knew she shouldn’t really be doing this, because given everything she knew about Beau, she had a feeling heartbreak was on the horizon. But for once, she would ignore that feeling.

She quickly changed into leggings and one of the tank tops that she most definitely had not realized had been driving Beau wild, washed her face, pulled Beau's hoodie on, and ran back downstairs. She knew she should hang back, not be too eager, go down in thirty minutes instead of the twenty that she'd said. She didn't care.

Beau was already in the TV room, setting something up on the coffee table. He looked up when she walked into the room.

A slow smile spread across his face when he saw her, and his eyes roamed down her body. She felt a shiver go through her.

"Hi," he said.

"Hi," she said. She suddenly felt shy. "Do you need any help? With dinner."

He shook his head as she walked toward him.

"Everything is heating up, I'm just waiting for the timer to go off. But I . . ." He looked down for a moment. Was *he* blushing now? "I didn't ask you what you wanted to drink, but I thought, maybe . . ."

Izzy came closer and saw what was on the coffee table. A champagne bottle and two glasses.

He'd done this, just for her? Beau wanted to celebrate as much as she did?

Her smile got bigger. She didn't even try to hide it.

"You thought maybe what?" she said. She wasn't going to let him off the hook here, no matter how sweet the moment was. She wanted to know what the rest of that sentence was.

He took a breath. "I thought maybe tonight was a good occasion to bring out some of my grandfather's champagne."

"I think that was a great idea." She sat down on the couch, in the same place she sat all the time. But it felt so different now.

He picked up the bottle, unwrapped the foil from around the top, and then slowly twisted off the cage around the cork. He poured the champagne into two glasses and handed one to her before he sat down next to her.

"Cheers," he said. "To a day of making up for lost time."

Izzy touched her glass to Beau's and took a sip of the champagne. And then she stared at the glass for a moment.

"I think your grandfather's wine is going to spoil me for wine for the rest of my life," she said.

Beau laughed. "This champagne is incredible, right? Perfect for the occasion."

They smiled at each other again. He took the glass out of her hand and put it on the table. Then he leaned forward and kissed her again.

She wrapped her arms around him and pulled him closer. She felt greedy, like she wanted all of him. Like she had to hold on to every touch, commit every caress to memory, absorb every moment into her bloodstream.

He kissed her hair and laughed softly. "I've been wanting to kiss you since that very first day, you know," he said.

She sat back and rolled her eyes. "You did not. You just wanted me out of your house."

He laughed. "Well, yes, at first I did. But the thing was, when you seemed so confident, so unafraid of me, when you refused to let me intimidate you, I was intrigued." His finger trailed from her cheek, down her jaw, to her collarbone.

She slid her fingers into his hair. "Mmm, were you really?"

He nodded as his hands moved down her body. "I was."

She pulled him close. Just as she was about to kiss him again, his phone alarm went off.

He laughed. "Dinner." He shook his head and stood up. "Perfect timing."

A few minutes later, he came back into the TV room with a tray full of food.

"I don't know how it's become my job to bring you food all the time," he said.

She beamed at him. "I don't know either, but I like it a lot." She glanced at the tray. "Ooh, baked Brie? Where did that come from?"

He lowered the tray to the coffee table and sat down. "I found it in the back of the freezer—pretty exciting, right?" He gestured to the bowl on the table full of crackers. "That's what these are for."

She leaned forward and cut into the Brie.

"You think of everything. See, this is why the food is your job. I wouldn't have thought of crackers!"

He narrowed his eyes at her. "That, my friend, is absolute bullshit, and you know it."

Izzy giggled. "I was *trying* to praise you, okay?"

Beau put a stack of salami slices on his plate and a handful of crackers. "Oh, did I miss where you were telling me how you've wanted to kiss *me* since the first day?"

Izzy looked sideways at Beau. He was smiling but a little shyly. She could tell he wanted a real answer.

"Well. Not since that first day. Then, I just thought you were an asshole. But after that day by the pool . . ."

He sat back against the couch and grinned. "Really? You seemed wholly unaffected by me!"

She rolled her eyes. "Come on. When you were parading around half-naked like that?"

He laughed. "I mean, I was *trying* to impress you, I just didn't know I'd succeeded."

She turned her whole body to face him. "You were trying to impress me?"

Beau didn't answer, and reached for his plate.

"Beau."

He looked like he was concentrating hard on spreading Brie on a cracker. Finally, he shrugged. "I guess . . . it depends . . . on what you mean by 'trying.' Did I know you were sitting by the pool when I walked outside to take a swim? I suppose the answer there is yes. Did I do the butterfly to show off a little? Perhaps also yes." He grinned at her. "I hadn't done it in years. I was glad I remembered how."

Izzy couldn't believe that he'd come out to the pool on purpose, just to see her. She put her hand on his and let it trail up his wrist, his forearm, to finally rest on his shoulder.

"You also, by the way, seemed wholly unaffected by me," she said. "I thought you didn't even like me."

Beau laughed. "Oh, trust me, I've been *very* affected by you from the first moment," he said. "And I've liked you more and more every single day that you've been here. I just wasn't . . . am not, probably, all that great at showing it."

This was one of the most unusual conversations Izzy had ever had with a guy. Usually, with guys she'd dated, they'd fenced with each other for a while with random flirtation and occasional insults. But then, after they hooked up for the first time (or the second time, and usually even the tenth time), everything was vague, up in the air, about when—or whether—they would see each other again, what was going on between the two of them, how they felt about each other.

But she and Beau had already talked about so much in the past few weeks that it felt natural for them to talk about this, too.

Maybe that meant she could ask him the question she kept wondering about.

He nudged her. "What is it?"

He knew her too well at this point for her to hesitate.

"If you've been wanting this since the beginning, why didn't you kiss me before?"

He put his plate down on the table and reached for her hand. "Izzy. You're living in my house. We're working together. This whole situation is already weird. I know I can be a real jerk sometimes, but I didn't want to be that kind of jerk." He smiled softly at her. "I came so close. That time in the kitchen. And in the line for ice cream. But I didn't want to do anything you didn't want to do."

She leaned forward and kissed him again. She really loved the way he kissed her, how he moved from gentle to passionate in seconds, how he touched her, like every part of her body was special to him.

And they had three more weeks together. What was going to happen after that? No. She wasn't going to let herself worry about the future right now.

Finally, she sat back. "I don't want the Brie to get cold."

He laughed and picked up the remote. "We can't have that. This is not a house where we waste cheese."

He put his arm around her as he turned on the TV, and she leaned against him to watch. After one episode of their show, he went back to the kitchen, returning with brownies and ice cream.

"I forgot to ask," he said. "Did you get good work done today? Oh, and did you get the tea for Michaela?"

In all the excitement about Beau's visit with his mom, and then everything that happened between the two of them, Izzy had almost forgotten about the hours she'd spent that day reading her manuscript, and what she'd realized.

No, that wasn't true, she hadn't forgotten—it had been a quiet, happy hum underneath everything.

"Yeah," she said. "To both things. I got Michaela her tea. And I got good work done." She smiled at him. "I read through my book. The one that I wrote, before."

He sat down right next to her. "I didn't realize you were going to do that. How did it go?"

He slid his hand into hers. She knew he really cared about her answer.

"I wasn't sure I had the courage to actually do it. I was scared that I would realize how bad it was, that it would make me feel like I shouldn't keep going. But I decided that if you could go see your mom today, I could face some words on a computer screen." She couldn't hold back her smile. "But I still love it. Obviously, it has its faults, it's not perfect—"

Before she could finish her sentence, Beau wrapped her in a bear hug. "Oh, Izzy, I'm so glad," he said. "And of course it's perfect, it's yours."

He sounded so happy for her. So confident in her. She nestled closer to him, hid her face in his chest so he couldn't see the tears escape and slide down her face. After a little while, she sat up and reached for her dessert.

"Thank you," she said. "For being so happy for me. I'm really happy about the book, too. I still don't know what I'm going to do with it—if I'm going to try to find an agent with this book, or just move on to writing the next one, or what, but at least I know that I can write. That I can do this. It makes all the difference."

He brushed her tears off her face with his thumb. Okay, so she hadn't managed to hide those from him. Somehow, she didn't mind.

"Of course it makes all the difference," he said. He pulled her close, and she leaned her head against his shoulder.

Izzy wondered what would happen at the end of the night. As perfect as today had been, as much as she loved being this close to Beau, she wasn't sure if she wanted their relationship to escalate beyond that, at least, not yet.

Well, no, she knew she wanted it to, that wasn't in question. Not when he was kissing her, when she was kissing him, when their bodies were pressed together, when his big, strong hands held on to her and moved slowly up and down her body. It was just that everything had changed so fast. It was so good, she was so happy, that it scared her. She had no idea if she was right to trust him, to let herself fall into this with him. Which is why she didn't want to let it go any further tonight, at least.

Late that night, after they did the dishes, Beau walked with her to the foot of the stairs. She wondered if he would expect to come up with her, but she shouldn't have worried.

"Good night, Izzy," he said. He leaned down and kissed her hard, and then took a step back.

"Good night, Beau," she said.

She was halfway up the stairs when he stopped her.

"Izzy."

She turned around and looked down at him.

"Today was the best day I've had in years," he said.

She let herself smile at that as much as she wanted to.

"Same here," she said.

CHAPTER TWENTY-FIVE

Sunday morning, when Izzy walked into the kitchen, Beau was standing in front of a waffle iron with a big bowl of batter next to him.

"Oh, thank goodness you're up," he said. He flipped open the top of the waffle iron and poured a ladle full of batter inside. "I didn't want to wake you up, but I also wanted waffles, so I was having a real quandary."

Izzy poured herself coffee and sat down at the table. "You could have started without me, I wouldn't have minded," she said.

She hadn't been sure what to expect this morning, after everything that happened. She'd fallen asleep so happy the night before, but this morning, she'd questioned everything, wondered if she'd imagined the way he'd looked at her, smiled at her, kissed her.

Beau shook his head. "But I would have minded." He gave her a slow, very sweet smile.

She hadn't imagined it.

"Plus," he said, "I don't know what you like with your waffles. I wouldn't want to use up all the whipped cream and strawberries and leave none for you."

She shook her head. "You can have them. Butter and maple syrup for me, please. And bacon."

Normally, she would have said, "If you have those" or "I'll take anything," or something like that. But it had only taken her a few days in this house to know there was always literally anything she wanted inside this kitchen. There was no point in not asking for exactly what she wanted.

Beau gestured to the oven.

"Bacon is staying warm in there, butter is right here on the counter, and I'll get the maple syrup."

She took the bacon out of the oven, transferred it to a plate, and put it on the table for them. Beau set a bottle of maple syrup in front of her.

"Here you go, straight from Vermont, a place I've never been. But I've been told maple syrup grows on trees there."

Izzy tried not to smile at that but failed.

He went back to the waffle iron, flipped it open again, and turned a huge golden waffle onto a plate.

"Come and get your waffle," he said. He ladled more batter into the waffle iron.

Izzy walked over to him. "Shouldn't we share that one? Now I'll be starting without you," she said.

He shook his head. "By the time you get your waffle all appropriately buttered and syruped, mine will be ready, don't worry." Then he slid his arm around her waist. "Mmm, wait a second. There's something I forgot to do."

He pulled her close, and she twisted her arms around his neck. Would she ever get tired of the way he held her like this? Had anything ever felt so good? Then he kissed her, and she stopped thinking about anything. Finally, he released her with a long sigh.

"Your waffle is getting cold," he said.

She smiled at him. "I don't really care."

He shooed her toward the table. "Okay, but *my* waffle is going to burn. We can't have that."

Izzy sat down with, she was pretty sure, a smug smile on her face exactly like the one on Beau's. She put butter and syrup on her waffle, and two slices of bacon on her plate. And sure enough, by the time she picked up her fork and knife, Beau slid across the table from her with a heap of whipped cream and strawberries on top of his waffle.

"See," he said. "What did I tell you?"

She shook her waffle-laden fork at him. "Excuse me, but it wouldn't have taken so long if it hadn't been for your delay tactics."

His smile grew even more smug. "I think you like my delay tactics a lot."

She let her smile get bigger. "You might be right about that," she said.

They grinned at each other for a few seconds before they dove into their food.

She was only halfway through one waffle when Beau got up to make a second one.

"Do you want another?" he asked her, before he ladled the batter into the waffle iron.

She shook her head. "Not now, maybe later," she said.

He turned to her after he closed the waffle iron. "Speaking of later. I was thinking maybe we could get our work done early today, and then maybe this afternoon, we could go hiking, or something?"

Izzy raised her eyebrows at him. "Do you go hiking around here a lot?"

He nodded. "Oh yeah, I've gone like . . ." He lifted a finger, and then a second, like he was counting. "Absolutely zero times in the past year."

Izzy burst out laughing. "Then why—"

"Look," he said. "I was trying to come up with some sort of date-like thing that wasn't just you and me sitting on the couch in the TV room eating dinner! Because as much as I love that—and I do, don't get me wrong—I thought maybe today we could do something different."

Oh. That was really . . . sweet.

He stared down at the waffle iron, and her smile got wider. Was he embarrassed? Maybe she wasn't the only one who had felt a little uncertain today.

"What about this?" Izzy said, when Beau sat down across from her with his plate. "Maybe after we write this morning, we can hang out by the pool this afternoon? I have to get some reading done, anyway."

He smiled. "That's a great idea. And what if we went out to dinner tonight?"

She raised her eyebrows. "You mean, eat dinner across from each other at a table, instead of on a couch?" She smiled. "That sounds great."

Izzy took their plates to the dishwasher when they were done.

"Let me run upstairs and get my stuff and I'll meet you in the library."

Five minutes later, Izzy walked into the library, but she didn't see Beau at the table. She jumped when she heard his voice. She turned and saw him, leaning against the door. Waiting for her.

"What took you so long?" He took one step and pulled her against him.

"I had to find my charger," she said as he moved his mouth closer and closer to hers. "I didn't bring it with me yesterday, so my laptop battery is fading."

"Mmm." His lips were almost against hers as he talked. She closed her eyes and listened to the rumble of his voice. "I suppose that's an acceptable excuse. But I'm going to need to do this before we sit down to work."

Then his lips were on hers, and her hands were in his hair, and his hands on her back pressed her closer to him, and her whole body strained toward his. They'd just kissed in the kitchen, but that time it had been different, a little tentative on both of their parts, more of an Are-we-actually-doing-this?-Yes-we-are, morning-after-the-first-kiss kind of kiss. This kiss was enthusiastic, assured, confident. It was all she could do to stay standing. His lips on her skin made her forget everything, want everything.

Beau slid his hands up underneath her tank top and spread his fingers across the small of her back. God, the way he touched her made her shiver. He made her feel like he valued every single inch of her, like every second he spent touching her, kissing her, mattered to him. She wanted to ignore the laptop in the bag hanging off her shoulder, ignore his book, the whole reason she was here, and stand here and kiss him forever.

She forced herself to take a step back. "Beau Towers. We have work to do."

He took a step toward her and reached for her again. "Mmm, I know," he said. "We've barely gotten started. I need to know if you like being kissed here . . ." He kissed her under her ear. "And here . . ." He kissed her collarbone. "And here . . ."

Izzy put her finger on his lips. "Okay, you've forced me into this. There's a new rule: No kissing in the library." He shook his head, but she kept talking. "Actually: No *touching* in the library." She dropped her finger and stepped away from him.

He glared at her. "No touching? At all? This is cruel!"

She walked over to the table and sat down at her seat. "You left me no choice. This room is for working. We have the whole rest of the house for kissing."

She thought about that. How it would feel to kiss him all over the house. In the living room, on one of those big, long couches. In the kitchen again, up against the refrigerator, where they'd almost kissed before. In her bedroom . . .

She looked up at him, and she could tell he was thinking about that, too.

"Well, I've never been so inspired to get my work done for the day," he said, and sat down.

She pushed his notebook across the table at him, and he flipped it open to the first empty page.

"Okay, setting the timer now." She opened her laptop.

At first, it was hard to concentrate. She'd write a sentence or two, then glance up at Beau to see if he was writing or looking at her, and then look back down. But after a few minutes, she forced herself to pretend he wasn't there. It only sort of worked, but after a while, she got deep into this thing she was writing. This thing she'd been too scared to call a book, because the last time she'd done that, it had led to heartbreak. But after the past few weeks of working on it, of thinking about it, it was becoming real to her. Now she could see the characters, the story, the shape of the rest of it. The rest of the book.

When the timer went off, she typed in a flurry for about thirty more seconds and then took her hands off the keyboard. She looked up to find Beau smiling at her.

"You don't have to stop on my account, you can keep going," he said.

She shook her head as she saved, then closed her laptop.

"It's okay," she said. "It's good for me to end sort of in the middle of something. It makes it easier for me to pick it back up the next time. If I start at the beginning of a scene, it takes me so long to get back in the flow of things."

Beau pushed the notebook back across the table to her.

"That's smart," he said. "You're so good at this."

Her cheeks got warm as she stood up. "Thanks," she said. "But it's just—"

"It's not just anything," he said. "It's just you, being good at this."

Maybe she needed to learn how to take a compliment. She hadn't had many opportunities to do so in the past few years.

They walked out of the library together. As soon as they stepped over the threshold, Beau turned to her and slowly backed her up against the wall.

"We aren't in the library anymore," he said.

She fought back a smile as she looked up at him. "You're right," she said. "We aren't."

He put his hand on the curve of her waist and moved his thumb slowly up and down.

"Do you know what that means?" he asked her.

"What does it mean?"

He propped his other hand against the wall, trapping her there with him. But there was nowhere she'd rather be.

"That I can do this." And then he bent down and kissed her. It was long, and slow, and gentle, but full of heat. He kept himself at a distance, and when she reached for him, tried to pull him closer to her, he stayed right where he was. She could feel him smile against her lips, but he just kept kissing her slowly, until she felt like she might go wild. After a long time, he pulled away and looked at her, that smile still on his face.

"Meet you by the pool?" he asked.

She breathed in hard. "The pool." Why did he . . . Oh right, that was their plan for the afternoon. "Yes. Meet you there in a few minutes. I'll just go change."

She ran up the stairs to her room, still dazed after that kiss. He'd known it, too, the jerk. She smiled as she walked into her room.

She reached for a sundress to change into and then remembered something. In a fit of optimism, or courage, after Marta had said she could stay longer, she'd ordered a bikini online. She'd tried it on when it arrived on Friday; it was blue-and-white striped, and she thought she looked cute in it. But did she feel comfortable enough in it—and comfortable enough with Beau—to wear it today? He usually dated models and actresses, after all. No, maybe she shouldn't wear it.

And then she heard Priya's voice in her ear.

"WEAR THE BIKINI!!!"

Izzy laughed out loud. "Fine, Priya, you win. I'll do it."

She felt like she had to obey invisible Priya, since she hadn't told her about yesterday with Beau. She wanted to—she'd almost texted her last night, after she got back up to her room. But everything with Beau felt so good right now, so perfect, almost magic. It felt like telling someone, anyone, about it might break the spell.

Beau wasn't there when she got out to the pool. The rose garden was just beyond the pool, and the roses were starting to bloom—she could smell them all the way over here. She set up one of the pool chairs so it reclined at just the right angle and leaned back. A few minutes later, he came outside, a bag in one hand and two towels draped over his shoulder.

"I thought we might get peckish out here," he said. "So I brought a few snacks."

He pulled out a bowl, which he set on the table next to Izzy. Then he took out a bag of chips, which he poured into the bowl. And then he took out a jar of salsa, which he poured into another bowl.

"You know," Izzy said. "One of the things I've always liked about you is your commitment to snacks."

He grinned at her as he took bottles of Topo Chico out of the bag. "Can you believe I was just thinking the same thing about you?"

He draped one towel over the back of her chair and another over the back of the chair next to hers. "I'm going to swim a few laps before I snack. Be right back."

Izzy watched him walk to the pool and get in. And then she just stared, as his arms cut through the water, as those muscles in his back flexed. This time, she didn't have to pretend to look away.

She looked down at her dress. She was nervous, so nervous, about wearing the bikini. But she knew, somewhere in New York City, Priya was shouting at her to take the dress off without even knowing why.

So she pulled it over her head and sat there, on the lounge chair, in the bikini.

She looked down at her e-reader and tried and failed to concentrate on this manuscript. Eventually, Beau pulled himself out of the water and turned toward her. And then he stopped, slowly walked over to her.

He stood above her and blocked out the sun as his hair dripped onto her legs. She looked up at him.

"You said that you didn't have a swimming suit here," he said, an accusatory tone in his voice. "Isn't that why we had to get you one for surfing?"

"I didn't," she said. "Then."

His eyes raked over her body. God, did that look on his face make her feel good.

"Well." He sat down across from her, still staring at her. "Wherever you got that from, God bless them, that's all I have to say."

She laughed, half in joy, half in sheer relief. "Oh, do you like it?" she asked.

"Do I like it? I have a feeling that you know exactly how much I like it," he said.

Her smile got wider. "You're welcome to tell me, though."

He stood up again, and then joined her on her lounge chair. "Oh, I'll do better than that," he said.

She got very little reading done by the pool that day.

CHAPTER TWENTY-SIX

When they got into the car after dinner, Izzy looked over at Beau. "So that was weird, right?"

Beau sighed. "I forgot. You've never seen that before, have you?" He started the car. "We haven't really gone anywhere together where anyone has paid attention to me. No one at the beach cares who I am, if they even know. All surfers care about is how good the surf is that day, that's why I like them. But that waiter definitely knew."

She looked at him sideways. "He seemed kind of . . . scared of you? Am I making that up?"

Beau shook his head. "No." He stared out at the street as he started the car. Izzy thought he would be angry at how hostile their waiter had been toward him, but the look on his face was more resigned than anything else. "I got a reputation when I was younger, and it never really went away. After that bar fight, and that car accident, and everything. No one will ever believe this—especially after what I did to my mom at the funeral—and I'm not trying to pretend I'm perfect, but a lot of that reputation was undeserved. The bar fight was just me defending my friend Madison. Some guy grabbed her ass, so I punched him. It probably wasn't the most appropriate way to handle it, but people always did that to her, and I knew how sick of it she was. And then the car accident, I was driving another friend home—he was *very* high and grabbed the steering wheel because he thought it was funny." He turned and looked at her. "I was totally sober that night."

She put her hand on his arm. "I believe you."

He smiled at her. "Thanks. So anyway, it became a whole thing. How I was the angry, bad one, of our whole group, you know." He looked over at her when he stopped at a light. "I was also the Black one."

She nodded. "Yeah." She raised her eyebrows at him. "Are you writing about all this?"

He sighed dramatically. "She has a one-track mind over here, doesn't she?" He grinned at her. "I'm going to write about it. It's on my list. I just haven't gotten there yet. I've been going a little out of order. Someone once told me I could do that."

She elbowed him, and he cackled.

She turned to him as they drove home. "Have you talked to any of your friends? Since you've been here?"

He shook his head. "They texted me for a while, checked in on me. Well, my good friends did. But I ignored them. And now it feels too late."

She put her hand on his. "If they're good friends, it's not too late."

He swallowed. "Yeah. I guess."

She wouldn't push it.

When they got in the house, Beau stopped her by the door again and bent down to kiss her. She still couldn't believe this was happening. This whole weekend had felt almost magical.

"You know," she said, "starting tomorrow, we're going to have to stop kissing in the hallway like this. Michaela will be around. We don't want to make her uncomfortable."

He pushed her hair back from her face and leaned forward to kiss her again. "Mmm, good point," he said. "I guess that means we have to take advantage of this while we can."

Finally, a while later, she pulled away.

"I have to get up early tomorrow, so . . ."

Beau slowly let go of her. "See you tomorrow, Izzy."

She smiled at him before she turned to go upstairs. "See you tomorrow, Beau."

As she walked to the kitchen in the morning to get coffee, she heard his laugh from down the hall.

"What's gotten you in such a cheerful mood this morning?" Michaela asked him, right as Izzy walked into the kitchen.

"Oh, you know, the weather was great this weekend, it's probably that." Beau turned when she walked in. "Good morning, Izzy."

She tried to smile at him like normal, in the same way she'd done before. How exactly had she smiled at him before? She couldn't remember now. At first it had been her fake cheerful smile, she knew that. But at some point, it had changed. And then it had changed again. She knew she couldn't smile at him the way she wanted to, the way that said "I had a great time kissing you all weekend, and if Michaela wasn't just a few feet away, I'd be kissing you right now," especially since Michaela was looking right at her. She hoped she just looked sleepy and walked straight to the coffee maker.

"Morning," she said, trying to direct her greeting to both of them.

"How was your weekend?" Michaela asked.

Izzy could feel Beau's eyes on her as she moved to the fridge for milk.

"Oh, good," she said, without looking at him. She poured the milk into her coffee and replaced it inside the fridge. "Apparently, there was a snowstorm in New York this weekend, so I feel very smug about being here, obviously."

Beau and Michaela both laughed.

She looked over at the baked goods corner. There were lemon poppy-seed muffins, and Izzy put one on a plate. "Okay, well, I'd better go back upstairs. I um, have a call in a few minutes." She started to leave the kitchen.

"Izzy."

She turned back around at the sound of Beau's voice. His eyes looked so warm. "Yeah?"

"Two thirty? In the library?" His smile was tiny, but she could feel it all the way across the room.

"Yeah," she said. "Two thirty in the library. See you then."

When she walked into the library that afternoon, Beau was already there, sitting at the table, his laptop open.

"Finally," he said when she walked in. "I've been waiting forever."

She pursed her lips. "First of all, I'm only five minutes late, I had a call that ran over. Second, we usually meet at three, so I'm actually twenty-five minutes early."

Beau grinned at her. "I know. But I couldn't wait that long today." He took the notebook that she pushed across the table to him. "Also. Before we start work, I'd like to request a slight amendment to the rules."

She tilted her head as she flipped her laptop open. She was pretty sure she knew what was coming.

"Mmm, that might depend on which rules we're talking about," she said.

She liked that look in his eyes. But then, she was realizing that she liked almost every look in his eyes.

"The rules about the library. And what we can—and can't—do here."

She tried to keep a straight face. "I see. What kind of amendment are we talking about?"

He tented his fingers together and looked at her over them. "Well. I think that when we—or rather, when you—made this rule, we—you—didn't consider that on weekdays, Michaela would be around, and so this time in the library would be our only time alone during the day. So *I* think we should at least get to bookend work time with . . . other time. Say, five minutes at the beginning and at the end, to do . . . whatever we want while we're in here."

She grinned at him. "Nice try. But this is our work time. Work only in here."

He let out a sigh. "I knew you would say that. But I had to try."

She laughed at him and set the timer.

When they walked out of the library Beau looked from side to side. Then he grabbed her hand, tugged her across the hall into the TV room, and closed the door behind them.

"You had better not try to tell me," he said, as he leaned down, "that there's no kissing in *this* room."

She put her arms around his neck and pulled him closer. "I believe this room is actually the shut-up-and-kiss-me room, as a matter of fact."

He smiled. "Well, I'd guess I'd better do what the room says."

On Wednesday morning, a few hours after she'd gone downstairs to get coffee and one of Beau's latest baked goods, she heard a knock at her open bedroom door. She looked up with a smile, expecting it to be Beau. Instead, Michaela was standing in the doorway.

"Oh, hi, Michaela," Izzy said. Why had she thought it would be Beau? He never came up here. Maybe she'd just been hoping it was him.

"Hi, Izzy. I hope I'm not interrupting anything?" Michaela smiled at her. "I have a favor to ask."

Izzy waved her in the room. "Sure, come on in. Just trying to reply to an annoying email, no big deal."

Michaela grinned at her. "Well, then, I'm glad I rescued you." She sat down and looked around the room and then out the window. "This really is a great room. No wonder Beau put you in here."

Izzy looked around the room, too. "Yeah. I love it."

Michaela turned away from the window with a smile. "I was wondering if you had time to come shopping with me later."

It made sense that Michaela would need an extra set of hands sometimes for all the food stocked in this house.

"Sure, I'd be happy to," Izzy said. "I can't wait to see how the snack cabinet magic happens."

Michaela laughed. "Oh no—not food shopping." She made a face. "Clothes shopping. I'm going to a wedding this weekend, and I need a dress. Your clothes are always so cute, so I thought maybe you could help me find one."

Izzy was flattered. Her collection of sundresses *had* grown considerably since she'd been here. She was saving so much money living here, what with no commute, and no spending money on food or going out or basically anything else, that she'd let herself indulge a bit. Plus, she'd just gotten a save-the-date for a friend's wedding this summer; she probably needed to find a few dresses for upcoming weddings too.

"Oh, I'd love to, that sounds fun! Beau and I are usually done in the library somewhere around four thirty or five. Do you want to go then?"

Michaela stood up. "Perfect. Thank you, I really appreciate it."

"Thanks for coming along with me," Michaela said as they drove down the hill.

"Oh, it's no problem," Izzy said. "There's so much great shopping around here—though most of it is too expensive for my budget. I have found a few bargains, though."

Michaela stopped to let someone walking their dog cross the street. "Tell me about it. I'm willing to splurge a little, if I find something great, but who knows. This is the first real dressy kind of thing I've had to go to since I had Mikey, and the idea of shopping is kind of overwhelming. Especially since I've been working for Beau for the past year, which means that wearing anything other than an elastic waist makes me overdressed."

They both laughed.

"How did that end up happening?" Izzy asked. "You working for Beau, I mean." She'd wondered this since the beginning and somehow had never asked Beau.

"Oh, that's a long story," Michaela said. Izzy wondered if that was her way of blowing her off and not telling the story, but then she started talking again. "I knew his grandparents—my dad worked for his grandfather a long time ago, and they stayed close, so I've known Beau forever. I always liked him, even though he had a reputation as kind of a jerk. He was never like that here. His grandma and I always used to drink tea together, and she gave me a teakettle for a present one year for my birthday, and I was so excited. He teased me about it, called me Kettle, and it kind of . . . stuck." She laughed. "Anyway, after his grandfather died, the lawyers hired my dad to kind of keep an eye on the house, check on it every so often. And one day, one of the neighbors called my dad to say he'd seen someone coming in and out of the house, and just wanted to make sure it wasn't him, before he called the police. My dad thought it might be Beau, so he and I—and baby Mikey—went up to the house to check. When I walked into the kitchen, it was"—her eyes widened—"total chaos, and Beau was standing there beating something in a bowl and getting it everywhere."

Izzy smiled. Yeah, she could picture that.

"Was he furious that you were there?"

Michaela laughed. "I was going to say you can imagine, but you don't have to imagine. When he realized who we were, he calmed down. We left him our numbers, and a few days later he texted me to ask if I knew anyone who could cook for him and stuff, since he was tired of getting takeout. I'd always worked in restaurants, but I'd just had the baby a few months before and was dreading going back to that world, so I said I'd do it. At first, it was just dropping food off for him a few times a week, and then I started sticking around to cook there and do the dishes and stuff, and then he had the idea for the foundation—he told you about that, right?"

Izzy nodded and tried to keep her expression neutral. Beau had told her about the foundation before they were anything more than just working together.

It wasn't that she cared if Michaela knew there was something going on between her and Beau. But for the same reason she hadn't told Priya, she didn't quite want to say anything to Michaela. It felt good, for this to be between just her and Beau. At least for now.

"Anyway, he asked me if I could help him with that stuff, so somehow I ended up working for him full-time." She shrugged. "It's kind of a weird job, but it's super flexible with a baby—Beau doesn't care if I'm late some mornings if the baby has made it impossible to get out the door, or if I need an emergency day off because he's sick, or if I bring him some days for an hour or two if I need to, or whatever."

Izzy tried to imagine how Beau would have functioned for the past year if he hadn't had Michaela around. She couldn't.

"Well, thank goodness he had you," Izzy said. "He would have been a mess otherwise."

"More of a mess, you mean." Michaela glanced over at Izzy. "I was worried about him, you know."

"Oh?" Izzy looked at her, but her eyes were on the road. "Just in general, or . . . ?"

Michaela nodded. "Just in general," she said. "And or."

Yeah. Anyone who saw Beau every day would have been worried about him. At least, anyone who cared about him would.

"I knew he was anxious about this book, even though—maybe especially because—he never talked about it," Michaela said. "How's it going now, anyway? Good, it seems?"

Izzy smiled. "Really good. I'm not even sure if Beau realizes how much he's done and how far he's gone. He's worked so hard on it. I'm just really proud of him for everything he's done—I think the book is going to be great."

"Oh, that's so good to hear," Michaela said.

Izzy knew she was gushing, but it was true. He had worked so hard. But she really needed to stop talking about Beau before she said too much.

"Okay, tell me more about this wedding, and what kind of dress you're looking for. We need a plan of attack."

Michaela's smile dropped away. "Ideally, I'd like something that looks roughly like a tea cozy. Can we find that?"

Izzy laughed. "I'll see what I can do."

CHAPTER TWENTY-SEVEN

Friday, at the end of their library session, Beau closed his laptop and smiled at her.

"Want to go surfing tomorrow morning? It's supposed to rain, so it won't be that crowded at the beach."

Izzy raised her eyebrows at him. "I feel like this is one of the times when the crowds have a point. Won't it be freezing in the water? And won't the waves be too big for me?"

Beau shook his head as they both got up to leave the library. "I checked the surf report—the waves won't be that high. It's not going to be windy, just a little rain. Perfect weather for a novice." He reached for her shoulder as they walked toward the door but stopped himself. "Plus, I'll be there. You have nothing to worry about."

"Okay," she said. "Surfing tomorrow morning sounds great."

Was this a date? she wondered. Were they "dating"? Technically, they'd gone out on exactly one date. Also technically, it had only been less than a week since they'd first kissed, but then they'd spent all day together Saturday and Sunday, and then this week they'd spent as much time together as possible. It was sort of weird, to be dating someone you were living with.

She smiled to herself. Weird, but good.

They left for the beach at seven the next morning. Izzy had objected when Beau had proposed the time—he'd said that's when "real surfers" go out—but she was so used to getting up at six for work during the week that it was a halfhearted protest.

Once they were in the water, Izzy managed to stand up on the board after just the second time she tried. And she stayed standing up for five whole seconds before she fell off. She counted.

"Wow," Beau said, after she surfaced in the water. "I'm impressed. Someone looks like she's been practicing her balance."

She had been, actually.

"Great job," he said as he leaned toward her. Usually, when they stood this close to each other, Izzy felt so much smaller than Beau. But here, in the water, they were face-to-face. She liked it.

And it made her think of how it would be elsewhere, to be this close when they looked at each other, when they kissed each other.

They kissed in the water for a while, Izzy holding on to Beau with one arm, until someone swam by them and whistled, and they broke apart.

Beau motioned to Izzy. "Okay, let's try that again," he said. He had a playful look on his face. "But . . . I'm just . . . curious. Which swimsuit are you wearing underneath that wet suit?"

Izzy didn't try to stop the grin that spread across her face. "The striped one."

Beau closed his eyes and took a long breath before he opened them. "I was afraid of that. Okay. All right. Going to do my best to concentrate on this"—he gestured to the water—"and not that"—he gestured to her—"but it's going to be a challenge."

Izzy smiled as she pulled herself onto the board. She'd never been with someone who was so excited by her before. Guys had been interested in her, sure. But both excited and willing to show it? She didn't know if she'd even known that was possible.

She took a deep breath and stood up. As she looked out at the cold, drizzly, quiet beach, she realized something else. She was just as excited by Beau. Did he know that? She didn't know. She'd held herself back, and she knew why. She'd been nervous to trust him, to declare herself, to ask for what she wanted. Nervous that if she did, everything would fall apart.

But if she'd learned one thing from this whole experience in California, it had been that she wouldn't get what she wanted until she asked for it.

A wave lifted the surfboard and carried her all the way in to shore. She lifted her arms, triumphant, and before she knew it, Beau picked her up and swung her around.

"You did it!"

She threw her arms around him and kissed him. "I did it!"

After a long kiss, she slid down his body and back onto the sand.

"Hey, Beau?" she said.

"Yeah?" He smiled down at her.

"Let's go home."

He took her hand on the walk to the car, just like he had after they'd sat on this same beach and kissed for the first time. He kept her hand in his all the way up the hill to the house as they drove through the rain, which had started coming down harder since they'd left the beach.

"I just remembered something," Beau said, when they turned into the drive.

Izzy turned to him. "Yeah?"

He squeezed her hand. "It's Saturday. We have the house to ourselves."

They were all over each other as soon as they walked in the front door. Her arms were around his neck, his hands clutched her back, and they kissed like it had been weeks since they'd touched each other, months since they'd kissed. They kissed like their kisses were oxygen, like they needed them to breathe. Beau pushed the strap of her sundress down and kissed her neck, her collarbone, her shoulder, her arm. His lips on her skin made her gasp.

He straightened up, and she moved her hands up his chest. She took a handful of his shirt in her hand and pulled him closer. She could feel the smile on his lips as he kissed her again.

Finally, she pulled back and looked him in the eye. "Beau?"

"Yeah?" He was out of breath. So was she.

"Why don't we go to your room?"

He brushed his finger across her cheek. "Izzy. Are you sure?"

She nodded. "Absolutely."

He smiled and took her hand. He led her down the hall, past Michaela's office, past the kitchen, and opened the door at the very end of the hall. She looked around as she walked inside. Beau's room had light gray walls, a huge window that overlooked the rose garden, and a very big bed. Looking at the bed suddenly made her nervous.

"Do you know, until this minute, I had no idea where your room was?" she said.

He grinned. "Where else did you think it could be?"

She shrugged. "This house has many hidden secret rooms, it could have been anywhere! If you'd led me up to the third floor, I would have just nodded and been like, I always thought there were only two floors, but guess I just didn't see that other staircase."

He cupped her face in his hands and laughed. She laughed with him. She wasn't nervous anymore. She was glad to be here, with him.

"How in the world did I ever get so lucky as I was the day you walked into this house?"

And then he kissed her again. They stood there, kissing, until they were sitting on his bed, kissing, until they were lying down, kissing. And it felt so good, to be so close to him, to see him this way, to kiss him, to touch him.

He kissed her softly as he ran one hand up the side of her body. "Happy?" he asked.

She smiled and reached for him. "Very."

Afterward, they lay there together, warm, comfortable, happy. She rested her head on his broad chest and moved her fingers through the springy hair there. She turned her head and kissed his chest, and he took her hand and raised it to his lips.

"Hey, Beau?" she said.

"Mmm?" She could feel his chest vibrate against her.

"Do we have the ingredients for more of those waffles?"

He laughed and turned so they were face-to-face. "Are you telling me that after everything I've already done this morning, you want me to go into the kitchen and make you waffles?"

She traced his freckles with her finger. "That's exactly what I'm telling you," she said. "Remember, I like them with butter and—"

"Maple syrup," he finished as he threw the covers back and got out of bed. "I bet you want coffee and bacon with that, too, don't you?"

Izzy pulled the covers up to her chin and grinned at him. "Oh yeah. I definitely do."

CHAPTER TWENTY-EIGHT

They didn't work in the library that day, for the first time in over a month. They had too many distractions. The next day, though, Izzy turned to Beau after he'd brought her breakfast in bed again—pancakes this time.

"I feel guilty about yesterday," she said.

He raised an eyebrow at her, and she giggled.

"Not that part of yesterday. We didn't—"

"Oh, we can change that right now," he said, and reached for her. She put her hand over his mouth.

"Oh my God, no, that's not what I'm saying! We didn't do any work yesterday, that's what I mean. We both have work to do—I'm going to take a shower and meet you in the library in thirty minutes, okay?"

Beau's lips curved into a pout. Izzy forced herself to resist the impulse to kiss him.

"You mean the room I'm not allowed to touch you in?"

Izzy nodded. "That's exactly the room I mean. One hour. Maybe two. You can hold out that long. You did last week."

Beau put his hand on her hip and smiled at her. "Yes, but that was before," he said. "It's going to be a lot harder now that I know—"

Izzy jumped out of bed. "Finish that sentence after we leave the library."

They went out to dinner that night, to a small place where they sat in the garden in the back, surrounded by heat lamps and the smell of jasmine. The waiter smiled at them as he took their order—if he recognized Beau, he didn't show it.

"We've spent a lot of time talking about my book," Beau said, "but not much time talking about yours. Can I ask you how it's going, or do you not want to talk about it?"

Izzy liked the way he'd phrased that. "Yeah, you can ask," she said. "It might be just the honeymoon period, or I'm reenergized about writing because of working with you, or, I don't know, just being here, but it's really flowing, in a way that feels so rare." She tried to figure out how to explain what she meant. "I feel like I'm living with these people, not just writing them. Like I can't wait to see what they do next. I wake up in the morning happy that I'm going to get to work on the book that day. I've even been waking up a little early to work on it . . . well, except for today." They grinned at each other. "I guess I'm falling in love with it in a way, and it feels wonderful."

The waiter brought their appetizers just then, thank God, because Izzy could feel her last sentence hanging in the air. *Falling in love with it.* Did she have to use those *exact* words?

Had she used those exact words for a reason? Was she falling in love with more than just her book? She didn't want to think about that right now, with Beau sitting across from her, the candlelight from the table warm on his skin, his strong hands reaching for his water glass, his chuckle at a bad joke from the waiter making her smile.

The waiter walked away, and Beau put some of the salad they were sharing on her plate.

"That's great that it's going so well." She breathed a sigh of relief that he'd brought the conversation back to writing. "Are you working on the other one, too?"

She shook her head. "I made a bunch of notes for myself on it, but now I'm trying to let them marinate. I don't want to rush it." She grinned. "Plus, I've been a little busy this week."

He reached across the table for her hand, and they smiled at each other.

That week it got even harder to hide everything going on between them from Michaela, especially since Izzy woke up in Beau's bed every morning. Granted, she usually woke up well before Michaela arrived, kissed a sleeping Beau on the cheek, and then ran back up to her room to start work. But especially since her route back to her room took her past the kitchen, Michaela's office, and the front door, she was always afraid that Michaela would get to the house early one day, see her race by in a tank top and pajama pants, and know exactly where she'd come from.

She wasn't sure exactly why they were both doing so much to hide their relationship from Michaela—it's not like she didn't know what could happen when two people in their twenties lived in a house together. They weren't really hiding it from the world at large; they'd gone out to dinner together twice, they'd made out on the beach like teenagers multiple times.

Was it because neither of them wanted to—or was ready to—answer questions from Michaela about what was going on between them?

She didn't know what was going to happen once she had to go back to New York. She'd avoided thinking about it as much as possible. She usually liked to plan for the future, but all she wanted was to live in the right now as long as she could.

Izzy smiled as she walked into the library on Thursday. Just two more hours until Michaela left for the day, and she and Beau would be all alone. And then just one more day until they had the house to themselves for the weekend.

They both got to work quickly, and when the timer went off, Beau pushed his laptop and the notebook back across the table to Izzy. She read over what was on the screen. It was his revised, cleaned-up version of the day he'd discovered everything about his dad and his mom, and how he'd fled to Santa Barbara, how he'd tried and failed to write for months. She stared at it for a while as she thought about what to say.

"You have that look on your face again," he said. "Like something's wrong."

She looked at him and tried to smile, and he made an exaggerated grimace.

"Okay, please never make *that* face again. That was some weird kind of half-frown-half-fake-smile hybrid, and it was terrifying."

She laughed, and he did, too, for a second.

"Come on, Izzy. What is it?"

She sighed. "It's not that—"

"Yes, yes, I know, it's not that something's wrong. You know what I mean."

She did know what he meant. "Yeah. Okay. This is super readable, you tell this part of the story really well, readers are going to be very invested in it. But the thing is, this book is your memoir, your story. People want to know about you. You don't say why you lashed out at your mom the way you did, how you felt about what you said to your mom when you discovered everything, or why it took you so long to reach out to her. The facts are important, sure, but the most important thing is how you felt about everyone, and about yourself."

He crossed his arms and sat back. That stony look was back on his face. "But you know all of that," he said.

She wanted to soften her voice, but she tried to keep it businesslike between the two of them in the library when they talked about work, so she didn't.

"Yes, *I* know all of that," she said. "But the reader doesn't. People can guess why, but they'll guess all sorts of things. Maybe you're planning to talk about it in a subsequent chapter, but if so, you should lay at least a little groundwork here so it doesn't feel like it's just . . . missing."

He looked angry. Again. She'd thought this conversation would be easier than it had been the last time, because of everything that had happened between them since. But it was just as hard. At least, it was for her.

He dropped his palms flat on the table. "I can't believe you would—" He stood up. "I need a break."

And before she could say anything else, he'd left the library.

Izzy looked after him, stunned. He was just going to walk out on her like that? She thought he would come back right away, but when he hadn't returned after ten minutes, she grabbed her laptop and notebook and walked up to her room.

She sat down on her bed, not sure what to do. Usually, after they left the library, Beau would pull her across the hall to the TV room, and then she would go up to her room and get more writing done, and then she would go back downstairs and hang out with Beau. They'd eat dinner, watch TV, curl up together on the couch, and end up back in his room. Now she wasn't sure what to do.

She opened her laptop and tried to work on her book, but she was too distracted. What happened when you had a fight with your boyfriend when you were living together? Was that even a fight? Was Beau even her boyfriend?

She wanted to cry, but she wasn't even sure what she was crying about. The look on Beau's face when he'd spat those words out at her in the library, the emptiness she felt about the idea of not having dinner with him tonight, the longing she felt for him right now—not the Beau who had left like that in the library, but the Beau who had woken up and kissed her this morning before she'd left his room.

She should have known these past two weeks were too good to be true. She had known, actually. Everything had been so good between them, so idyllic, with beaches and picnics and swimming and surfing and reading to each other in bed. She'd known it couldn't last.

She wanted to text Priya, ask for her advice, but since she hadn't told Priya about any of this, there would be a lot of catching her up first, and Izzy didn't have the energy for that. See, that's why she should have told Priya all this last week, in anticipation of something like this happening.

She went to the bathroom to wash her face. That always helped reset her mood. Then she sat back down at her computer. If she was going to feel all these emotions—this frustration, these pent-up tears, this sadness—she might as well use it. She opened her manuscript.

As she wrote, her frustration mounted, and her sadness turned to anger. See, this was better. She—and her main character—should get angry instead of so sad. What had sadness ever done for her? Nothing.

When she finally looked up, she realized the sun was already setting. She and Beau usually ate dinner by now; no wonder she was hungry. But she was so mad at him that she wanted to wait to eat until after he was safely out of the kitchen.

No. That was silly. She wasn't going to sit in her room and hide from him.

She got up and went downstairs.

The kitchen was empty when she walked in, and she felt a mixture of relief and disappointment. She opened the refrigerator door to see what Michaela had left for them tonight. She hadn't done this in a long time, she realized. Beau was always in charge of getting their dinner ready.

"Hey."

She turned around, and he was standing there, leaning against the kitchen door.

"Hi." She took a salad bowl out of the refrigerator and set it on the counter.

"I wasn't sure if you were coming down," he said. He took a few steps into the kitchen.

That was really all he was going to say?

"Oh, are you done with your break?" she said.

Beau winced. Okay, yes, she'd sounded kind of bitchy—okay, very bitchy—when she'd said that, but what did he expect?

"I'm really sorry about earlier in the library," he said. "I should have led with that. But, Izzy, I'm trying here. This is all hard for me, you know that. Yes, of course, what you said today made perfect sense. But it was hard for me to hear, hard to realize I have to do it, to reveal to the whole world more of the hard parts of myself if I want to make this book any good. And I hate that I still miss my dad, despite everything. I started to get mad at you in there, and I realized I had to stop and take a breath. So instead of lashing out at you, instead of saying something I knew I would regret, I told you I had to take a break. Please don't be mad at me for that?"

Oh.

She should have realized that's what he was doing. He'd basically told her, but she'd been so freaked out by their first fight after they'd become . . . whatever what they were . . . that she hadn't bothered to think about it from his point of view.

She uncrossed her arms. "I'm sorry, too. You did the right thing. I should have thought about it more from your side."

He let out a sigh. "No, it's okay. I came back to the library to apologize, but by then you'd left, and you'd forgotten your phone there, so I couldn't text you. And I couldn't come up to your room, so—"

"You can come up to my room," she said.

He shook his head. "I promised I wouldn't."

She'd almost forgotten that he'd said at the very beginning that he wouldn't come upstairs.

"Yes, but it's different now," she said. "I'm saying that you can."

He took over dinner assembly—a Caesar salad, with chicken and fresh croutons—while Izzy pulled out the dishes. She felt bad for getting carried away, getting so mad at Beau for something she should have understood.

Had she apologized well enough? Probably not. She should have explained better how she felt, how what he said made sense to her, why she'd overreacted so much.

But to do that, she'd have to explain how she felt about him, and she wasn't sure if she knew how to put those feelings into words. Or if she was ready to.

They went into the TV room with the food, Beau carrying almost everything, as usual. She'd tried once, but he could easily carry more than twice as much as she could, so she'd given up and let him do it. He was silent as he put the food down on the table.

When he sat down, she made herself turn to him. "Are you mad at me?"

He looked surprised. "No. Why would I be mad at you?"

"Well, I wasn't . . . I was kind of mean, in there. I should have given you the benefit of the doubt. I shouldn't have—"

Beau shook his head. "Yeah, but I'm not sure if I deserve the benefit of the doubt. I was a real asshole, the last time we went through this."

Izzy shrugged. "Yeah, but that was before."

He gave her a very sweet smile. "Yeah. That was before." He put his arm around her and pulled her close. They hadn't touched since she'd left his room first thing that morning. She'd missed this. "And no. I'm not mad at you."

She put her hand on his cheek. "Good." She looked up at him. "It's okay that you still miss your dad. He was still your dad—you're still grieving him. And you never got to be mad at him in person; you're grieving that, too." She turned his face to hers and kissed him. "And you do deserve the benefit of the doubt."

He smiled down at her. "Thank you. For all of that."

She wanted to say more, but for right now, it felt like enough to curl up on the couch with him, to eat dinner and watch their show and just be together.

CHAPTER TWENTY-NINE

The next morning, just after nine, an email popped up in Izzy's personal account.

Hi, Isabelle—
I hope all is well with you; it was great to run into you in February. A position of assistant editor here at Maurice just came open, and I immediately thought of you. I'm not sure if you're looking to leave TAOAT, but I thought I'd reach out just in case. We'd like this process to be relatively accelerated, so please let me know if you're interested as soon as you can. I'd love to bring you in for an interview next week, if that's possible.

Thanks so much,
Josephine Henry

Izzy stared at her phone for a full minute. Was she imagining this? She took a screenshot of the email and texted it to Priya.

IS THIS REALLY HAPPENING???

Priya texted back seconds later.

YES YES YAYYY YESSSSSS

Izzy typed her response in a flurry.

Hi, Josephine—
Thanks so much for reaching out! I'm definitely interested in an assistant editor position at Maurice! Please let me know what else you need from me, and what the next steps are.

Best regards,
Isabelle

No, too many exclamation points. She took them out.
Wait, now it seemed too stilted. Almost unfriendly.
She sent it to Priya.

HELP ME DRAFT THIS REPLY PLEASE THERE WERE TWO EXCLAMATION POINTS BUT I TOOK THEM OUT AND NOW IT SEEMS WRONG, ALSO IS "BEST REGARDS" TOO COLD???

Oh, and should it be "Hi, Josephine," or just "Josephine"???

Priya texted back right away.

No exclamation points, hi, best regards is fine. I know I know the periods all look wrong but she doesn't have any exclamation points so do what she did

Izzy went to press send but stopped herself. Josephine's first email had mentioned an interview next week.

An interview in New York next week.

She would have to leave California.

Izzy left the email in her drafts and went to go find Beau.

Luckily, he was in the first place she looked: the kitchen. Unfortunately, Michaela was there, too. Not that she usually minded Michaela being around, but right now she needed to see Beau alone.

She poured herself more coffee and tried to catch Beau's eye, to get him to realize by, like, ESP or something that she had to talk to him. But he wasn't looking at her.

Michaela *was* looking at her, with a little smile on her face. Izzy looked back down at her coffee. She should have texted him before rushing out of her room, but most of the time he didn't have his phone on him, so that probably wouldn't have done any good. She'd just have to say something.

"Um, Beau?" Beau immediately turned and smiled at her. "Marta asked me a question about your book, and I wanted to check in with you before I answered her. Can you meet me in the library so we can talk it over? It should only take a few minutes."

"She did?" Beau suddenly looked nervous. Oh no, she should have come up with some other story to get him out of the kitchen. "Okay. Now?"

"Yeah, but it's nothing bad, or anything," she said, in an attempt to fix her mistake. Nope, he still looked stressed.

He stood up. "I'll be right back," he said to Michaela.

Michaela nodded, still with that smile on her face. "Sure, no problem."

Izzy shut the door of the library as soon as Beau walked in.

"Marta didn't ask me anything about your book," she said right away. "Sorry, I just had to get you alone to talk to you about something, and it was the first thing I could think of."

Beau looked relieved. And then he grinned. "Well." He took a step toward her. "What a nice surprise. Couldn't wait until later? I like it. Does that mean we've suspended the library rule?"

Izzy laughed. "No, not that either."

He looked at her closely. "Something good happened?"

She bit her lip and nodded. "I think so? At least, it has the potential to be good. But also, it's . . ." She tried to come up with a word to describe how she was feeling right now. Excited? Terrified? Worried? Conflicted? Thrilled? She didn't know.

Beau walked over to the table and pulled out her chair. "Sit down."

She sat, and then he walked around the table and sat across from her. "Now. Tell me."

She tried to figure out what to say. "Okay. Do you remember how I told you that a long time ago, I applied for that job at Maurice, working with that editor I really respect, and I didn't get it and how I have always sort of wondered what if?"

He nodded. "Of course I remember. Why, what happened?"

She still couldn't believe it.

"She emailed me this morning. That editor, Josephine Henry. She said they have another opening, for a job that would be a promotion for me. She said she thought of me immediately, and she wants to bring me in for an interview."

Beau's face lit up. "Izzy! That's fantastic news. Congratulations."

He looked so happy for her. That look on his face made her want to leap across the table and throw herself into his arms, but she held back.

"Thanks," she said. "I can barely believe it. Granted, it's just an interview, but—"

He brushed that off. "You'll be fantastic," he said. "When's the interview?"

She took a deep breath. Would it matter to him? Would he care? Suddenly, she felt weird about rushing downstairs to tell him.

"She said she wants it to be soon. Sometime next week, but I'm not sure what day. So that means—"

"You'll have to go back to New York," he said. His voice was flat.

"Yeah. I'll have to go back to New York. I haven't . . . I didn't email her back yet. I wanted to tell you first."

He didn't say anything for a moment. "Okay," he said. "Obviously, you don't want to tell Marta that you're going back early for a job interview. Why don't you schedule the interview, and then I can tell Marta I don't need you here anymore, and you can just let her think you're going back to New York a day later than you actually are, so you can go the day before the interview. Does that work?"

Oh. He'd thought the reason she wanted to tell him first was to help her deal with Marta. That was nice of him. But she hadn't even thought about Marta until he'd brought her up. She'd only been thinking about him.

He'd tell Marta he didn't need her anymore. Why did that sting so much? Maybe because it came to him so quickly. She tried to shake that off.

"Yeah," she said. "That works great. I'll email her back right now." She took her phone out of her pocket, read over her draft email, and pressed send.

"Okay." Beau stood up. "Just text me when you hear back. I'll email Marta when I hear from you."

Izzy stood up, too, and walked to the library door. "Yeah. Okay. That sounds great. Thanks for your help."

That sounded so cold and businesslike. But it suddenly felt so businesslike between her and Beau.

No, she was being silly. They were in the library, remember? She was the one who had made the work-only-in-the-library rule. And he was helping her. He'd probably assumed she came to him because she needed help with the Marta part of the problem. Which she did, actually. She was overreacting again.

When they walked out of the library, Beau looked both ways, then grabbed her hand and dragged her into the TV room.

"Okay, now that we're out of the library," he said, "I can congratulate you for real."

He enveloped her in his arms and kissed her so thoroughly she couldn't think about anything at all.

By the time she got up to her room, Josephine had emailed her back.

> Hi, Isabelle—
>
> Thanks so much for your quick reply. Are you available for an interview Monday afternoon, by chance? If not, I understand—just let me know what works for your schedule next week. I'm going on vacation the following week, and I'd love to meet with you before I leave.
>
> Best,
>
> Josephine

Monday. Butterflies fluttered around her stomach. That was so soon.

To make it to the interview by Monday, she would have to leave California the day after tomorrow. Probably the smart thing would be to actually leave tomorrow so she'd have time to settle in at home, unpack, and prepare. But there was no way she could leave so soon. The whole idea of it made her feel panicky.

Everything was going so well between them. They'd only had a few weeks together, like this. She wanted more. And she had no idea what was going to happen when she left.

They'd never talked about that. Their relationship had been purely present tense. Everything between them had centered around her living here, in his house, working together in the library once a day, being together every day for hours, rarely texting, because why would they, they were right there together. Even this morning, it hadn't occurred to her to text him when she had news; she just walked around the house to find him, like she always did. The night before, when they'd had that not-quite-a-fight, they'd had an actual conversation about it and figured it out. How would it have gone if he'd just texted her and she'd sent him some bitchy text back, like she knew she would have? Not very well, probably.

But then, this situation wasn't forever. She'd known that from the beginning. She'd tried to ignore the ticking clock for the past few weeks, but she'd felt it all the same. Beau was probably right when he said, that he didn't need her anymore. He could write the rest of this memoir on his own and send it on to Marta. If she didn't get this job at Maurice, she'd still be involved with it, as Marta's assistant. Just at a distance.

Would that hurt, to still be involved in everything about Beau's book, from her desk at her cubicle in the TAOAT building and not from her seat across from Beau in the library? To be cc'd on emails with him and his agent and Marta, to write him polite, professional notes reminding him to send in his copy edits?

Izzy dropped her head into her hands. She knew the real question was whether she would still be involved with Beau romantically. Whether this thing between them could or would survive when she left. Or was all the magic between them here, in this enchanted house, in the rooms where they'd talked and worked and fought and kissed and loved each other?

No. It was too soon for that word. She was just getting emotional, that's all. She was freaked out about this interview, that this was all happening so fast, that she could finally get away from Marta and TAOAT and land the job she'd been dreaming of for so long. So instead of worrying about that, she was heaping all her stress onto leaving

California and leaving Beau. She needed to pull herself together and reply to Josephine's email.

> Hi, Josephine—
> Monday afternoon works well for me, thanks so much. Please let me know the timing and any other details. I look forward to seeing you then.
>
> Regards,
> Isabelle

Then she texted Beau.

> Interview is set for Monday afternoon!

He texted her back a few seconds later.

> Great. I'll email Marta now. Michaela can get you a ticket to fly out on Sunday.

And now it felt all business again. How else was it supposed to feel when he had his assistant book her plane ticket back to New York?

She tried to push the thought aside—Michaela was probably far more efficient at this than Beau was; it was a business expense, after all—but the curt tone of Beau's text didn't help. That was probably just how he always texted. It's not like she was all that familiar with his texting voice.

And then she stood up and started to pack.

CHAPTER THIRTY

Saturday morning was their last session in the library. Izzy pushed that out of her mind the whole time they worked so she wouldn't cry. At the end, Beau took his laptop back from her and slid his notebook across the table to her like he always did.

She took a deep breath and slid it back to him.

"I, um, should leave this with you," she said. "I think it's safe now, don't you?"

He looked down at the notebook for a long time. Finally, he looked up at her. "Right," he said. "I forgot. And yeah, I think so." He closed his laptop. "I can't believe I've managed to write some of this book. You're a miracle worker, Izzy."

She shook her head. "You've written most of the book, actually. And thank you, but I can't take all the credit here. You've worked really hard."

She was so proud of him, of how much he'd accomplished, of how hard he'd worked to break through everything that had been holding him back.

He smiled at her. "I did work hard, but so did you. With me, and your own work. I can't wait to read all your books someday. Someday soon."

She *had* worked hard. She was proud of herself, too—of all the work she'd done with him, for the skills as an editor she'd gained, for all the writing she'd done on her own work. She hadn't written most of a book while she'd been here, but she'd started one. And she had a newfound belief in the one she'd already written.

"I can't wait for that, too," she said.

She wondered, though: On that imaginary future day when he would read her book, would it be because she gave it to him and he read it sitting next to her? Would they still be together? Or would he see it in a bookstore, years from now, and remember her?

She knew she should ask him. But the words died on her lips.

Beau stood up and tucked his notebook under his arm.

"I told Michaela not to make us dinner tonight," he said. "I thought we could go out."

Dinner tonight. Their last night.

"That sounds great," she said.

She was glad—and touched—that Beau had made plans for dinner tonight. The past day and a half had been so rushed that she'd barely thought about anything not on her to-do list.

Of course, she'd thought constantly about Beau, but her thoughts were all jumbled, with no clear shape. She wanted to stay here with him, she wanted to get the job at Maurice, she would miss him, she knew he would miss her. But would he just miss her because he would miss the company, and not her specifically? Was this just one of those summer camp kinds of romances, hot and intense and so real in the moment, but quickly fading away as soon as they were apart?

The night before, when they'd watched their show together on the couch in the TV room with his arm around her, and then later, when he'd kissed her so tenderly in his room, everything had felt so perfect, so right between them. But now she wondered if it was all in her head. After all, they'd always known she'd be leaving soon, but he'd never made any reference to the future. To *their* future, after she left.

No, she couldn't think about any of this today. Not on their last day.

As soon as they walked out of the library, he pulled her to him and kissed her, so hard it made her breathless. When the kiss ended, she clung to him. Why did she suddenly feel like crying?

"I'm going to miss you, Isabelle Marlowe," he said in her ear.

Damn it. Now she knew she was going to cry.

"I'm going to miss you, too, Beauregard Towers," she said. And instead of crying, they both started laughing.

Saturday night, her last night in California, Izzy got dressed for dinner with Beau. She was flying out of LAX the next morning at nine, which meant she had to leave Santa Barbara by five. Her suitcase was totally packed—when she realized earlier that day how much extra stuff she'd acquired while she'd been here, she'd run out and bought an overnight bag for the overflow. She'd finish packing it when they got back tonight.

She put on the long bright yellow sundress she'd bought on that shopping expedition with Michaela. This was the first time she'd worn it.

She walked down the staircase to meet him, the long dress trailing behind her. He stood at the foot of the staircase and watched her the whole way, a soft smile on his face.

"Hi." He reached out a hand to her when she got to the bottom step. "You look beautiful."

She took his hand and held on tight. "Thank you." She stood on her tiptoes and kissed him.

They were quiet as they drove down the hill for dinner. She hadn't even asked him where they were going, she realized as he parked not far from the beach. He took her hand and steered her down the street.

"Where are we going?" she asked.

He pointed up ahead. "That Mexican place, it's right near the water. I thought it would be nice, since you're going back to cold weather."

She smiled up at him. "I actually missed the bulk of the cold weather this year—according to Instagram, it's spring in New York now. The snow is all gone, flowers are out, I might not even need my coat when I get off the plane."

He grinned. "Is it going to be warm enough for you to be able to wear that dress?"

She laughed. "Not for a month at least."

They sat down, ate chips and salsa, and chatted about nothing important as they looked at the menu. How Michaela's salsa was better than the salsa here, how Beau was going to try making croissants again from a different recipe he'd found, how Beau was going to get someone to restore some of the chairs in the library.

"Oh," Beau said when the waiter brought their margaritas. "My mom is coming next weekend."

"Wow, that's great," Izzy said. Had he planned on purpose for his mom to come after she left? No, she wasn't going to spoil their last night with thoughts like that. "I'm sure it'll be really good to see her again. And for her to see the house."

He nodded. "Yeah, that's what I thought. And to get to see Michaela, meet the baby. "

Beau looked so happy at the thought of seeing his mom again. Now Izzy felt guilty for her momentary resentful thoughts. She reached for her drink.

"What time do we have to leave tomorrow morning to get you to LAX on time?" he asked.

Izzy looked up from her drink. "You don't have to drive me," she said. "I can—"

Beau shook his head. "You can just stop talking now, because I'm driving you."

Izzy opened her mouth to say something else and then closed it. For once, she would obey a stop-talking-now directive. She lifted her glass and smiled.

After dinner, they walked down to the beach. Izzy slipped her sandals off and tucked them in her bag. There were other people on the beach, a few small groups, other couples walking hand in hand like them, but it felt quiet, peaceful. The only sounds were the waves crashing in to shore, and the faint music coming from somewhere farther down.

Beau held her hand firmly. She wondered what he was thinking. He'd said that he would miss her, and she knew it was true. She would miss him, too, so much. She thought, again, about asking him what would happen between them when she left. Would they keep this up? Would they keep in touch? Was this the end of everything?

But she hesitated. Everything between them had been wonderful for the past few weeks, better than any relationship she'd ever had before. But was it real? Was this one of those limited-time, fairy-tale romances, one of the ones that happened because of a castle and a curse and lots of magic, but that would vanish when real life started again? She hoped not. But she didn't know.

But God, she didn't want to leave the next morning. She knew that for sure.

The music got louder as they walked down the beach and she saw a string quartet playing outside at a restaurant.

Beau stopped and turned to her. "Dance with me," he said.

She looked up at him. She could barely see his face in the darkness, but she knew he was smiling. She dropped her purse and put her arm around his neck.

They danced together on the sand, moving in a slow circle, the wind blowing the full skirt of her dress, his hand on the small of her back, as the music and sound of the waves soared around them. Finally, the music stopped, and she rested her head against his chest. They stood there together for a long time. Finally, Beau leaned down and kissed her, slowly, gently. She cupped his face in her hands.

"Let's go home," she said.

He kissed her once more. "Yes, let's go home," he said.

The next morning, they woke up to her alarm. It took everything in her not to cry when she realized this would be the last time she woke up with him like this. Instead, she cleared her throat and sat up.

"I'm going to go take a shower and bring the rest of my stuff down, okay?" she said. Beau had already brought her suitcase downstairs the night before.

Beau blinked at her sleepily and nodded. "Right. Okay." Then he seemed to suddenly realize what she was saying, and sat up. "Yes. Get your stuff. I'll get in the shower, too."

She ran up the stairs to her room. She walked into the bathroom, this perfect bathroom that she'd loved so much. She felt silly about it, but she said goodbye to the bathtub that had felt like her only friend here at first, to the shower where she'd had so many good ideas, to the perfect selfie lighting at the mirror that she'd taken full advantage of. Then, after she'd showered and said her goodbyes, she pulled on her jeans and black T-shirt and Beau's hoodie, threw all her toiletries into her new bag, and zipped it up.

"Okay." She looked around the room from the doorway. So much had happened to her here in such a short amount of time. She'd arrived angry and uncertain and burned out; she was leaving refreshed, with a renewed sense of purpose and a new belief in herself. She was so grateful.

"Thank you," she said out loud to her room.

As she turned to leave, she was almost sure she heard a tiny "You're welcome."

Beau was waiting at the foot of the stairs when she came down the staircase.

"Ready?" he asked. "I put your suitcase in the trunk already, and I have coffee for us in the car." He reached for her duffel bag, and she handed it to him.

"I keep wondering if I'm forgetting something," she said. "But Michaela can send me anything if I did."

Beau nodded. "Yeah."

As they left Santa Barbara, Izzy looked out at the water and saw surfers on their way in to shore.

"We never got to go surfing again," she said.

Beau squeezed her hand. "At least we got to go back to the beach last night," he said.

She realized she'd wanted him to say that they'd have plenty of chances to go surfing together again. He hadn't.

There wasn't much traffic that morning, not until they got closer to LAX, where cars were all jammed up for the five miles approaching the airport. He reached for her hand as they inched along the freeway, and she held on tight.

When they finally got to the airport, it all went too fast.

Beau took her bags out of the car. She swung her tote bag over her shoulder and set the new duffel bag on top of her suitcase.

"Okay," he said. "I'll text."

She nodded. "Yeah. Okay." Her eyes suddenly filled with tears. "Beau."

He took one step and pulled her close. "Oh, Izzy."

They stood there together on the sidewalk for a few moments, the bustle of the airport loading zone around them. She managed to push the tears back. She didn't want to cry, not now. Finally, she stepped back.

"You should go," she said. "Before someone yells at you to move the car."

He looked around. There was an airport security car just a few yards away. "Yeah," he said. He stepped back over to the car and opened the door. Then he lifted a hand to her. "Bye, Isabelle Marlowe," he said.

She held her tears back, and smiled at him. "Bye, Beau Towers," she said. And she turned and walked into the airport.

CHAPTER THIRTY-ONE

Izzy hadn't paid attention to her plane ticket other than to note the time and airline, so it wasn't until she got to the ticket counter to check her suitcase that she discovered her ticket was in first class.

"Oh, Beau," she said under her breath.

"What was that, ma'am?" the ticket agent asked her.

She shook her head. "Nothing." She took the baggage claim ticket he handed her. "Thanks."

She managed to hold it together as she went through security, as she walked through the airport, as she waited for the plane to board, as she got on the plane and tucked her bags away, as she nestled herself into her enormous reclining window seat. The flight attendant came by and offered her a mimosa, but she declined. She'd never flown first class before, and she felt like she should take it, but right now, she didn't feel the slightest bit celebratory.

It wasn't until the plane took off and she saw the Pacific Ocean beneath her that she started to cry.

Thank God for first class, where she could stare out the window and let tears stream down her face for as long as she wanted, and no one would be close enough to see her. She was suddenly convinced she'd never see Beau again, that the hug outside the airport was the last time he'd ever hold her, that when she'd squeezed his hand as they pulled apart was the last time she'd ever touch him. Oh God, they hadn't even kissed goodbye. They hadn't even kissed this morning when they'd woken up. Their last kiss had been an accidental last kiss, a sleepy, quick good-night kiss the night before. Why hadn't she made sure to kiss him goodbye?

She told herself to stop crying, that she was overthinking everything, that she needed to stop thinking about Beau, to prepare for her interview. But then she realized there was a packet of tissues at her elbow. She reached for it and saw the flight attendant nod at her. That made the tears well up again. She wrapped herself in Beau's hoodie and cried until she fell asleep.

When she woke up, there were a few more hours of the flight left. She took a deep breath. Okay. She'd had her cry; now she had to pull herself together. She was flying back to New York for this interview, and she couldn't waste the opportunity. Izzy pulled out one of her notebooks and started brainstorming interview questions and answers.

The flight attendant came over to check on her.

"Would you like a glass of wine, dear? Some cheese and crackers? Maybe some tea and cookies?"

Izzy smiled at her. Her name was Angela, Izzy saw on her name tag. "That all sounds great, thank you."

She checked her phone when she landed. But Beau hadn't texted.

When she walked out of the airport, there was a shout.

"Isabelle!"

She turned, and her dad jumped out of his car. She smiled so big she thought her face might crack. She hadn't realized just how much she'd missed him.

"Dad!"

He gave her a huge hug, and she hugged him back.

He grabbed her suitcase in one hand and her overnight bag in the other.

"Oh, honey, it's so good to see you," he said. He touched her cheek. "You're as brown as you usually are in the middle of the summer."

She laughed. "Santa Barbara is beautiful," she said. "I got to spend a lot of time outside. But don't worry, I got a lot of work done, too."

He tossed her bags in the trunk and opened the car door for her. "I wasn't worried about that," he said. "It's good that you had a bit of a break. You were having a hard time before you left."

She looked over at him. "How did you know?"

He laughed at her. "Isabelle. I'm your father. You think I don't know when you're having a hard time? You didn't seem to want to talk about it, so I didn't pry, but I could tell something was off. And I was pretty worried about you when you first started this project in California, but after a week or so, you seemed so much happier than you had been." He smiled at her. "I'm glad. Now. Tell me about this interview."

Izzy reminded him about Josephine, and told him all about the job at Maurice.

"Ah, so this would be a promotion, that's fantastic. So . . . does this mean that if you got this job, you might be able to move out?"

There was a suspiciously hopeful tone in his voice. Wait.

"Oh, did you and Mom like being without me that much?"

He looked guilty. "We missed you! We did! But—"

She had to laugh. She'd felt guilty for how much she'd enjoyed being away from her parents, and it turned out that they'd enjoyed her absence just as much.

Her mom had a big dinner ready for her when they got home, and Izzy told her stories all over again, showed them pictures of California, talked about her interview. She'd been so tired of her parents before she'd left, stifled, like she needed to escape. But it was great to see them again. She already felt better about being back home.

But Beau still hadn't texted.

He said he'd text, but that didn't mean she couldn't text him, right? She pulled up his name on her phone and saw their last texts there, the ones about the interview, then just above, the selfie of the two of them he'd snapped when they were together by the pool one day the week before. Before she knew she was leaving, when the sun had been shining down on them and he'd just made her laugh about something and they were so happy. Just looking at that picture filled her with that same longing she'd felt on the plane. It felt like she was homesick, she realized, even though she was back home now. She'd never realized she could feel homesick for a person before.

Did he feel this way, without her there?

She wasn't his type, she'd known that from the beginning. She wasn't like the other people he'd dated. The tall, thin, famous ones. She'd known she couldn't get invested in him, let herself fall for him. Maybe he'd just liked her because she was there, because she was convenient. Not because of *her*.

Maybe that "I'll text" was what he said because he couldn't think of another way to say goodbye.

She scrolled to Priya's name on her phone instead.

> I'm back! Interview is tomorrow at 2, wish me luck!!!

Priya immediately texted back.

> GOOD LUCK. You're going to be fab! Can't wait to hear all about it.

That was better. If she texted Beau, it would just make her cry again. She didn't need to be sad like this, going into her interview. She needed an uncomplicated pep talk. Beau was a lot of things, but there was nothing uncomplicated about him.

The next morning she woke up at nine—six, California time—after tossing and turning most of the night. She reached for her phone. Nothing from Beau. That's just what she'd expected, wasn't it? That's why she'd been so sad on the plane, because she'd known that she was going back to her real life, it was all over between them. She'd been right not to text him the night before.

Being right didn't make her feel good.

She ate the breakfast her dad left for her, took a shower, did her makeup, told Priya she needed the biggest pep talk she could manage. That all helped a little, especially Priya's multi-text pep talk calling her many things, including "not only devastatingly beautiful but a veritable princess of books."

Izzy looked at herself in the mirror after she got dressed for her interview. Okay. It was time to give herself a pep talk.

"Isabelle Marlowe, you're going to be GREAT at this. You can do this job—you know that now. You're a good writer, you're a good editor, and you're going to fight for your books and your authors to succeed. And today, you're going to walk into Josephine Henry's office and wow her."

The Izzy in the mirror smiled back at her. She was right. She was going to be great at this.

CHAPTER THIRTY-TWO

Josephine glanced at her watch.

"Oh my goodness, I didn't realize we'd been talking so long." She smiled at Izzy, and Izzy smiled back. This interview had felt good since the first moment, when Josephine had walked into the lobby to get her, a huge smile on her face. And it had only gotten better from there. "If you have a few more minutes, I'd love to introduce you to some of the other people you'd be working with here at Maurice."

Izzy smiled and stood up. "I'd love that."

This felt like another good sign.

Josephine walked her down the brightly lit halls. There were books everywhere here, too, just like at TAOAT, and Izzy didn't know why it felt so different. Maybe because everyone looked friendly instead of stressed, maybe because she just needed a change that badly.

But no, it was more than that. She'd lost track of time, too, talking to Josephine. It was less an interview than a long conversation—yes, Josephine had asked her about her career goals, her strengths, the kinds of books she wanted to work on, but she'd also listened to her, told Izzy some of her own goals, told her things she'd wished she'd known when she was Izzy's age and at that point in her career. They'd talked about editing and writing, and Izzy had told her—without going into detail about who or where or how—that she'd been working on a project with an author, and how much it had made her think about the role of an editor, how inspiring it had been for her.

Izzy had even told her about her own writing, something she'd never told Marta. Josephine had seemed excited and said she couldn't wait to read her work when it was ready. And yes, sure, that was a thing sometimes people just said when you told them you were working on a book, but Josephine really seemed to mean it.

She was aware she couldn't count on actually getting this job—she knew as well as anyone that publishing could be unpredictable—but now she also knew something she hadn't known for sure this morning: The rushed trip back from California had been worth it.

She shook off thoughts of California when Josephine stopped at an open office door.

"Hi, Scott, do you have a minute? There's someone I'd like you to meet."

Izzy smiled at the spectacled, bearded, pleasant-looking white man sitting behind a desk. He looked vaguely familiar, but then, most men in publishing were white and bearded and wore glasses. He stood up as they walked in.

"Thanks for interrupting, I was about to start my expenses and I'll take any excuse to avoid those."

Josephine laughed. "I know how that is. Scott, this is Isabelle Marlowe, she's applied for the open assistant editor position; she's currently an editorial assistant over at TAOAT. Isabelle, this is Scott Tobias, he's another editor here."

Izzy shook hands with Scott. Now she knew why he looked familiar. She'd seen him at a few different publishing events; he'd edited a handful of her favorite books.

"Nice to meet you, Scott. Actually, I think we met briefly at a book event for *Then Somebody Bends*, though I'm sure you don't remember, it was packed in there."

He looked at her for a moment, then smiled. "I do remember you! You asked that question about how she pulled off the three points of view. I remember because the author was so thrilled to get that question."

Oh wow, she couldn't believe he remembered that.

"That was me," Izzy said. "It was a great event."

Scott turned to a box stacked by the door. "Wait, these just came in. . . ." He grabbed a book and handed it to Izzy. "Interested in an advance copy of her next one?"

Izzy gasped and reached for the book. Josephine and Scott both laughed.

"Looks like she's definitely interested," Josephine said. She took a step backward. "Well, I'll let you get to your expenses, but I'm glad you two got to renew your acquaintance."

Izzy dropped the book in her tote bag. "Thanks so much," she said to Scott. "It was great to meet you again."

Scott smiled at her and went back to his desk. "Great to meet you, too, Isabelle. Hope to see you again soon. Talk to you later, Josephine."

Josephine walked her to the elevator.

"Thanks again for being able to come in on such short notice, Isabelle," Josephine said. "Like I told you, I'll be on vacation next week, but I'll keep you posted about our timeline."

They shook hands, and Izzy smiled at her.

"Thank you," she said. "I've had a wonderful time talking to you."

Josephine smiled. "Likewise."

Izzy walked out of the Maurice building and turned her phone back on. She had a bunch of texts from Priya—thank goodness she'd remembered to turn her phone off before she'd walked inside. But nothing from Beau.

He'd known when her interview was. He'd definitely known.

He hadn't texted her to see how her flight was or to say good luck on the interview or to ask her how the interview went. Nothing.

The texts from Priya were great. But she knew she wanted to share this with Beau; to celebrate with him; to hear his familiar, deep, warm voice rumble in her ear.

She made herself click over to Priya's texts.

I bet you're doing great in there!

Text me as soon as you're out

How was it???

Izzy had better answer her immediately or else Priya would melt down.

I'm out! It was great. I thought I wanted it before I walked in the door, but now I want it soooo bad. Josephine's really great, everyone there is great, the books are great . . . Ahhhhh

Priya responded right away.

And YOU are great!

Izzy grinned at her phone. She could always count on Priya.

Okay, but also—wanted to make sure you saw this article, if you haven't already. Have you heard any of this from Marta? Is it true?

Izzy frowned down at her phone as she clicked the link Priya had texted. What could this be about? Was what true?

She scanned the article, something about a new Hollywood memoir recently acquired by TAOAT. Acquired by Gavin, ugh. But why had Priya texted her this? What would she have heard about from Marta?

And then she found it.

> This acquisition was all the more important for TAOAT since Beau Towers's memoir—acquired by Marta Wallace over two years ago—won't be published next year. A source within TAOAT says Towers's manuscript is far overdue and that the likelihood of Towers actually turning something in is "slim to none." "Towers is a liability," our source said. "He's uncooperative, has significant anger management issues, and frankly, isn't all that bright." It's clear that TAOAT has given up on that book.

Won't be published next year? Given up on it? Isn't all that bright? What the hell?

Izzy felt enraged, betrayed. How could they do this to Beau? How could they do this to her? He'd worked so hard. Marta knew how hard he was working, he'd told her! To hit him out of nowhere, insult him like this, with just an anonymous quote in some gossipy publishing piece, felt cruel.

And she'd worked so hard with him. Did none of that matter? Had they just let her keep working with him after they'd given up on Beau, after they'd realized they didn't want his memoir anyway, just for busy work, because they'd given up on her, too?

Did he know about this? No he couldn't know, he would have asked her about it. Maybe he thought she knew and didn't tell him, and that's why he hadn't texted her?

If that was why, then she was furious at Beau, too. How could he think that she wouldn't tell him about this? How could he think she wouldn't be on his side?

She should text Priya back.

No—I didn't know any of this

Ok, let's talk asap tomorrow. Can't wait for you to be back in the office!

I can't wait, too!

That was a lie, but what else was she supposed to say to Priya? She didn't want to go back to the office at all—even though she was angry at Beau for not texting her, for not trusting her, she was just as angry at Marta for doing this to Beau.

She had to talk to Marta about this. Even though she didn't think she'd ever see Beau again, even though their relationship might be over, she still believed in his book. While she'd been in California, she'd learned how to fight for herself and her dreams. She was going to keep fighting. For her dreams, and for Beau's.

CHAPTER THIRTY-THREE

On her walk to work the next morning, Izzy smiled as she looked around. When she'd left the city less than two months ago, the world had been gray, dreary, hopeless. Now the sun was out, there were flowers everywhere, and birds chirped all around her. She was actually happy to be here. To be back. And she was happy about more than just that. She was nervous about today, about walking back into the office for the first time in so long, and about confronting Marta about that article. And she missed Beau, so much she could barely think about it, so much she knew she would have to guard her facial expression when she talked to Marta about his book. But she also felt hope for the future, for her future. She loved books, she loved writing, she loved publishing, and she knew she had a place in that world. She wasn't going to let anyone take that love from her again.

A few minutes before nine, she walked into the TAOAT offices. It took her much longer to get to her desk than usual—everyone stopped her on the way, smiled at her, said how much they'd missed her, gave her hugs, handed her advance copies of books they'd been saving for her. She hadn't realized how many people here knew and liked her.

Marta's office was still dark when Izzy got to her desk, but she'd known it would be. She had a stack of mail on her desk; that would help keep her busy while she waited for Marta. She glanced at her email inbox, but the number of new messages was overwhelming. She was already stressed about this upcoming conversation with Marta. The email could wait.

After about half an hour, Gavin walked by. "Isabelle, welcome back."

She wasn't going to let him destroy her good mood today. "Thanks, Gavin."

He, apparently, was in a good mood today, too, if his insufferable grin was any sign. "You finally gave up on Beau Towers, huh?" he asked. "Don't worry, it's okay. I'm sure you'll have more—and better—opportunities eventually."

She knew Gavin was dying for her to ask him what he knew about the status of Beau's book and to bring up that other memoir he'd acquired, but she refused to give him the satisfaction.

"Thanks!" was all she said. Just that moment, her desk phone rang, and she turned to answer it. Gavin walked away toward his desk.

"It's just me," Priya said, from five desks down. "I saw you were here and was going to come over for a hug, but then I saw Gavin talking to you and I had to rescue you first. Coffee?"

"Oh definitely," Izzy said in her most professional voice. "I'll be sure to pass along that message."

Priya laughed. "Text me." She hung up, and Izzy grinned as she reached for her phone.

> Coffee, yes! But not until after Marta gets here. I need to find out the deal about that article. I'll fill you in when I know
>
> Yes, keep me posted. I have some info on that, too; I have to talk to Holly about it. We will DISCUSS
>
> Also, thank God you're back! I got so much WORK

done when you weren't here, can you imagine???
But wait, why are we still texting, I'm coming over for
a hug right now

Izzy laughed as she stood up to greet Priya. She'd missed her so much.

Twenty minutes later, Marta walked in and went straight to her office, staring at something on her phone. Izzy wasn't sure if Marta hadn't noticed she was there, or if she had just forgotten that Izzy had been gone. Either way, she forced herself to give Marta time to settle in for the day.

She'd made herself a list of talking points for this conversation with Marta, but were they good enough? Would Marta listen to her? Would Marta be furious at her for pushing back about this? After ten minutes, she couldn't take it any longer and knocked on Marta's open door.

Marta looked up from her phone. "Isabelle, you're back. Excellent."

Izzy took a step inside. "Thanks, Marta. There was something I—"

Marta waved her to a chair. "This whole thing with you in California worked far better than I thought it would. You managed to get an actual book out of Beau Towers, which I didn't think was possible."

Izzy took a deep breath. "I wanted to talk to you about—" Suddenly, she realized what Marta had just said. "Wait, what did you just say about Beau Towers?"

"Oh, I assumed you knew, since you were cc'd," Marta said. "He sent in his manuscript this morning."

He'd sent Marta the manuscript this morning? The whole manuscript?

"I started reading it on the subway on the way here," Marta went on. "When he sent those pages a few weeks ago, I could tell it was going to be good, but this is far better than I expected."

He'd sent Marta pages a few weeks ago? He hadn't told her he was going to do that.

"Um—yes, he worked really hard on it. It blew my expectations out of the water as well."

Marta looked very smug. "Sales is going to go bananas for this one. That was a great idea you had, to go talk to him."

Great idea *she* had? Now Izzy was very confused.

"I . . . Thanks, Marta," she said. "But I saw that piece yesterday, and I thought that TAOAT was planning to cancel the book?"

Marta gestured to her. "Shut the door."

Izzy got up, shut the door, and sat back down.

"Don't pay that piece any attention." She could almost see Marta grind her teeth. "I don't know who that source was, but when I find out . . ." Marta smiled. It was the scariest smile Izzy had ever seen. "I reached out to both Beau Towers and his agent as soon as I saw the article. They know it's bullshit. We haven't decided how to handle it publicly here yet—now that we have the manuscript, we might just let it stand until we have a cover, surprise the world some, that's always a good splash. Ooh, or this might be fodder for a new chapter. Publicity will die at that promo material."

Izzy had no idea what to say. She'd spent the last eighteen hours gearing herself up for this confrontation, but Marta already loved Beau's book, TAOAT was on his side, and Marta had congratulated her?

"I give you a lot of credit for how good this book is," Marta said. "Good job."

As amazing as it felt for Marta to say that, she couldn't take all the credit. "Thank you, but Beau is a great writer. I did a lot, yes, to help him figure out how to write a memoir, but the writing is all his."

Marta waved that away. "Yes, yes, that's what being an editor is.

The writing is always all theirs, but that makes our work even more important. His proposal for this memoir was a nightmare. I could see there was a good writer in there, but I knew it would take a lot for me to pull a book out of him. You did a lot of that work for me already."

Today was not at all turning out to be how she'd expected. Should she do something else that she hadn't planned on? She didn't stop to change her mind.

"Thank you, Marta. Actually, there's something else I'd love to talk to you about. I've wanted to move up to assistant editor for a while, but it didn't seem like that was possible for me here. But recently, Josephine Henry over at Maurice reached out about an assistant editor position. I had an interview over there yesterday."

Marta nodded slowly. "Yes. That sounds like a great place for you."

Izzy's mouth didn't quite drop open, but only because she caught it in time. "I tried here, you know. Because of the budget cuts last year, we couldn't add any new assistant editors, and I was worried that I might lose you. To be honest, I was waiting for you to ask about it."

But Gavin said . . .

Gavin said her book was no good. Gavin said she didn't have potential here. Gavin said Marta didn't believe in her.

None of that was true.

Before Izzy could really absorb this, Marta spun to face her computer. "I have Josephine's number. Let me give her a call about you now."

Izzy just stared at her.

Marta glanced at her and laughed out loud. "I'm only going to tell her great things about you, not that there's much else to tell." She thought for a moment. "Well, you're not very good at tooting your own horn. Work on that."

Classic Marta: telling her one of her faults, ordering her to get better, not recognizing or thinking about all the reasons why it was difficult for her to acknowledge or brag about her accomplishments. Ahh, the world felt a little bit more normal now.

"Okay" was all she said. "Thanks, Marta."

Marta reached for her phone, and Izzy stood up.

"Josephine, hi," Marta was saying by the time Izzy opened the office door. "This is Marta Wallace. How's business?"

Izzy closed the door gently. Of course Marta would ask "How's business?" instead of "How are you?" To be fair, to Marta the two were likely one and the same.

She walked back to her desk and then shook her head and went to the elevators. She couldn't sit down at her cubicle after what had just happened. She had to go somewhere and be alone to process that conversation.

She'd expected Marta to be curt, dismissive, tell her in so many words that her two months in California had been pointless, to Beau, to TAOAT, for her career. And yes, Marta was curt, she always was. But everything else had been different.

When she walked outside into the brisk spring air, she finally let herself think about one of the most unexpected things Marta had told her. Beau had turned in his manuscript this morning.

He'd done it, the thing he thought he couldn't do, the thing he'd told her, less than two months ago, that he knew he couldn't do. He'd written the book. He'd fought and struggled and worked so hard on his writing and himself. And he'd done it. She wished she'd been there when he'd pressed send; she wished she could give him a big hug; she wished he knew how happy she was for him. How proud she was of him.

She missed him so much. She wanted to see him, congratulate him for this, ask him how he felt, tell him about the interview, ask if he'd known about that piece before he'd gotten Marta's email about it, hug him again.

Then she stopped in the middle of the sidewalk, causing someone walking behind her to yell at her, a curse she barely even heard.

Why couldn't she do all of that? She'd convinced herself they were done, she'd never see him again, they couldn't have a happy ending, that's how it had to be.

Just because he hadn't texted her for two days? She hadn't texted him either.

And why had she thought he would be mad at her because of the article? Beau would never, for one second, think she had anything to do with that.

She'd convinced herself she couldn't ask for more. That what she and Beau had wasn't real. But that wasn't how she felt. That wasn't what she wanted. She'd fallen in love with him, as they'd worked together in the library, as they ate dinner on the couch, as they fought and made up in the kitchen, as they kissed on the beach. And she hadn't told him that, any of it. She hadn't even been able to admit it to herself.

Maybe he didn't feel the same way about her as she did about him. But she'd been so careful over the past few days to hide her feelings from him, from herself—to prevent disappointment, to keep herself from getting hurt, to keep herself from getting her hopes up, that she hadn't allowed herself to truly admit what she wanted. She hadn't allowed herself to dream about how it would feel to get it.

She had to ask for what she wanted. And what she wanted was Beau.

She reached for her bag to grab her phone, and found neither. Right, her bag—and her phone—were at her desk, back in the office. She'd left the office so impulsively after talking to Marta she hadn't stopped to get either.

She turned around. She had to go get her phone. She had to call Beau.

CHAPTER THIRTY-FOUR

When Izzy got to her desk, there was a slim overnight package sitting on top. She pushed it aside to reach for her bag, but the strong, bold writing on the package caught her eye. And then she saw the Santa Barbara return address. She tore it open.

Inside was a thick black spiral notebook. When she picked it up, her eyes filled with tears. She traced the little marks on it with her finger, the stains, the dents, all of which she remembered so well. This was Beau's notebook.

The one he'd written in almost every day for weeks, the notebook they'd passed back and forth across the table, like a ritual, at the beginning and end of every one of their sessions in the library. The notebook she'd returned to him, at the end of their last time in the library together. And now Beau's notebook was here.

That splash of coffee, there in the corner, from when she'd gestured too enthusiastically and knocked over her coffee cup. That little orange smudge along the side, from that day they'd snacked on Flamin' Hot Cheetos. That swelling on one side, from the day they'd worked by the pool and Beau had accidentally dripped water on it.

Read Me, said the Post-it note on top.

She flipped it open.

She said if I didn't know what to write I should write about how annoyed I am that she's making me do this, so fine, that's what I'll do. I'm very annoyed about it. I'm also very annoyed about how much I like her.

Beau wrote about her? She closed the notebook. She couldn't read this here.

She glanced at Marta's open office door. Just then, Priya's boss, Holly, walked into Marta's office, a grim look on her face, and closed it behind her. Perfect timing.

Izzy grabbed the notebook and raced for the elevators.

She walked to the tiny park a few blocks away, where she and Priya often met to eat lunch and gossip on nice days. Thank God the weather was with her today.

She sat down on her favorite bench, took a deep breath, and opened the notebook.

> *She said if I didn't know what to write I should write about how annoyed I am that she's making me do this, so fine, that's what I'll do. I'm very annoyed about it. I'm also very annoyed about how much I like her.*
>
> *I absolutely don't want to do this. I thought when she said she'd help me with the book, we were going to start slow, but instead, boom, she set a timer and told me to go. And even worse, I can't believe I got myself into this situation, living with this woman I'm wildly attracted to who has every reason to despise me, sitting across a table from her every single day for a month. This is going to be a nightmare. And it's all my fault. Will I actually get a book out of this? Doubtful.*
>
> *She's just sitting there looking down at her phone as I*

write this. I looked up at her for a while, just now, but she didn't even glance at me—she's smiling away at something on her phone. I wonder what it was—a friend of hers? Someone she's dating? I wish I knew how to make her smile like that. I've done it accidentally, but I have no idea how to replicate it. I used to be better at this. At least, I thought I was. But first my dad died and I was furious at the world, and then I was furious at myself, and then I locked myself away in this house for a year, and now I barely know how to talk to any other human beings, let alone a gorgeous, smart, slightly caustic woman.

That was from their first day in the library. He'd thought this way about her from the very beginning? He'd told her that, but she hadn't really believed him.

Gorgeous, smart, slightly caustic. Wow, what a great description. No one else saw her like that.

She kept reading.

I guess I should be writing about why I'm so furious at myself. Yes, probably, but I can't do that today. Baby steps. Maybe I'll start with why I came here, to this house. Why I've been here since that night I found out everything. Oh God, writing about how annoyed I am that Isabelle made me do this led me to do exactly what she wanted me to do. So fine, Isabelle, you win this round.

She skimmed the rest of that entry—it was a much messier version of that first chapter he'd given her to read, weeks after that first day together in the library. She flipped to the next page.

I can't believe I let her have this notebook. When I gave it to her, yesterday before we left the library, I kind of forgot what I'd written about her at the very beginning—on the very first page. But she promised she wouldn't read it, and I think she kept her promise, because she isn't acting weird to me today or anything.

Well, not weirder than usual, since, you know, she sort of thinks I'm a monster.

Not that she's wrong about that, but still.

Can I trust her to take the notebook again? On the one hand, I am sort of terrified that if I keep it I'll delete everything and that I'll rip out those first pages I wrote. Not for the same reason as I did the first time. The first time I deleted everything, it was because what I wrote was terrible, untrue, dishonest. It made me hate myself when I read it later. Izzy says I shouldn't have done it, that I should have saved it somewhere, but I needed to do it, to help myself get rid of the person who had written those words, who'd thought he had all the answers, who was so confident and wrong.

No, now I'm afraid I'll rip out those pages because they're too honest, and I'm not sure if I'm ready for that. So I guess that's why I need to give them to her, for safekeeping. I guess I need to try to trust her.

Izzy remembered a few times that week, Beau had looked at her strangely as she'd pushed the notebook across the table to him. She hadn't really thought anything of it at the time; he always looked at her kind of strangely back then. But now she realized why: He was trying to see if she'd read his notebook. If he could trust her.

She flipped to the next page. And then the next, and then the next. At the beginning of almost every entry, Beau had written about her.

> *We had dinner together again last night. Me and Isabelle. Izzy. We had a good day working together—at least, it seemed good to me. She seemed upset about something at dinner, and I asked her what was wrong. She seemed surprised that I knew something was wrong with her, and I don't know how I could tell, but I could. Eventually, she told me it was some jerk she works with who made everything difficult for her today. I think talking to me about it made her feel better. I hope it did.*
>
> *And it definitely made her feel better when she made fun of me for not washing my dishes. To be fair, I kind of deserved that.*
>
> *Okay, more than kind of.*

A different day.

> *I'm sure Izzy hasn't opened this notebook once in the entire time she's had it. I wonder if she has any idea how every night, when we sit on the couch together and watch TV, I have to fight to keep from leaning over to kiss her. I won't do it—I don't think I'll ever be able to do it—but, God, I want to.*
>
> *Every day I like her more. It's not just that I'm more attracted to her—that, too, obviously, especially when she wears those little tank tops down to dinner—I just like her. Last night when we ate dinner, she went on this extended riff about how she was really sure the snack cabinet was*

talking to her one day, and I laughed harder than I've laughed in . . . over a year, actually.

Izzy remembered that night at dinner. That was a fun night. A few days later.

We went surfing yesterday. I needed a break from writing. It was sort of an impulsive decision, but a really good one. It seemed like she needed a break, too, because I expected her to argue with me about where we were going and what we were doing, but she didn't, at all, and came along to the beach, and even let me start to teach her how to surf. It was a lot of fun—for me, but I'm pretty sure for her, too. I mean sure, she fell off a million times, but we laughed about that a lot. I think we both trust each other more after yesterday, even though that wasn't my goal.

I think we both like each other more after yesterday, too.

The problem is I almost kissed her last night. It was after dinner; we were together in the kitchen, cleaning up; we'd each had enough wine to be not quite drunk, but somewhere on the way. She was kind of giggly; it was cute. Anyway, she slipped, and I caught her. And then I didn't let go. And she just relaxed against me. And we stood there like that for a while. And my God, it felt so good. And then suddenly, I knew that if I stayed like that with her for one more second, I would kiss her, so I made myself drop my hands and take a step back.

I can't stop thinking about the way she smelled, still faintly of the ocean, but with that floral scent in her hair.

She could still feel that first embrace, in the kitchen. How solid, comforting, warm he felt. How she didn't want to let go either.

The next week.

I showed her my writing for the first time yesterday. She even liked it—I know she did, because she seemed surprised at first when she told me it was good, so I know she was telling the truth. I didn't really tell her this, but part of the reason it was so hard for me to start this memoir—or, this version of it, anyway—was that the idea of other people reading it terrified me. I'm really glad that Izzy is the first person to read any of this.

And then, later that week.

Izzy's friend is in town. She came over yesterday—Izzy said she wanted to see the house and asked if she could come. She seemed kind of nervous to ask me that, which irritated me, that she's still nervous around me, but whatever. Anyway, when they were here, her friend said something about how Izzy's going back to New York in just over a week. I sort of forgot she's leaving so soon.

Whatever. It doesn't matter.

Later that day. She almost didn't want to read this.

Well, shit. I fucked everything up now, didn't I? I was such an asshole to her today. Yes, a bigger asshole than the first day, if anyone can believe that, which I don't know if anyone can, but it's true. I was such an asshole that she walked out of the library, took the car, and drove away. I'm sitting in the kitchen now, writing in this thing because I don't know what else to do, while I wait for her to come back. Though I don't blame her if she doesn't.

I said really shitty things to her. I don't even want to write them down. If she comes back—and who knows if she will—she'll probably just go straight up to her room, pack, and leave. I guess I'm just sitting here because I want to be able to apologize to her before she does that.

I thought writing all this, thinking about all this, was making me less of an asshole. I guess not.

I should wait outside for her.

That was the worst day.

She came back. She's still here.

I didn't think she'd come back. I didn't even try to convince her to stay, I didn't think it would do any good. Even though it's what I wanted, more than anything.

I apologized, and she blew me off, and I did it again, and she listened, only sort of, at first. And then she told me that I hurt her, and even though I knew it was true, hearing her say the words felt like a punch in the face. It made me realize how much I care about her, how important our . . . friendship, I guess, is to me, because now I know that I never want to do anything to hurt her ever again.

I told her everything. About my dad, my mom, me. What I did to my mom. The stuff I haven't been writing about, not even in here. The stuff I've skipped over. And she listened. And she's still here.

She told me to write it down, everything I told her tonight, and I'm going to do that, in just a second, but I just had to write this first.

I promised Izzy I'd never do that to her again. I don't know if she believed me, but I swear, I'll keep that promise.

He'd kept that promise.

Izzy told me about her own writing. The unbelievable part is that when I encouraged her to start again, to write again, she listened to me. I'm sure it wasn't just me, she said she'd already sort of started while she was here, I think she just needed a tiny push to get her to really do it, but I'm glad I could be the one to give her that push. So now she's sitting across from me, writing, too.

Izzy was glad he was the one who gave her that push to write again, too.

I texted that therapist, the one I used to see. I'm going to talk to him tomorrow morning. I'm nervous as hell about it.

She hadn't known that.

Izzy is supposed to leave at the end of this week. I really want her to stay longer. I think I might ask her if she will, if I get the courage. Wish me luck.

The next day.

She's staying. An extra three weeks.

Marta said that for Izzy to be able to stay, I had to send her some pages—to prove, I guess, that I've gotten work done. She said that it was nonnegotiable.

Now another thing made sense. She'd *known* Marta had said something else to him at the end of that call.

I didn't tell Izzy that part—she knows how terrified I am for anyone but her to read what I've written. I thought if I told her, she'd realize how important it was to me for her to stay. And that she'd realize how I felt about her.

At first I thought I was just attracted to Izzy in the same way that I've been attracted to lots of women. I thought it was just that this one felt different, because I knew I couldn't do anything about it. Then, as she stayed longer, as we talked more, as we got closer, I thought it was because we were friends now, and her friendship was important to me.

But now I know I'm really starting to fall for her. Does she think about me in any way other than a friend—sort of—or a work project? I have no idea.

All I know for sure is it's getting harder and harder not to let her know how I feel.

Izzy remembered how she felt, back then. At that point, she'd been trying to pretend her feelings for Beau away. At least he'd admitted his feelings to himself.

We kissed yesterday, on the beach. She kissed me first, and then I kissed her back, and then we just kissed each other, for a really long time. My mom still knows me so well, after all that time—she could tell, just from how I talked about her, that I'm falling for Izzy. She told me to go for it—I can't believe I'm getting woman advice from my mom, but she was right, wasn't she?

Izzy and I didn't talk about much. I told her that I've been wanting to kiss her since the beginning, and she seemed surprised, almost like she didn't believe me at first. I almost told her to just flip open this notebook and she'd know for sure, but then I caught myself.

And then, a week later, just a few lines.

Izzy woke up in my bed this morning. I think, for the first time in a long time, I'm actually happy. I think she is, too. She's smiling, across from me, as she writes. I just realized I'm smiling, too.

God, she missed him.

She's leaving. I knew it was coming—we both knew it was coming—but we thought we had more time. She's leaving the day after tomorrow.

This morning she pulled me in here and told me she has an interview for another job, a job I know she really wants. I'm thrilled for her, of course I am, she tries not to talk about it too much, but I know she's really struggled at her job for a while. She needs this. I wanted to tell her that I don't want her to go, to please not go, but I stopped myself. I don't want her to feel guilty. I can't hold her back.

I did tell her I'm going to miss her, though. I couldn't help it. Because my God, I'm going to miss her, so much.

It wasn't until her tears dropped down onto the notebook that Izzy realized she was crying. She turned the page.

It's our last time, here in the library. The last time, with her sitting across from me like this, pressing her lips together when she's concentrating, taking her hair down and putting it back up and then taking it down again every five minutes, smiling at me when she looks up from my laptop like she's proud of me, grinning at me when I grab her as soon as we walk out of this room. Fuck. I hate this. I'm going to miss her so much.

And then just one more page.

She left yesterday. I'm sitting in the window seat in the library—I couldn't bear to sit in my regular chair and look across the table and not see her, but I also couldn't bear to not work here in the library, where it's like I can feel her here with me.

I've been sitting here for hours, writing. I'm almost done with the book. I think I can send it to Marta soon, even tomorrow. I wrote all night, mostly just to give myself something to do. I didn't want to go to bed, I knew I would miss her too much.

I didn't tell her how I feel about her, before she left. I wanted to, the words were on my lips, but I stopped myself. At first I told myself it was for her, that I didn't want to hold her back, that I didn't want to distract her from the interview, that I didn't want her to think I wanted her to stay with me instead of following her dream.

But now I realize that was just an excuse. I was scared to tell her how I feel about her, scared she doesn't feel the same way, scared she was relieved and happy to go back to New York and her old life there and leave me behind.

And maybe it's true. Maybe she does feel that way.

But I have to know for sure.

I'm going to make myself send this notebook to her. I realized when she gave it back to me before she left that I'd always thought of it as hers. That I've always been writing all of this to her.

I've always been writing this to you, Izzy, if you're reading this, if you've gotten this far. This has all always been for you.

CHAPTER THIRTY-FIVE

Izzy closed the notebook and wiped her eyes, even though it didn't do any good. The tears just kept coming.

She looked around for her phone. She had to call Beau.

Oh God. She'd left her phone at her desk again? She'd gotten so used to not taking her bag—or her phone—everywhere with her when she'd been in Santa Barbara. She was out of practice. She had to get back to her desk to get it.

She walked the few blocks back to the office as words, phrases, sentences from the notebook ran through her brain. She couldn't believe he'd been writing about her since the beginning. All this time, when she hadn't known how she'd felt, he'd known how he felt. All this time, when she hadn't been sure of him, he'd been right there.

He hadn't told her he wanted her to stay, because he didn't want to hold her back. That might be the most romantic thing she'd ever heard.

As she reached her desk, Gavin disappeared into Marta's office and the door closed again. Marta was having a whole lot of closed-door meetings today.

Well, that was convenient, since whether Marta's door was open or closed, she was just going to leave again. There was no way she could make this call from her desk.

As she walked away, she heard raised voices from Marta's office. At any other time, she would have lingered to see what was going on, but not now.

She went outside. She couldn't go back to the park, that was too far away; she couldn't wait that long. She walked around the corner, just to get some distance from the building, and finally called Beau.

The phone rang, and anticipation built up in her chest. Where was he? she wondered. In his bedroom? In the kitchen? In the library? She hoped he was in the library.

The phone rang again and again. And then it went to voicemail.

Voicemail? Was he kidding her with this? He'd sent her this emotional grenade of a notebook with just a Post-it note on top and then let her call go to *voicemail*? He probably hadn't even turned his ringer on that day, or he'd left his phone on the other side of the house, or something.

She couldn't wait to yell at him for this.

"Hi, Beau, it's Izzy. I got the notebook. I read it. Call me. As soon as you get this."

She hung up and then stared at her phone for a few minutes, willing him to call her back. Now, right away. But five minutes went by, and her phone was still silent.

She'd pushed her luck as much as she could on her first day back. She had to get to her desk.

She walked into the TAOAT building and toward the elevators, her mind in a daze. How could she possibly get any work done today until she'd talked to him?

She was almost at the elevator when she heard her name. She turned and stared at the security desk, as if in a dream.

"Yes, Isabelle Marlowe. No, I don't have an appointment. I know you said she's not answering her phone, can you try it again? She should be there."

"She's here," Izzy said. And Beau turned to face her.

He'd gotten a haircut, he had a bouquet of roses in one hand, he looked like he hadn't slept in days, but Izzy didn't notice any of that at first. All she could see was that it was Beau, it was really him, he was here, in New York. And he was here for her.

They walked toward each other. Beau's eyes were locked on hers. He had that nervous, uncertain look on his face that she remembered from that first time he'd asked her to read his work.

"Hi," he said. "I . . ." He stopped. "Did you—"

Someone jostled his arm, and he looked around. At the same moment, Izzy realized they were in the lobby of her office building, with lots of people—lots of people she knew—walking in and out.

"Let's go outside," she said.

Once they got outside and around the corner, she turned to face him.

"Beau," she said. "You're here."

He smiled at her. God, she'd thought she'd never see that smile again. "Yeah," he said. "I'm here. I sent you—"

Before he could finish the sentence, she pulled the notebook out of her bag. "I read it," she said. "I read it all."

He swallowed. "There's something I realized I didn't say in there." He took a step closer to her. "I love you."

She let herself smile just as big as she wanted to. "I love you, too," she said.

She'd barely gotten the words out when she was in his arms. He crushed her against him, and she held on to him, just as hard. She felt his warm chest, his breath on her ear, his lips in her hair. The fragrance of the roses, still clutched in one of his hands, surrounded them.

"I wanted to tell you, before you left," he said. "But I kept putting it off. I was scared, I think. But my God, Izzy. I love you so much."

Then it wasn't enough to just hold him, be held by him, and she pulled his face down to hers and kissed him. She felt him smile against his lips as he kissed her back. They stood there kissing for a long time, with the sounds of New York around them, her hands in his hair, his arms holding her tight against him.

When they finally stopped kissing, Izzy laughed against his chest.

"I really hate to say this, but I have got to go back to work," she said.

He looked down at her and smiled. "I'll be here waiting, when you get off. I'm staying at some hotel nearby." He started to let go of her, then stopped. "Oh! I turned in my book today, did you know?"

She pulled him down to her and kissed him again. "I know. I'm so happy. I'm so proud of you." She made herself pull away, and they turned back toward the building. "Marta told me she started reading it on the subway on the way to work and that it's great."

He beamed at her. "Really? Oh wow. Oh! How was the interview? I should have texted, I'm sorry, I was just—"

She grinned. "That's okay. I have so much to tell you. The interview was good, really good. Wait, but did you—"

Izzy heard a commotion behind her and turned.

It was Gavin.

"She's going to regret this!" he shouted as he walked out of the building, with a security guard on either side of him.

What was going on?

Then he saw Izzy staring at him.

"You. It was you who told her it was me, wasn't it? I bet you're happy now, aren't you? Well, you're going to regret this, too."

Izzy narrowed her eyes at him. "What the hell are you talking about, Gavin?"

He moved closer to her. "Oh, you're going to do your little innocent smiley girl act here again, hmm? Just rainbows and sunshine over there, aren't you? *Someone* apparently told Marta that they overheard me on the phone with that reporter. I can't believe she fired me over that. But then, I can believe you did this to me."

Gavin. Of course.

"But how could I have told her that? I wasn't even—"

Gavin took another step toward Izzy. "I know it was you. I've never been fooled by you. You've been gunning for my job since the first moment, I knew."

Beau turned to her with a grin.

"This guy has great timing." He handed her the bouquet of roses. "This is going to be fun."

Beau stepped in front of Gavin. "Hi, Gavin," he said, in a very cheerful voice. It was very . . . gratifying to see how Beau loomed over Gavin. "I'm Beau. So nice to meet you. Just FYI, if you ever talk to Isabelle like that again . . . actually, no, let me restate that—if you ever talk to Isabelle ever again, at any time, in any context, I will make it my life's work to destroy you. And I just turned in my book, so I have a lot of free time on my hands."

Gavin stared up at Beau, open-mouthed. The security guards grinned.

"Now." Beau pointed down the street. "Go." Gavin hesitated. "Go. NOW." Gavin turned and ran, his messenger bag bumping against his hip as he stumbled away.

"There." Beau wiped his hands as he walked back to her side. "I found that very satisfying. Didn't you?"

Izzy grinned up at him. "My hero." She threw her arms around his neck.

He grabbed her by the waist, and pulled her in for a kiss. "You'd better believe it."

EPILOGUE

One year later

Izzy opened her eyes, and smiled as she looked out the window.

It had been a busy, exhausting, wonderful year. Marta had offered her the assistant editor job at TAOAT, after Gavin's departure had left an opening, but the offer from Maurice had been too good for her to turn down, especially after she'd flexed some negotiation skills of her own. Plus, even though it was incredible to discover Marta actually had faith in her, she was happy to get a fresh start, and to have a boss who was willing to give her positive feedback on a regular basis. Priya—who, as it turned out, had been the one who told her boss, and then Marta, that she'd overheard Gavin talking to that reporter—had been promoted, which thrilled both Priya and Izzy.

She and Beau had managed to see each other a lot—Maurice was very liberal with remote work, and Beau had been spending a lot of time with her in New York these days, too, at the apartment that she and Priya now shared. But it so good to be back in Santa Barbara now, actually on vacation and with a whole week to just be together.

She turned over to smile at him, but he wasn't there. Why was she alone in his bed?

Then she heard his footsteps.

He pushed the bedroom door open with his bare shoulder and walked in the room, holding a very laden tray.

"What's all this?" Izzy asked as she looked at all the food on the tray, along with a bottle of champagne and a badly wrapped present. “It’s your book release day. I was going to do this for you.”

He set the tray on the bed and picked up the bottle of champagne. “I know you were, that’s why I got up early, so I could do it for you instead.” He grinned at her. “Plus, I’m a better cook than you are.”

Izzy picked up a piece of bacon. “Okay, you have a point there, but I strategized with Michaela about this.”

He laughed as he twisted the cage from around the top of the champagne bottle. “I know,” he said. “Fun fact: Michaela works for me.”

Izzy laughed. “You and I both know that Michaela does whatever she wants around here.”

Beau grinned at her. “That’s definitely true.”

Izzy thought about what Michaela had told her when she’d arrived the day before.

“I think it’s safe to tell you this now,” Michaela had whispered in her ear. “That first day you were here: I didn’t really sprain my ankle.”

Izzy pulled away. “What?”

“You heard me.” Michaela grinned at her. “I had a feeling about you.”

Izzy still couldn’t believe it.

So fine, she’d forgive Michaela for this one.

“You can cook for me on the day your book comes out next year,” Beau said. “That’ll give you some time to learn how to cook.”

She laughed and looked down at the tray. “What’s that?” she said, pointing to the gift there.

Beau’s smile got wider. “Open it,” he said.

She picked it up. It was shaped like a book, but why would Beau get her a book? Not that she didn’t constantly come home with new books for herself, but he knew she did it so often that he’d have no idea which books she actually owned. Was it rare? Or maybe something from the library that he wanted her to keep?

"You know," he said as she turned over the present in her hands, "it's easier to figure out what it is if you open it."

She rolled her eyes at him and finally tore at the wrapping paper.

It was his book. His picture was on the cover, one the photographer had taken one day last summer, when she'd come for a long weekend. The photographer had snapped the shot of Beau looking at Izzy on the beach, though only the three of them knew who Beau was looking at.

Izzy loved that picture. But why was Beau giving her his book?

She looked up at him.

"The Post-it," he said.

She looked down at the book. There was another *Read me* Post-it note. There must be tickets inside. Her favorite play was coming to LA in a few months; she kept meaning to tell him they should go together. She smiled and flipped to the page.

But there were no tickets. She read the page and then looked up at him, her eyes full of tears.

> *To Isabelle. I never would have been able to write this book if it wasn't for you. I love you.*

She'd assumed he'd dedicate it to his mom. She'd been sure of that, for months now. She'd never even thought this might happen.

"You didn't know?" he asked. She couldn't say anything; she just shook her head. Her heart was so full.

He let out a sigh of relief.

"I wanted to be the one to tell you, but I was so nervous that somehow you'd find out first. Marta said she'd keep it a secret, but everyone over there knows you, so I was worried."

"I had no idea," she said. She should say more, but she didn't even know how to say what she felt right now. Shock, joy, pride, amazement, all at once. But mostly, love.

"I love you so much," she said.

He handed her a glass of champagne.

"I love you, too," he said. He sat down next to her and touched his glass to hers. "To you, Isabelle Marlowe, the woman who walked into my house one day and changed my life."

And then she kissed him.

ACKNOWLEDGMENTS

There are so many people who supported me with their actions, their friendship, and their love as I wrote this book, and I am so very grateful to all of them.

To the entire team at Hyperion Avenue, thank you so much for trusting me with this story, and for everything you've done to help this book become a reality. Jocelyn Davies, thank you for your thoughtful edits that made this book so much better, and for loving Izzy and Beau as much as I do. Marci Senders and Stephanie Singleton, thank you for this incredible book cover that I fell in love with immediately. Elanna Heda, Cassidy Leyendecker, Sara Liebling, Guy Cunningham, Jody Corbett, Martin Karlow, Meredith Jones, and Marybeth Tregarthen, thank you for all of your hard work in turning my manuscript into this beautiful book. And thank you so much to Lyssa Hurvitz, Seale Ballenger, Danielle DiMartino, Holly Nagel, Ian Byrne, Marina Shults, Monique Diman, Nicole Elmes, Michael Freeman, Loren Godfrey, Kim Knueppel, Vicki Korlishin, Meredith Lisbin, Vanessa Vazquez, and Samantha Voorhees for ushering this book out into the world and helping it find its readers.

Holly Root, you are a true gem. These past two years have been immeasurably easier because of you; this book is only a book because of your advice, your support, and your many, many pep talks. Thank you, so much. And thank you to everyone else at Root Literary: Alyssa Moore and Melanie Figueroa, thank you so much for all of your hard work on my behalf. Taylor Haggerty, many thanks for all of your excellent Santa Barbara advice! Kristin Dwyer, what a joy it is to work with you. Thank you for being exactly you.

Amy Spalding, thank you for all of your advice about this book, for being such a great research travel companion in Santa Barbara, and for your friendship. Akilah Brown, thank you for your advice, honesty, and friendship. Kayla Cagan, thank you for your brilliance, your humor, and the cheese balls. Thank you to Sara Zarr, who said "If you write, then you're a writer" to me at a time when I absolutely didn't think I deserved that title. Many thanks to Josh Gondelman, the king of pep talks. And thank you to the many other writers who gave me advice, companionship, and support throughout these past two years: Jami Attenberg, Melissa Baumgart, Robin Benway, Alexis Coe, Nicole Chung, Mira Jacob, Ruby Lang, Jessica Morgan, Julie Murphy, Samin Nosratt, Helen Rosner, and Emma Straub.

It's not just that I wouldn't have been able to write this book without my friends; I wouldn't have made it through these past two years of a global pandemic without my friends. Nicole Clouse and Simi Patnaik, I love you so much. (Simi, I hope you're happy now.) Jill Vizas, I don't know what I'd do without you. Janet Goode, I miss you so much; I can't wait to see you again. Kimberly Chin, here's to many more meals together, and many more years of friendship. Sarah Mackey, thank you for helping me name all the things. All my love and gratitude to Joy Alferness and the entire Alferness family, Nanita Cranford, Nicole Cliffe, Jenée Desmond-Harris, Rachel Fershleiser, Alyssa Furukawa, Alicia Harris, Jina Kim, Danny Lavery, Kate Leos, Lisa McIntire, Caille Millner, Runjini Murthy, Maret Orliss, Samantha Powell, Jessica Simmons, Sara Simon, Melissa Sladden, Christina Tucker, Dana White, and Margaret H. Willison. I am endlessly grateful to all of you for making me laugh and cry, for all of the hugs, both in person and virtual, for always being there for me, for all of the phone calls and video calls and many many text messages.

Thank you to Meghan and Harry, for showing me all of the places a real princess would go in Santa Barbara. (Just kidding.) (Or am I???)

Thank you to my family, I love you all so much. I cannot list you all by name because we'd be here for four or five more pages, but know that I love you all so much, and I appreciate all of your love and support. Special thanks to my parents, who have always been there for me. Mom, you're the greatest (I know you know that, but I have to say it). Dad, I love you so much.

Thank you to all of the libraries and bookstores who have worked so hard over these past few years to get books to readers. Special thanks to East Bay Booksellers and the incredible staff there, and to Chaucer's Books in Santa Barbara, which makes a little cameo in this book. And a thousand thanks to every teacher and librarian who encouraged and indulged my love of reading; I'm grateful for every single one of you.

And thank you to all of you reading this. Whether this is the first book of mine that you've read or the seventh, I am enormously grateful to you for taking the time to read my books. To anyone I gave a pep talk to over these past two years, thank you, you helped me even more than I could have possibly helped you. And for those of you who told me that my books helped you through these past two very hard years, I can't thank you enough; you helped keep me going.

And if you'd like to read more of my writing, or see what comes next, go to JasmineGuillory.com!